1

ISOBEL

A MALLERY & HOBBS MURDER CASE

BY

A.J. GRIFFITHS-JONES

For My Sister, Jenny x

CHAPTER ONE – A NEW ARRIVAL

Isobel Gilyard leaned gently back against her ailing Volkswagen Beetle, sucking hard on a filtered cigarette and enjoyed the heat of the early May sunshine tickling her cheeks. Tossing her lighter into the opened handbag on the passenger's seat, she surveyed the beautiful French countryside around her, a far cry from the busy Manchester streets that she'd left behind.

She knew her old car more intimately than any of her relatives and felt confident in its ability to recover swiftly from the long journey behind them. Another half hour of exposing the overheated engine to the slight breeze and she could be on her way again, of this she was certain, and Isobel closed her eyes for a moment or two.

The sound of a vehicle pulling onto the hard shoulder behind her shook Isobel from her reverie, daydreams of new beginnings and forgotten talents, causing her to turn and wait as the driver of an old Citroën van alighted.

'*Qu'est-ce qui ne va pas?*' the unshaven middle-aged man called out, as he strode closer, wiping greasy palms on creased trousers.

Isobel looked around, slightly unnerved, the rumble of passing traffic buffering the sound of the Frenchman's voice.

'*Chaud,*' she replied, pointing to the VW's boot which sat exposing its internal workings like a gaping mouth at the dentist. 'It's hot.'

'*Ou allez-vous?*' he continued, now near enough for Isobel to smell stale sweat and grime, her nostrils twitching at the repugnant stench.

Quickly translating the question, Isobel smiled as politely as her face would allow and said, 'Bordeaux, Saint Margaux.'

The man nodded, his greasy fringe falling across one eye as he did so, satisfied that the old motor would indeed make its destination.

Isobel waited, wondering how to defer his assistance and then took a step forward before dismissing him with a simple, '*Merci, Monsieur.*'

The man didn't move, but instead eyed her with something verging on lust, his white-tinged tongue flitting briefly across cracked lips as he appraised Isobel's trim figure. His gaze moved to the rear window of her vehicle where a myriad of multi-coloured suitcases filled the back seat. An untidy eyebrow lifted questioningly. Of course, it was money he wanted she suddenly realised, glancing at her open handbag with its contents brimming for all to see. Could it really be that simple?

Isobel Gilyard stood her ground, trying to remember if there was anything in the Beetle that she could use to defend herself, but apart from a pair of flip-flops and a can of warm Cola, she could think of nothing. She conceded that her best bet was to run towards the busy road and wave down a passing car should the stranger come any closer. Thankfully, the moment of panic passed as hastily as it had appeared, and the Citroën driver shrugged his shoulders in mock defeat.

'*Au revoir, Mademoiselle.*'

Isobel could hear her heart pounding in her ears and relief washed swiftly over her as the man turned away, spitting on the ground as he went. She watched him slowly slide back into the driver's seat of his unwashed van. He turned the key and she kept her eyes fixed upon him until the back of the vehicle disappeared into southbound traffic, its orange indicator fading out of sight as the Frenchman sped away.

'Jeez,' Isobel whispered under her breath, stamping out the cigarette with the toe of her sensible loafer, 'he made my skin crawl.'

Realising that her own armpits were now drenched in perspiration, Isobel reached through the rear door and pulled a clean t-shirt from one of the cases. Traffic was still passing at a steady pace, so she hunkered down in the footwell of the passenger's side to avoid being seen and rapidly changed, rolling up her dirty denim shirt and pushing it into the glove-box. A quick spray of deodorant later and she felt fresher and ready to leave.

'Right, come on, old girl,' she told the VW, slamming the boot shut and starting up the old banger. 'Let's do this.'

The remainder of the trip was uneventful but incredibly scenic. The little car skirted the surrounds of Bordeaux town, heading through idyllic countryside towards the smaller community of Saint Margaux. By 4 pm, Isobel could glimpse the sandstone walls of the monastery and knew that her journey would soon come to an end. Two more miles and she would reach the pretty French town that would serve as her new home.

Maurice Fabron gave a start as the pale blue Volkswagen backfired outside his traditional boulangerie. The baker smiled, pleased to see that his new employee had arrived safely and in good time, despite her very rusty and ageing mode of transport. He had been on tenterhooks all afternoon waiting for this moment. Now, as a mop of blonde hair emerged from the driver's side, Maurice called out to his watching customers.

'Here she is, my new baker. You will see, she is amazing.'

Three faces peered out of the shop doorway, eager to catch their first glimpse of the Englishwoman who had been able to stir such excitable emotions in Maurice Fabron. The baker was already on his feet, however, before the customers could utter a word in response.

'Isobel!' he called cheerily, discarding a white floury apron and rushing outside. '*Bonjour.*'

'*Bonjour*, Monsieur Fabron,' she replied, kissing the man on both cheeks in traditional French fashion before stretching her arms animatedly.

'Is a good journey, *oui*?' Maurice enquired, ushering Isobel in through the wide double doors. 'May is such pleasant weather to travel.'

Isobel nodded, taking in her new surroundings as the baker pulled out a chair close to the window. Three perfectly coiffed women sat drinking tea at a nearby table and they immediately tilted their heads in unison as they stared inquisitively at the newcomer. Isobel raised her hand in a friendly gesture and then turned her attention back to her new employer. The women resumed their tea-drinking, whispering amongst themselves as they finished their cream pastries.

'Some tea?' Maurice was asking, putting a hand on Isobel's arm. 'And something to eat? How about a chocolate éclair? '

She glanced at the glass cabinet display of pastries behind her, now almost empty as the day came to a close, but resisted temptation. 'Just a black coffee please, Monsieur Fabron.'

'Hey, hey, if we are to be working together, I insist that you call me Maurice,' the baker grinned.

'Then you should call me Izzy.'

Maurice nodded enthusiastically before turning to call through a half-open door, 'Telo, Telo, *deux grands cafés noirs.*'

Izzy sat watching as a very handsome but sullen-faced young man appeared from the back room, his eyes mere slits as he guarded his vision from the bright sunlight reflecting through the bakery window. It took just three or four seconds to feel the man's hostility towards her, wrapping around her like an invisible shroud, but she forced a greeting and pasted a smile on her lips. Telo Fabron was the spitting image of his father.

There was a shuffling of chairs as the three onlookers craned their necks to get a clear impression of the scene unfolding before them, unperturbed by their brazen inquisitiveness. Isobel wondered if all the residents in Saint Margaux were so forthright.

'Telo, Izzy,' Maurice introduced, waving his hands between the pair before lowering his voice. 'Telo is my son, Izzy. He is a little, how to say, simple? But I'm sure you'll get along. He's a good boy.'

Isobel was slightly taken aback. Monsieur Fabron's wording was peculiar, as Telo appeared to be at least twenty years of age. At her one and only visit here some weeks previously, the baker hadn't mentioned that he had a son, let alone that Telo was working here. She remembered Maurice saying that his wife had passed away, hence the need for assistance with the baking, a role that Izzy felt she could fulfil more than adequately, but she supposed there had been no reason for her new employer to explain about his son to a virtual stranger.

The sound of Telo clattering cups and saucers brought Izzy back into the moment, realising that the baker was bombarding her with questions.

'Would you like Telo to take your luggage up to the apartment? Shall I ask him to park your car at the rear?'

Isobel reached into her jeans pocket and swiftly pulled out the set of keys, nodding eagerly. 'That would be great, I'm absolutely exhausted.'

In a flurry of French, Maurice instructed his son on how to assist, his dark eyes shining excitedly as he took the keys from Izzy's outstretched hand. He then took a small brass key from a hook near the door, which Isobel presumed would be to unlock the apartment upstairs.

Telo pushed two steaming cups of coffee across the table and took the VW keys and smaller Yale key from his father's nimble fingers, glancing down at Isobel's furry pompom keyring but avoiding the Englishwoman's gaze completely. There was something innocent about the young man, but it was tinged with anger, too, if she wasn't mistaken.

'So, welcome to Saint Margaux,' the baker announced proudly, as much for the benefit of his curious customers as for Isobel's, and then raised his white china cup to clink gently against hers.

'*Merci*,' Izzy giggled, already starting to feel relaxed in her new surroundings. 'I think I'm going to be very happy here.'

Outside, Telo had started up the Beetle. As the gears crunched under his unfamiliar touch, Isobel was once again reminded of the unsavoury character that she'd met at the roadside earlier that afternoon and gave an involuntary shudder.

'You are cold?' Maurice asked. 'I can shut the door.'

Isobel shook her head, but the motion went unnoticed as, at the same moment, the trio of ladies had chosen to leave. Amidst great ceremony, the baker took the proffered Euros and ushered the women out into the late afternoon sun, relishing the opportunity to explain how Izzy would now be here to provide exquisite English bakes and wonderful occasion cakes, should they find themselves requiring sweets for special events.

One of the three looked back to where Isobel was finishing her coffee and frowned, an expression that, in itself, relayed the woman's doubts as to the capability of Maurice's new employee. Isobel Gilyard was oblivious to the watchful eyes upon her, being preoccupied instead with the fuzzy sensation of new beginnings that was settling upon her, and sat back in her seat with a grateful sigh, as the heady aroma of fresh coffee permeated her senses.

Coming back inside and preparing to close up for the day, Maurice Fabron smiled at Izzy, who had her head thrown back in the chair, studying the ancient plasterwork that decorated the boulangerie ceiling. Light reflected off the watercolour cherubs, reminding her of a trip to Rome that she'd taken with the school many years before.

'Those are three of our regular customers,' the baker explained jovially, stepping behind the counter. 'The little blonde lady is Cecile Vidal, she owns the local vineyard. Dominique Fabre runs the gift shop, she's the one with reddish-coloured hair and has a passion for fresh cream cakes, and the woman with short black hair is Simone Dupuis. Simone has the flower shop next door. I'll introduce you properly next time, as now it's time to shut our doors, and the ladies are on their way home.'

'No doubt I'll get their names completely mixed up,' Izzy confessed, trying to get the women's descriptions straight in her mind. 'They're all so… chic.'

Maurice laughed and shrugged his shoulders as if it were natural that every French woman looked like a Vogue model.

'Tonight, you should rest well,' he commented, 'and tomorrow explore the village. If you need anything at all, let me know, I am just across the street.'

Pointing to a rather grand 'Maison du Maitre' with pristine blue shutters and window-boxes brimming with delicate blooms, Maurice indicated his home's close proximity to the boulangerie. It struck Isobel that Monsieur Fabron would be quite a catch, should someone happen to be looking for love.

She straightened up and yawned, running a hand through her unruly hair. 'I will, Maurice, thank you.'

Each studied the other briefly. Isobel was a woman in her mid-thirties, short, slender and pale with cropped bleach-blonde hair like a schoolboy, while Maurice was ten years her senior, tall, handsome and tanned, slightly greying at the temples. Both were attractive in their respective ways, while not being each other's typical 'type', per se. However, if any untoward thoughts had crossed either of their minds at that point, they were abruptly cut short by the arrival of a rather portly flustered gent wearing a dark blue uniform.

'Ah, Maurice,' he panted, '*Vous avez des croissants?*'

'Jean, *bonjour*,' the baker chuckled, '*Oui. C'est tout?*'

The men chattered in French for a few minutes whilst Maurice wrapped the last of the day's croissants in paper, adding a complimentary pain au chocolat for good measure. Shortly afterwards, the animated character left, giving Maurice's new assistant just a slight nod before bustling down the street as fast as his short legs would carry him, leaving Izzy to look on in bewilderment.

'That was Jean,' Maurice explained, 'he works at the local railway station. He's a funny man. Instead of coming first thing in the morning when the croissants are fresh from the oven, he comes after work, preferring to eat them with supper!'

'Does he come in every afternoon?' Izzy asked, amused at the comical interruption.

'Oh yes,' Maurice countered, 'Although he'll be going on holiday to Switzerland soon. No doubt croissant sales will fall rapidly while he's away.'

The baker pulled a face, pretending to pout at the thought of lost business.

Isobel stifled a giggle, trying to be polite, but Maurice had already started chuckling and before long the pair were in fits of laughter as they watched poor Jean hurry home with his cold pastries.

'I think working here is going to be fun,' Isobel commented, helping the baker to lock up for the night. 'Thank you for having faith in me, Maurice.'

That evening, feasting hungrily upon freshly baked bread, soft melted Camembert cheese and delicate slithers of ham, Izzy reflected upon her decision to move to France. This was probably the most life-changing point of her thirty-five years, but she truly believed that you had to grasp opportunity with both hands if you wanted to make a successful path.

'Why France?' her younger and more sensible sister, Vivien, had pressed. 'Your French isn't even up to scratch, and you're not a qualified baker.'

Isobel had flinched at the harsh words, feeling the insult as sharply as if it had been a slap across the face. Still, she had risen above her sibling's jealousy, for that's what it was, and had continued with her plans to relocate.

'It's a fresh start,' she'd replied smugly, continuing to fold bright dresses and pastel-coloured cardigans into a large suitcase as Vivien looked on, 'a brand new adventure and I might not even come back!'

Her parents had been no more encouraging, their lack of enthusiasm grating on Izzy's nerves like nails scraping a chalkboard.

'So where will you be?' her mother had fussed at the last minute, realising that to argue with Isobel would be futile. 'You haven't given us your new address or phone number. What if there's an emergency? Suppose your dad was taken ill, God forbid. Izzy, please, we're just worried about you.'

'I'll let you know once I'm settled,' she'd said flippantly, secretly having no intention at all to stay in touch with any of them. 'I'll write.'

Isobel Gilyard had driven away with the determination to succeed, telling herself that it was quite ironic how those closest to her were now showing their concern for her well-being. It hadn't always been that way. Vivien had been deemed the brighter of the two, completing her exams without stress, never causing so much as a stir as they battled teenage hormones and conflicting interests.

'Why can't you be more like our Viv?' their father had raged, after another of Izzy's outbursts. 'You could do well to take a leaf out of her book.'

At the time, it had seemed faintly amusing. Isobel Gilyard had no intention of being like her sister, then or now. Vivien had a sensible job, the same stagnant position in the local bank that she'd joined on leaving school, and a sensible husband who earned just enough as a salesman to drive a middle of the range car. They lived in a nondescript house with magnolia-coloured walls, on an estate where net curtains twitched but nothing notable ever occurred. The couple's one, very diligent and polite, child was doted on by her grandparents and life for Viv was altogether very agreeable.

Isobel poured another glass of local Chenin Blanc as she chuckled to herself. The thought of her sister, in her tidy box of a lifestyle, could bring not one iota of envy. She wouldn't trade places with Viv if her life depended upon it. Admittedly, the past decade would have been simpler had she been in her sister's shoes, but it also would have been uneventful and stifling. She wondered what Viv was up to right at that moment; no doubt she was spending her Saturday night catching up on the latest episodes of her favourite soap while dutifully ironing her husband's shirts. She imagined Vivien's husband sprawled across the sofa, snoring his head off after an afternoon of football and beer.

Izzy raised a glass to Vivien and her family. 'Here's to not being like you,' she laughed. 'Poor sad, ridiculous, unaccomplished Viv!'

Having finished her supper and settled in a comfortable armchair by the open window, Izzy appraised the village below, where neat wooden benches framed a central square. A few residents walked the main street with their dogs, stopping to chat as they passed one another, a sure sign that Saint Margaux was a warm and friendly community. In the distance she could see the bell-tower of the local church, grey and ominous against the early evening blue sky. The scent of wild flowers, freshly cut grass and food cooking wafted upwards, allowing Isobel to breathe in Saint Margaux one lungful at a time. She took out her lighter and lit an after-dinner cigarette, placing it between her lips in the manner of a seasoned Hollywood actress. On the opposite side of the street, a light burned brightly on the upper floor of Maurice Fabron's house and Isobel strained her eyes out of curiosity to see who occupied the room.

Telo Fabron sat hunched at a desk, a long slender finger following the written words in his battered French copy of *Lord of the Flies*. Behind him, the young man's father nodded approvingly as he listened to his son read aloud with the concentration of a professional orator, hanging on Telo's every word.

The bedroom was neat, not a single item out of place, just as the sole occupant liked it, and needed it to be. Tidiness and the obsession with everything having its own unique place was an essential element of daily life for Telo Fabron. If so much as a pencil were out of place on his writing bureau, the young man would know. Hence, nobody was allowed in here, except for his beloved father, as Maurice understood how things had to be for his son. He instinctively knew the triggers that caused anxiety in Telo, the need to be in control and the love that the boy was capable of should he choose to allow you into his world.

'*Tres bien*,' Maurice said finally, patting his son on the shoulder. '*Lait froid?*'

Telo nodded as the baker padded back downstairs to get him the glass of cold milk that he ritually drank before bed.

'Papa,' he ventured on his father's return, '*je n'aime pas* Isobel.' I don't like Isobel. The words were as innocent, yet damning, as could be.

Monsieur Fabron sighed, easing himself down onto the single divan as the youngster returned his book to the antique oak shelf. The baker had felt this moment looming for the past few hours but had hoped that his son's instinctive dislike of the Englishwoman would have dissipated by now. Maurice collected his thoughts, carefully choosing words, before explaining to Telo that Izzy would be staying because he needed her help.

'*Mais bien sûr.*' But of course, the young man conceded begrudgingly, acknowledging for the umpteenth time that his own skills didn't stretch to baking, before sipping at the cold milk like a sulking child. He wished, as he did every night before turning in, that his mother was still here. She would take her son's side, soothe his worries, tell the stranger to go away. It didn't occur to Telo that if his mother had still been alive, Isobel would not have come.

Maurice Fabron kissed his son's head, ruffling the soft dark hair with the tips of his fingers, and left him alone with mixed feelings. He sincerely hoped that Isobel Gilyard would prove herself to be a fine employee, but Telo rarely took a dislike to someone so instantly, which certainly caused concern. It was usually his son's excellent judgement of character that kept the baker alert to any insincere newcomers. Maybe, when Monday arrived, the baker mused,

Telo's negativity would be forgotten. Isobel might even win him around with one of her special bakes.

Upstairs, Telo carefully placed the empty glass on his bedside table, a rim of milk clinging to the sides, and sauntered over to close the shutters. He counted to ten, as he always did, before reaching out to pull at the slats. Directly across the street, he could see the stranger sitting at the window, looking straight into his room, his private space. The young man eased the wooden slats to with a bang, intending to send a message to those prying foreign eyes.

Go home, Isobel, Telo chanted over and over in his head, *you don't belong here*.

Isobel watched as Monsieur Fabron's son shut himself away for the night and then reached for the last of the white wine. 'I might as well finish it,' she told herself. 'No work tomorrow, just a lazy Sunday to explore my new surroundings.'

Still, despite her relaxed mood and slightly intoxicated train of thought, Izzy felt unnerved by the way in which the baker's son had glared at her that afternoon, and now, too, she was certain that there was a certain spitefulness in the violent way that Telo had closed those heavy shutters.

Her thoughts returned inexplicably to the Frenchman in the Citroën van, his uncouth manner and roving eye somehow in unison with Telo Fabron's hostility. Perhaps she was becoming too sensitive as she hurtled towards forty, she told herself; a prerequisite to menopausal angst, no doubt. No, Telo was just a bit slow, Maurice had explained that himself, therefore she must allow them both a while to become properly acquainted. Time will conquer all, Isobel smiled, and time is something that I have in abundance.

Before retiring to bed, Isobel reached to the back of the closet and felt for the battered shoebox that had become a fixed part of her material world. Rubbing her hand across the sagging cardboard, she felt the familiar ridges, knowing them better than any line on her own face. She didn't need to take out the contents, nor lift the flimsy lid, but simply yearned for the reassurance that it was still there, where she'd left it earlier. The box, containing everything that Izzy needed to recollect her past life, had travelled here wedged under the driver's seat of her beloved Volkswagen, away from prying eyes, safe from those who had no right to enquire as to its contents.

CHAPTER TWO – A SECOND STRANGER

Inspector Maxime Mallery swung from left to right in his office chair, causing the underside of the seat to squeak, his feet up on the desk in a relaxed posture, as if to test its durability. The police officer paused for a second to inspect a miniscule blob of fluff on the tip of his brown Oxford brogues and then, satisfied that it was merely dust from the unkempt office, resumed his monotonous motion. Seconds later, a manicured finger hovered over Max's mobile phone, sorely tempted to redial the number that had called him three times this morning already. Best not, he admitted to himself, not yet.

Having moved to Bordeaux the previous month, Mallery was already bored with the lack of excitement. Save for a few overdue parking fines, some teenage graffiti and a missing cat, the extent of his caseload was nothing compared to that of his former position in Paris where serious crime was on the rise daily. It wasn't as though he'd had any choice in the matter; if he were honest, it was all self-inflicted, but he wouldn't have changed the circumstances leading up to his relocation for the world.

Mallery peered gloomily into the empty mug on his desk and then landed both feet on the floor with a thud, intending to refill the receptacle with a beverage from his state-of-the-art coffee machine. Hovering between vanilla latte and macchiato pods, he was interrupted by a knock, followed by a slight cough in the doorway.

'Excuse me, sir,' the young female *policier* smiled, her French polite and well enunciated,'there's an Englishman here to see you.'

A dim light went on inside Mallery's head as he probed his brain to recall why there might be a foreigner asking for his attention. The recollection flickered, turned warm and then pressed an alarm bell in his memory.

'*Oui, un moment,*' the Inspector nodded, appraising the woman's shapely legs and tightly fitted pencil skirt as she retreated. '*Merci.*'

Abandoning the coffee, Max Mallery turned to the pile of papers on his desk, rifling through them impatiently before pulling out a memo from the Commissioner.

'*Merde*!' he cursed, scanning the document with fervent eyes, the memo had lain forgotten for almost two weeks. He remembered pushing it to the bottom of the 'In' tray in the hope that it would mysteriously disappear. It clearly hadn't.

The contents left no room for doubt as to the message. Inspector Mallery was to be given a new recruit on his team, one with a reputation for using his initiative and being a real team player. On the surface, the new addition seemed ideal – that was, until you took into consideration that he was from Yorkshire in England. At first Max had thought it a joke, that the Commissioner was testing his resolve after relocating Max to what he deemed to be the back of beyond. But, on delving further into the matter with a few heated phone calls and an internal profile search, it seemed that the request was legitimate, due to the Englishman's move abroad with his French wife.

Mallery rolled the memo into a ball and then tossed the paper expertly into the waste bin. He shrugged on a navy blazer, checking his appearance in the reflection of the glass-panelled door, always the epitome of professionalism where work matters were concerned. Satisfied that his pale pink shirt was without creases and not a hair on his head sat out of place, Max strode out of the office, stopping only to polish the brass nameplate on the outside of the door with the sleeve of his jacket.

In the ground floor lobby of the *Poste de Police*, dressed in a black suit and white shirt, sat a ginger-haired man in his early thirties. Jack Hobbs was well aware of the fact that he was twenty minutes late arriving at the police station but hoped that his explanation of a newly born baby in the household would tug at the Inspector's heart strings. As it was, he didn't have to wait long to find out.

'*Bonjour*. Inspector Maxime Mallery,' Max introduced himself as soon as his feet touched the bottom step, before pushing back a cuff to look at his watch. 'You are Jacques?'

'Hi, erm, yes, well, Jack actually, Hobbs. Sorry I'm late, sir, new baby.'

Max nodded, angling his head towards the upstairs offices. 'Okay, this way.'

Lifting a small rucksack onto his left shoulder, Jack followed the Inspector up two flights of stairs and then to the end of a long corridor with high ceilings and parquet wooden flooring. He noted the other man's smart yet casual appearance and chided himself on having turned up looking like a funeral attendee.

The Inspector ushered him inside the office and then kicked the door closed.

'So,' the slightly elder of the two enquired, 'What brings you to Bordeaux.'

Jack looked the Frenchman in the eye and said openly, 'My wife is French, and her father is a Judicial Police Officer in Toulouse. He, erm, pulled a few strings to help my transfer from Leeds Crime Squad.'

'Pulled a few strings,' Max repeated, pressing the tips of his fingers together to form a steeple. 'Like a puppet.'

Jack Hobbs was confused. Was the Inspector intending to make a joke or to mimic him? He wasn't sure of the vibes coming across the expansive desk.

No sooner had Inspector Mallery appraised his new recruit from head to toe than he was heading for the coffee machine again.

'Cappuccino? Espresso? Americano?' he offered, holding back from offering the Englishman his own personal favourites.

'A cappuccino would be great, thanks.' Jack grinned, his cheeks flushing pink.

Mallery breathed out slowly and inserted the capsules into his prized possession, allowing questions to silently form in his astute mind as he studied the freckled young man sitting before him.

'So, tell me,' Max began, pushing a plate of plain biscuits across the desk, which the newcomer started devouring hungrily, *parlez-vous Français*?'

Hobbs nodded but replied in English nevertheless. 'A little and Angélique, my wife, is teaching me new words every day.'

'So, I suppose you're incapable of writing a report in French, or requisitioning support from other divisions, or even reading a criminal their rights?'

Jack blushed, pulling at the collar of his shirt as he became flustered under the scrutiny of the very suave senior officer.

'I'm a fast learner,' he countered, 'and my track record back in Leeds was exemplary. I've got a letter of recommendation from my commanding officer.'

'Very well, may I see?'

Unzipping the rucksack and taking out a white envelope with sticky brown edges, Jack frantically rubbed to erase the offending marks. However, before he could do so completely, Mallery had lifted the letter from his fingers and slid a paperknife under its sealed edge, wrinkling his nose as he did so.

'Treacle?' he asked, lifting an eyebrow.

'No, sir, it's Marmite. Must have come from my sandwiches, they're in the bottom of…'

The Inspector held up a hand as he started to read the reference, impressed with its contents, but not so much with the manner in which they had been delivered.

'It seems Commissioner Chirac has left me no choice but to welcome you to the team,' Mallery sighed, after an uncomfortable silence in which he mulled over the dilemma in his mind, 'although I presume that this is a temporary measure until a more suitable position can be found for you elsewhere. As a detective used to investigating murders, drugs and suchlike, you will no doubt find Bordeaux a terribly boring place to work.'

'I'm happy to help out in whatever way I can, Inspector Mallery. Just being here in France is change enough for now.'

'In that case, welcome.' Max shrugged.

'Yes, thank you, sir,' Hobbs replied, his gaze still lingering on the dishevelled looking envelope. 'I won't let you down, Inspector Mallery.'

'And Hobbs,' he added, shaking his head at the few crumbs that remained on the china plate, 'tomorrow, be sure to eat breakfast before you start work.'

Jack reddened again, feeling like a child under reprimand. 'Yes, sir, I will.'

For the remainder of the morning, Jack Hobbs sat at an allocated desk two doors down from his new boss. He shared the room with the rest of the team and had enjoyed a pleasant welcome in response to Mallery's introductions.

'Luc takes care of IT, CCTV, and other technology-related matters,' the Inspector had explained, 'while Gabriella and Thierry are what I like to term as my foot soldiers. They go out on the streets of Bordeaux and keep their eyes and ears to the ground.'

Hobbs nodded, greeting everyone in turn and desperately trying to memorise names and roles.

'Our current caseload includes three unpaid fines, some rather artistic but anonymous graffiti in the rear courtyard of the tobacco shop, and the case of poor missing eight-year-old Claude.'

'A missing child?' Jack questioned, perking up at the idea of some proper investigative work.

'*Non*,' giggled Gabriella, tossing her sleek ponytail over one shoulder, 'Claude is a black and white male cat.'

Jack's shoulders sagged. Perhaps this wasn't going to be the opportunity of a lifetime after all.

'I don't understand,' he ventured. 'Why are the police getting involved in the search for a cat?'

Thierry clapped Hobbs on the back and whispered in his ear, 'It's the beloved station cat.'

'I see...'

Mallery turned a stern eye on the newcomer and pointed at Luc. 'I'm sure Luc would appreciate your help in the search, *oui*?'

At this point, Max Mallery returned to his office, perplexed at what else he could possibly find for Jack to do. Although, he reminded himself, Bordeaux was a large town and there would surely be some hint of criminal activity at some point, whether the young man would be there long enough to assist was another matter entirely. It was virtually unheard of, an Englishman working with the French police, and one with hardly any local language at that!

Max lifted the Englishman's file from the bottom drawer, where he'd absentmindedly pushed it as soon as the folder had arrived on his desk. Hobbs hadn't been overly smug about his track record, it was all there in black and white, making interesting reading. Three years as a Constable in Leeds City Centre before being promoted to Sergeant, and then another three years before the final transfer to Detective. In the following few years, Hobbs had been involved in no less than six murders, three armed-robbery cases and a drugs racket, all of which he'd come out of with glowing reports from his seniors.

'So, Jacques,' Mallery muttered, lighting a cigarette, 'I'm afraid you are going to find our quiet French town very dull indeed.'

By noon, Jack Hobbs had procured some stationery from the well-stocked cupboard and arranged everything in his desk drawers. He had then spent the next couple of hours helping Luc to search CCTV footage in the hope that the errant Claude would be spotted on his feline travels. They were just scrolling through black and white images of nearby alleyways when Mallery returned.

'Jacques,' he announced, hands on hips in a decidedly animated manner, purposely putting emphasis on the French version of his new employee's name, '*Le dejeuner*. Lunch.'

'Oh, I'm alright thank you, sir, I've brought my own…'

'Not *your* lunch,' Max interrupted, obvious distaste at the thought of Hobbs' Marmite sandwiches written across his face. 'Could you go to the boulangerie and get some for us?'

'Yes, sure,' Jack agreed, jumping out of his seat. 'Where's the nearest bakery?'

'In the next street,' Gabrielle interjected helpfully. 'I'll come with you.'

'Thanks, that'd be great.'

Max dug deep into the pocket of his designer jeans and pulled out a crumpled twenty Euro note. 'Today, it's on me. Treat yourself, too, I'm sure the local baguettes are much more tasty than what you brought with you.'

Having quickly asked for everyone's order, Jack followed his team mate downstairs and on to the bustling Bordeaux street.

'Does he mellow after a while?' Hobbs asked tentatively, glancing at the woman at his side. He guessed she was in her late twenties but daren't ask.

'Mellow? Sorry, I don't understand…'

'You know, does Mallery chill out, relax a bit,' Jack prompted.

'Ah, *détendre*.' Gabrielle smiled, showing perfect white teeth. 'To be honest, I don't know. Inspector Mallery, Max, has only been here about a month, so we haven't really become, how to say, erm… familiar with him yet.'

Jack was surprised. He'd got the impression that Mallery had his feet well and truly under the table, something which usually came with time.

'Do you mind me asking where he was before?'

Gabrielle opened her hands, palms up. 'In Paris, but why he would want to give up the excitement of the capital city for here, I have no idea.'

Jack Hobbs stored the information in his brain for later. It might, or might not, be relevant that Mallery was also new to the area, but it seemed rather a big coincidence all the same.

'The boulangerie is here,' his colleague nudged. 'Hurry up.'

Later that afternoon, Luc tapped on Mallery's office door with a purring cat in his arms.

'*Inspecteur*,' he said, grinned broadly, '*Claude est ici.*'

Max was on his feet in seconds. He'd taken rather a shine to the fat furry creature on the first week of his arrival and was glad that at least one mystery was solved.

'*Très bien*,' the officer smiled, stroking the cat's head before turning to his team member. 'Excellent, Luc.'

It took a few minutes for the lanky techie to explain that it had actually been Jack Hobbs that had located and brought Claude in, causing Mallery to stride down the corridor to offer his congratulations.

'It seems you've made a great start at cracking our most difficult case to date,' Max joked, slapping Jack on the shoulder. 'Put on your jacket, we're going out.'

Nudges and winks behind him raised suspicion that perhaps the newcomer was to be reprimanded for his early success. Perhaps Mallery thought he needed taking down a peg or two.

Bewildered, Hobbs did as instructed, struggling with the sleeves of his jacket until Thierry offered a helping hand, and then followed his boss out to a bright red sports-style BMW.

'Wow, nice motor,' Jack commented. 'Where are we going Sir?'

Revving the engine before releasing the brake, Mallery checked the mirror and pulled into the street. 'A short drive,' he explained, 'to show you the area of our jurisdiction. There are some truly beautiful villages in this area, and I haven't even seen them all myself yet. So, this afternoon, we will do what you English call "see the sights".'

'Sight-seeing,' Jack corrected, wishing immediately that he'd kept quiet. 'Sorry, sir, just a habit.'

'Mm,' Mallery grunted, indicating into the fast lane. 'Enjoy the ride.'

Passing sleepy hamlets and fields of wheat, barley and wild flowers, the car turned down a side road and Max pulled into a farm gateway. Tall cypress trees stood either side of furrowed tracks, marking the territory of the local landowner. From the entrance, the men could see for miles across lush green countryside, smelling the gentle aroma of fruit and flowers. Gesturing to Jack to join him, the Inspector got out and went to stand at the gate, immediately lighting up a cigarette.

'*Fumer?*' he asked, offering the pack to his colleague.

Hobbs shook his head. 'Erm, no, I've given up, because of the baby.'

Mallery tossed his head back, blowing smoke out of his nose. 'Ah well. I suppose it is a good thing with a little one in the home. Congratulations, Jacques. Now, if you look across there, a little to the right, you can just see a church tower rising up out of the valley, yes?'

Max spread his arm wide, indicating the dip in the rolling countryside as it curved slightly. A grey stack could be seen in the distance, with a sandy-coloured larger building shadowing it slightly from afar.

Jack strained his eyes and nodded.

'That, my friend, is the beautiful village of Saint Margaux. Beyond, you can see a majestic monastery. Then, if we turn to the left, we can see the vineyards where they make the best wine in all of France. A little further to the south are Riberon and Salbec, both also quiet and beautiful. You like French wine, *oui*?'

Jack blushed, scratching the back of his head nervously. 'I'm more of a beer drinker to be honest with you, sir.'

'Ah, so do you like our Stella Artois?'

'To tell the truth, I'm more of a Boddington's man,' he confessed.

The Inspector frowned, having no clue as to what the other man was talking about but also lacking the inclination to follow up that particular line of questioning.

Hobbs breathed in the fresh country air, glad to be out of the office and discovering new places. He wondered whether Angélique knew these villages and if they might explore them together on his next day off. Glancing at the man next to him, Jack could see that Mallery was more relaxed out here, too. There was something about being at one with nature that brought out the best in people. He'd loved walking the Yorkshire Dales and exploring the Lake District with his parents as a youngster. It was a pity that Angélique couldn't see the benefits of having such areas of natural outstanding beauty on their doorstep, but he understood her need to come back home, too. If their roles had been reversed, Jack would have wanted to be close to his family as well.

There was a loud buzz, followed by the ringtone of a popular Abba song, as Max snatched the mobile phone out of his blazer pocket. Without a word, he stepped a few yards down the lane, looking furtively behind him, and answered the call.

'*Oui, ma chérie,*' he murmured, only just audible to an inquisitive Jack Hobbs, who recognised the endearment immediately. He bent down, pretending to busy himself with an undone shoelace as Mallery continued his conversation.

'*Avec qui?*' Max was asking, before listening long and hard. Seconds later, the call was finished and he returned to the car looking much more flustered than before.

'Your wife, sir?' Jack ventured, his natural cheeky charm now coming to the fore. 'Needs you to pick up some wine for dinner by any chance?'

'I am not married,' Max replied curtly. 'Anyway, Jacques, we've seen enough for today, I think it's time we got back.'

'Sorry, sir, I didn't mean to pry,' Hobbs explained, as soon as the car was back on the main highway to Bordeaux, weaving its way through slower vehicles. 'I just presumed that you were married.'

'It's fine, you did not know. Anyway, for the record, Jacques, I am very, very happily single.'

Jack sniffed at the use of the French pronunciation of his name. Mallery had done that several times already and it was only Hobbs' first day on the team. He wanted to know more about his boss, no matter how temporary the arrangement was to be.

'So why the move from Paris?' he asked casually, trying to steer the subject onto neutral ground. 'Seems we're both new to the area.'

'Ah, you've been asking questions,' Mallery answered, tightening his grip on the steering-wheel, eyes fixed on the road ahead. 'A typical English detective.'

'No. Actually, Gabriella just happened to say that you hadn't been here long. Sorry if I spoke out of turn.'

'No matter.' Max sighed, rubbing at his temple with a free hand. 'Yes, I'm new here too, needed a, erm, what do you call it, change of view?'

'Change of scenery, sir.'

'How about you?' Mallery questioned. 'Was it your wife's idea to move here?'

'Yes. Angélique wanted to be closer to her family now that we've got our son. Seemed to make sense, really. Happy wife, happy home and all that.'

'Of course,' Max nodded. 'Family is very important to French people.'

Jack Hobbs had to agree. Besides, his homesick wife had hated living in Leeds.

Back in his office, Max Mallery closed the door and pressed the button revealing the last caller on his phone. He redialled, imagining the tempestuous woman on the other end smiling as his name lit up on the device's screen. He waited patiently, eager to continue the conversation that he'd ended abruptly only an hour before. Vanessa had said she was going away for a while, to visit friends in Belgium. As far as Max could recall, she'd never mentioned knowing anyone in that part of Europe. When the ringing stopped and it went to answer-phone, he pulled the swivel chair up to the desk and typed in a password.

Scanning for new messages, Mallery sat upright, his finger hovering over the mouse, partly afraid to open the email but wildly curious, too.

Subject: Vanessa, he read, suddenly feeling parched and sweaty.

Mallery clicked on the contents and read the single line on his screen. It was from the Commissioner, informing Max that his wife would no longer be available for communication.

Reading the line over and over, the Inspector sat as still as a marble statue, although the cogs in his mind were still churning with panicked thoughts.

What has he done? Where is Vanessa?

A dark cloud gathered outside the open window, reflecting Max's dark thoughts. He didn't think that the Commissioner was capable of harming his wife, but this was a proud man afraid of his spouse's indiscretion becoming public knowledge. Who knew what lengths a spurned husband would go to? Especially one with money and power at his fingertips.

Mallery automatically picked up his phone and tried the familiar number again, feeling his palms become sticky under the vibration.

The woman's voice was hurried, raspy as though out of breath, scared of being discovered. Yes, she explained, she was fine, but her husband was threatening to ruin Max's career if he contacted her again. This was it, she insisted, they must never speak again for both their sakes.

'Wait,' he wanted to say, realising that what had started as fun was now, for him, something much more serious, but it was too late.

The line was dead.

Max dropped the phone onto the desk, his stomach churning, head thumping.

So here he was, stuck in Bordeaux with his talent for detection slipping quickly down the *toilettes* and to add to the insult, it appeared that Vanessa was not going to keep her promise of warming his bed every other weekend after all. He understood, quite clearly as it happened, that the socialite and role model mother didn't want to lose the benefits of having such a lucrative marriage. If she carried on seeing Max, who, then, would provide the expensive beauty treatments and designer clothes, not to mention the trips to New York and Milan?

They'd successfully hidden their secret lunch dates, overnight stays when the Commissioner had been out of the city on business, and lover's trysts at every opportunity. But now, things were different. Real-life had dealt Mallery a blow and he had no choice but to take it, no matter the consequences.

If only he could turn back the clock, pick another woman, a different wife with whom to conduct an illicit affair. It had been so much fun, wining and dining the wife of the most senior law man in the whole of Paris. He couldn't even pinpoint the fatal lapse that had caused the Commissioner to put a tracker on his wife, to try to catch the man with whom she had become obsessed. It could have happened any time within the past six months. And now what? Stuck in this godforsaken town with less action than a senior citizen's Christmas party and, to make matters worse, he now had to babysit an Englishman into the bargain!

Merde!

CHAPTER THREE – A DINNER INVITATION

As morning sunlight probed through Isobel Gilyard's flimsy cotton curtains the next day, a lone figure sat below the window, hunched over and on a reluctant mission. Telo Fabron wrung his hands together, palms sweating, brows furrowed. His father had asked him to deliver a message to the Englishwoman – in person, he had specified – and now the youngster must wait until the idle stranger was awake.

As soon as Izzy pulled back the lilac drapes, she noticed the familiar young man sitting on a bench close to the boulangerie. She thought it strange and continued to look down. Suddenly, as if instinctively, like a fox sniffing out its prey, Telo was on his feet and gazing up at her with narrowed eyes and tightly buttoned lips. She waved, feigning a smile, but he simply reached into a shirt pocket and withdrew a note, which he then held aloft to show Isobel that it was intended for her.

Wrapped in a silk robe, Isobel padded down into the bakery, the red-tiled floor cold underneath her bare toes, and bent down to pick up the paper that had been pushed underneath the door.

DEAREST IZZY, the delicately looped handwriting read, *PLEASE JOIN US FOR DINNER TONIGHT, 6PM. MAURICE.*

Isobel smiled, grateful that she wouldn't have to seek out a restaurant for her Sunday night supper and took the invitation back up to her new apartment, grabbing a croissant from the covered remains of yesterday's bakes to sate her breakfast hunger.

The village was a great deal quieter than it had been the day before. Fewer people were out on the streets and the calm tranquillity of the place filled its new resident with a grateful satisfaction. The sounds flooding in through the apartment window, where Izzy now stood taking in the view whilst enjoying freshly brewed coffee, were merely natural. No buzz of cars, as would certainly have been the case back home in Manchester, no loud shouts of overexcited youths, not even a lawnmower to break the perfect peace.

Pulling a simple yellow sundress from the closet, Isobel showered and dressed, intending to explore her new surroundings on this most glorious first full day of her new start.

Having walked a few hundred metres out of the village, it soon became obvious where all the residents were hiding, as the dulcet tones of singing were now filling the air with a ghostly quality. The church in which the congregation had gathered was small and medieval, its ugly gargoyles out of place in such a rural idyll, mouths open in mock laughter as they guarded the turrets high above. The churchyard, too, was somewhat ancient in its setting, tombs green with lichen and moss, the inscriptions blurred with age. Izzy wondered if Maurice and Telo were attending the service. Perhaps she was the only one to be wandering the lanes whilst others gave thanks to God. Having never been particularly religious, Isobel didn't dwell on these thoughts, but continued her solitary stroll, eager to gain some insight into Saint Margaux and its environs.

Down the narrow lane, the opposite direction to the one which she had so carefully navigated the previous day, Izzy stood looking in awe at the tall monastery, its tiny windows giving the impression that the interior must be a very dark place, although perhaps that was indicative of the order of monks who resided there, she mused. Ancient sandstone walls loomed as the building perched upon a hillock, guarded from the outside world with an almost enchanted existence. Straining her ears, the Englishwoman could make out the faint tones of chanting and, in that moment, it seemed as though the whole of Saint Margaux were creating harmonious melodies without her.

Further, just a few minutes on, the road opened up slightly, widening towards a stone bridge. A slow-running stream trickled underneath, reminding the walker that she should perhaps have brought a bottle of water with her to quench her thirst along the way. She sat for a while, soaking up the sunshine and watching a rabbit scampering across the bank, until thirst prevailed, and Isobel retraced her steps back to the boulangerie.

Having passed the rest of the day unpacking suitcases and arranging books on shelves, Isobel Gilyard sat at the dressing-table and carefully applied pink lipstick. Her short, bleached hair had its limits, but a diamante clip added a feminine touch and Izzy appraised herself contentedly for a few moments before crossing the street to Résidence Fabron.

There was a loud echo throughout the white-washed house as the bell announced its guest's arrival, suggesting that the rooms were considerable and numerous, before footsteps could be heard coming down the hallway.

'Izzy, *bonsoir*.' Maurice grinned, kissing his guest earnestly on both cheeks, delighted to note that the young woman had made a special effort with her appearance that evening. 'You look wonderful. Please, please, come in.'

On crossing the threshold of the baker's home Isobel was taken aback by the opulent grandeur of the house. A wooden parquet floor showcased oil-paintings against brightly painted walls and a solid marble-topped table, dressed with a glass vase of fresh roses, ran along one side of the entranceway. It was the sight of the flowers that had the newcomer cursing her own negligence.

'Oh, Maurice,' she gasped, putting a hand to her mouth theatrically, 'I'm so sorry, I should have brought wine, or at least a little something…'

'Dear lady,' Maurice grinned, 'if you can find a shop open in Saint Margaux on a Sunday, then you are a… erm, a miracle worker.'

The baker's humour broke the ice and Izzy immediately relaxed, her shoulders visibly sagging as she followed the muscular figure through into a vast kitchen. Delicate smells permeated her nostrils as soon as they entered, a wonderful, heady concoction of herbs and fish wafting its way over from a large range stove.

'*Bonsoir*,' a woman chirped, sliding gently from a stool next to the kitchen island unit and putting out a hand. 'Lovely to see you, Isobel?'

Izzy recognised the perfectly presented lady as one of the women who had been at the boulangerie on her arrival.

'*Bonsoir*,' she smiled, shaking the delicate fingers. 'I'm sorry, but I don't think…'

'Simone, Simone Dupuis,' Maurice interjected. 'My fault, I should have introduced you both yesterday.'

'It's fine, Maurice,' Izzy smiled. 'Lovely to meet you, Simone.'

Furtive glances were exchanged between the two women as Maurice moved around the kitchen, pouring wine and expertly chopping herbs.

Isobel felt intimidated by the older woman, whom she presumed to be in her late forties, with her perfect dark bob and manicured red fingernails. Simone wore a pale blue dress which skimmed her slender hips in a flattering manner, the neckline revealing just enough cleavage to lure an admirer's eye. Isobel looked down at her own floral number and wished that she'd put on something newer and more refined.

'*Le poisson à la vapeur*,' Maurice explained, pointing to a long steel pan. 'You call it steamed fish, I think, Izzy.'

'Yes, that's right. It smells delicious,' Isobel enthused, leaning closer to breathe in the heady aroma. 'I'm looking forward to trying your cooking, Maurice.'

'Maurice is a most excellent chef,' Simone trilled, eyeing them both amusedly over the top of her glass as she gently sipped, 'but very modest.'

'We eat simply but healthily here, Izzy,' the baker explained, adding a handful of parsley to the pan, 'and I'm looking forward to trying your cooking, too.'

Simone looked at her watch and checked the time against the wall clock. 'I really should be going, I have such a lot to do.'

'Oh, aren't you staying for dinner?' Isobel asked, silently glad at the news that she might have the pleasure of Maurice's company alone tonight.

'*Non*, I am too busy, sadly. Perhaps we shall chat another time, Isobel.'

Izzy stepped back, expecting Simone to leave, but the woman continued to finish her wine, lips pursed like a contented cat.

'Can I do anything to help?' Izzy offered, feeling the need to busy her hands.

Maurice turned, smiling broadly. 'Perhaps if I show you to the dining room, you could help to carry a few things in for me, such as the bread-basket?'

Isobel took the handbag off her shoulder and tucked it onto the windowsill, before moving the bread knife from the board and adding the freshly sliced loaf to a wicker basket. It was still warm and smelled absolutely delicious.

'Lead the way,' she said, grinning.

Monsieur Fabron's dining room was no less grand than the rest of his home, the dark walnut furniture having been highly polished, and the table set with antique silverware. The linen was white and crisp, while the dinner plates were etched with navy and gold around the rim. None of these touches, and their obvious value, were lost on Isobel Gilyard as she took in her surroundings, curious as to how the village boulangerie owner came to live amongst such riches. Was there more to the handsome Maurice than met the eye, she pondered.

A painting of a handsome gentleman in riding attire caught Isobel's eye and she couldn't help commenting on the man's likeness to her host.

'A relative, Maurice?'

'*Non.*' The Frenchman smiled proudly, straightening up and looking at the canvas intently. 'My wife's great-grandfather. A wonderful man, so I'm told.'

'Did he also live here?' Izzy ventured. 'In this house?'

Maurice nodded. 'Absolutely. Seven generations of her family. One day, I will tell you the story of Valerie's ancestors, but now we must eat.'

Back in the kitchen, Simone was picking up her little bolero jacket and matching bag in preparation to leave.

'See you soon.' She waved to Izzy, before leaning forward to embrace Maurice. 'Have a lovely evening.' The words were smooth and silky but sounded slightly insincere.

'Back in a second,' the baker told Isobel, swiftly escorting Simone to the front door.

It was at that precise moment that Izzy felt a pang of jealousy and wondered if there was a physical relationship between her employer and the exotic woman. She imagined them lingering over a kiss in the hallway but in reality Maurice had returned far too soon for it to have been more than a peck on the cheek.

It wasn't long before dinner was served.

'Telo, Telo,' the baker called cheerily through the open door, '*le dîner.*'

Isobel tensed, very slightly, on hearing the young man's name. She noticed that her employer had directed her to a seat on the left-hand side, now taking up the head of the table himself, which meant that she would be facing Telo for the duration of the meal. The cause for Isobel's unfamiliar feeling of hostility was as yet unapparent, for the young man had done no more to insult her then a few sidelong glares and mumbled words, yet her skin prickled uncomfortably as he slid into his seat and glanced upwards. Telo had long, dark eyelashes, like those of his father, and they fluttered softly as he flicked his gaze towards their guest.

'A quick prayer of thankfulness,' Maurice was saying, pressing his palms together, but still his son looked upon the newcomer with intrigue, almost as though she were the main course in tonight's supper.

As soon as they began eating, Izzy mustered up the courage to test Telo's conversational skills, although she doubted if more than a few sentences would be forthcoming.

'*Parlez-vous Anglais*, Telo?' she ventured, hoping that the young man would answer in the affirmative, making the conversation easier, at least for the sake of their new working relationship.

Wild eyes shone as a knife and fork clattered onto the expensive china plate and Telo licked his lips in an exaggerated manner to remove the remnants of creamy sauce before spitting out the word, '*Non.*'

Isobel nodded, accepting the abrupt response with polite dignity before turning to Maurice and saying, 'I shall have to try very hard to improve my French then, won't I?'

The baker raised his perfectly tamed eyebrows, seemingly unaware of the tense atmosphere that his son had caused, and gave a slight shrug. 'I think it will come quite naturally, my dear. In time, you will speak like a native.'

Isobel sincerely hoped that time in Saint Margaux would be something that she would have in abundance and smiled contentedly at the thought of this beautiful place becoming her permanent home. A safe haven away from all that had happened at home, she mused.

'You haven't eaten very much, Maurice,' she commented, trying to lighten the mood. 'I'm afraid that Telo and I have eaten far more.'

'I dined with Cecile and Hubert at the vineyard earlier,' he replied, pushing the dinner-plate to one side. 'We had a little business matter to conclude and they were preparing lunch, so...'

As the man's deep voice trailed off, Izzy wondered what business it had been.

'Are you close?' she heard herself asking.

'Cecile is my sister-in-law. She is Valerie's younger sister. Together with her husband, Hubert, the vineyard produces some of the best wine in France. In fact, we are drinking one of their finest Chenin Blancs right now.'

Isobel joined the dots in her head. It made perfect sense that Maurice was still close to his dead wife's sibling. She also noted that he had used the present tense when talking about Valerie, something that a person might do when the loss is still hard to bear.

'You saw Cecile yesterday,' Maurice continued. 'She was taking afternoon tea with Simone. A tiny woman with beautiful natural blonde hair.'

Izzy instinctively touched her peroxide locks and blushed, as the comment reminded her that she really must buy some dye soon to cover up her dark roots.

'Ah, yes, I remember. There was another lady there, too, auburn hair, a little bit plumper.'

'Plumper?' Her host laughed, 'Don't let Dominique hear you say that! Although, in truth, she is very fond of chocolate cake.'

Maurice winked, allowing Izzy to breathe out after her obvious faux pas.

'Great, I make a mean chocolate fudge cake.'

'Talking of "*les desserts*",' Maurice announced, after asking his son to lend a hand with the dirty plates, '*Tarte au Citron*.'

Izzy's mouth watered at the thought of lemon tart and all previous thoughts disintegrated like fragments of dust.

'Now I will truly be able to test your baking skills,' she giggled, as the baker flitted out of the room. 'How delightful.'

Telo shot a backwards glance as he followed his father to the kitchen, his face a deeply lined scowl, portraying the knowledge that he had fully understood the Englishwoman's words and distrusted her every sentence.

Sitting outside, sipping at their wine in the magnificent walled garden, Maurice and Isobel chatted about how they would set about beginning their work together. Monsieur Fabron was open to new ideas and relished the thought of Izzy's younger, much more creative mind bringing elegant bakes to his very traditional boulangerie. Isobel fought the urge to light a post-dinner cigarette and chattered to keep her mind occupied and away from the craving.

Telo had asked to be excused and his father had hugged the young man tightly, saying to Isobel, 'His favourite television show is on, Telo never misses it.'

'Do you think Telo will come around?' she asked tentatively when the lad was out of earshot, setting down her glass for Maurice to refill.

'Come around? I'm sorry, how do you mean?'

'Well, it's just that he doesn't really seem to… approve of me being here.'

Maurice waved a dismissive hand, shaking his head in disagreement. 'Telo will be fine, it's just his way with strangers. Once you know each other better, all will be well. Trust me.'

Isobel wanted to agree, but there was still a nagging doubt warning her to tread cautiously around the baker's son, just in case. She changed the subject.

'Simone didn't leave on my account, did she?'

Maurice took a gulp of wine and shook his head. 'No, Simone and I are very old friends, she quite often pops in for a drink. I think secretly she worries that two men are not capable of running such a large house.'

Izzy smiled. 'Well, she'd be wrong. Your home is fabulous, as was dinner.'

'Thank you.'

Maurice's tired eyes lingered for a few seconds more than intended. He liked the fire inside his new employee, she seemed fun, forthright and honest.

'To new beginnings!' He smiled, evenly distributing the last of the white wine.

The pair clinked glasses and enjoyed the final moments of evening sun as it slid down behind the garden wall.

That night, as Telo sat up in bed reading aloud, Maurice patiently listened to his boy's narration. At the end of the chapter, he praised Telo and patted the bedcovers, signalling that it was time for sleep.

'*Très bien. Lait froid?*' he asked, offering to fetch the ritualistic glass of ice-cold milk that Telo enjoyed every night before going to sleep.

'*Merci*, Papa,' and then, '*Je n'aime pas* Mademoiselle Gilyard.'

Maurice sighed, placing both hands on his knees before rising. 'Telo, Telo, Telo.'

The man carefully navigated the steep curving staircase on his quest to fetch the drink, fretting about Telo's comment. He'd known all along that this new phase wasn't going to be easy for his son, but he hadn't anticipated quite so much negativity. Isobel hadn't even begun her duties in the boulangerie yet, in fact little more than twenty-four hours had passed since her arrival. Telo was unusually sensitive to strangers, normally prone to quite accurate estimations of a person's nature, but in Miss Gilyard's case he must be mistaken. Or so Maurice hoped.

Across the street, Izzy had tipped the entire contents of her handbag onto the bedroom rug, trying in vain to locate her cigarette lighter. She knew she'd had it earlier, having smoked just before brushing her teeth. She could have sworn she'd put it into the bag with her fags. And that was the strange thing; the cigarette packet was there, but no lighter. It must have dropped out, she cursed. She lay on top of the bed as it was too warm to slide under the covers yet, her eyes fixed upon the white-washed ceiling above. She felt that the evening had gone amazingly well considering, despite Telo's attempt at animosity. He reminded her of a boy that she'd known at school, the outsider, always on the edge of her group's conversations but never willing to join them. Or was it that they hadn't asked him? She couldn't remember now, it was so long ago, a lifetime of experiences had happened to her since then.

Despite the iciness between them, Isobel resolved to make an extra effort with Telo, for his father's sake and for her own peace of mind. It wouldn't bode well for her future here if there was continual tension, she told herself. Perhaps it would be prudent to enquire of Maurice the exact nature of his son's learning difficulties. After all, there had been more than a fragment of intellect in Telo's face as he had listened to her speak over dinner. Could it be that the young man had understood her? He had a distinct intellectual quality bubbling below the surface.

Unable to stave off her nicotine urge any longer, Izzy padded into the kitchen and lit a cigarette from the gas stove. She took the smoke deep into her lungs, savouring the taste; after all, it had been almost six hours since her last one. Moving over to the living room window in order to exhale into the night air, the young woman's thoughts turned this time not to Telo, but his kind, talented and handsome father. Isobel surveyed the grand house across the street, thinking of all the *objects d'art* inside, the sheer opulence of everything she'd seen. Maurice was undoubtedly a good catch, a wealthy widower who could cook, clean and hold an intelligent conversation. She calculated the age gap between them. It was surely no more than ten years. A decade was nothing if the right couple were attracted to each other, you only had to look at some A-list actors to figure that out.

Isobel wondered whether Maurice was ready for a new relationship yet. And where did Simone Dupuis fit into the picture? Were they on the verge of becoming lovers? Taking the last drag, Izzy stubbed out the cigarette end in an ashtray and glanced at herself in the mirror. She wasn't bad for thirty-five, although the bleached blonde cut had been a little drastic, a nod towards leaving her old life behind. Her figure was trim, perhaps too boyish for most men, and when she made an effort with make-up she could definitely be considered pretty. Tomorrow was the start of her new job and, perhaps, getting to know Maurice Fabron would be like a garden coming into bloom.

Telo Fabron switched off the Tiffany lamp at the side of his bed, pulling the sheets up over his shoulders more from customary habit than chilly air, and sighed deeply. He didn't know what it was about Isobel Gilyard that troubled him, and his brain would have certain difficulty in finding the right expressions to explain it to his father, but there was something weirdly uncomfortable about her presence. No matter now, though; the decision to employ her had been made by his Papa and he hoped that the Englishwoman would take up her new position without troubling herself to try and befriend him. If Isobel knows what is good for her, she will keep out of my way, he thought, with a grimace.

Maurice lay awake in the master bedroom, mulling over his son's words yet unsure of how to put the boy's mind at rest. He needed to know that Isobel wasn't the enemy. In fact, anything but. She would be an asset to the boulangerie, enticing new customers with her baking skills. It had been a bold move to employ an English cook, for that's how he saw her, rather than a qualified pastry chef who might demand a more considerable salary, but Maurice was confident in his choice. It would work out in the end.

'Ma chérie,' the baker whispered, kissing a silver-framed photograph of his wife and gently rubbing fingers over her smiling face, 'what would you do? Would you approve of Isobel?'

A faint breeze ruffled the chintz curtains, icy cold as it traversed gently across the room and came into contact with Maurice's exposed skin, causing him to look up.

'Valerie?' he whispered softly, yearning for a response yet knowing too that it would not come, not tonight, not ever.

One of the heavy wooden shutters banged loudly against its hinges, the rising night breeze causing it to pull free from the grasp of its hooks and Maurice heaved himself up to securely close them and, in doing so, shut himself away from the outside world in order to continue grieving.

'Just the wind,' he muttered, disappointed that there could be no supernatural cause for the cold air that had penetrated the bedroom. It was certainly not the spirit of his dead wife.

Settling back against the pillows and switching off the nightlight, Maurice Fabron struggled to bring the image of Valerie's beautiful young face to mind. Such an attractive woman, glamorous in the succinctly natural way that he believed only French women could be, Valerie had been the epitome of chic. Yet tonight, all alone here in the bed that they had shared for nearly twenty-five years, all the man could recall was the lank, thinning hair that had hung limply around his dying wife's shoulders, a mere shadow of herself, cheeks hollowed, skin ravaged by the terrible illness that had finally taken her. The boulangerie owner would fail to sleep well that night, tormented by the image of the shell that had become his darling Valerie.

CHAPTER FOUR – AN INTRUDER

As Jack Hobbs raced up the wide police station staircase, gloomily aware that he was already later to arrive than the rest of the team, Inspector Max Mallery came clattering down in the opposite direction, shoes polished to a high sheen.

'Don't bother going up,' he ordered, hardly stopping for breath, 'you're coming with me, Jacques.'

'Yes, sir.'

'And you can drive,' the senior officer added, striding out into the car park. 'Which one is yours?'

Jack pointed to a dark blue Ford Mondeo with British number-plates, looking decidedly forlorn amongst the array of newer, sportier cars in the parking lot, and flushed slightly. His boss wasn't going to be impressed with the ride.

'Let's get going,' Max sighed, shaking his head at the nodding dog ornament in the back window. 'God help us.'

The main route out of Bordeaux was fairly quiet for the time of day, as most of the traffic was headed in towards the town, buzzing along like a marching army of insects as commuters reluctantly drove to their offices, each and every one feeling the Monday morning blues. Jack considered himself a safe and cautious driver and navigated the unfamiliar roundabouts and turnings confidently, while his supervisor sat back and signalled to the westbound carriageway. It wasn't long before the sprawling town stood behind them and the surrounding countryside opened up to small hamlets interspersed with rural farmland.

'We're heading for Saint Margaux Vineyard,' Mallery revealed, desperately trying to mask his discomfort at sitting in a right-hand drive car. 'There's been a burglary, apparently, although nothing was taken. Might be a waste of time but it's a pleasant drive and gets us out of the office.'

'Any crime scene details?' Hobbs enquired, glancing across to where Max was fiddling with the car door.

'Not much, just that somebody broke into the safe, according to uniform. Now, where the hell is the button to open the window?'

Jack smiled. 'You have to wind the handle, sir, this is an old model.'

If ever there was an ideal place on earth to spend a Monday morning, it had to be the village of Saint Margaux. Surrounded by lush green countryside and picture-perfect houses, it was a thriving hub of activity, not only with locals but with regular visitors, too. Keen walkers hiked the rolling hills, those who enjoyed fishing tried their luck in the clear water of the gushing river and those in search of a tranquil place to escape the hubbub of city life rented the gîtes that stood waiting for their hard-earned Euros.

As Jack's Ford turned right onto a narrow lane, a signpost pointed to the village and Max gestured for him to continue along the route.

'About half a mile down here, you will see a sign for the vineyard.'

The Inspector was right. Announcing the entrance very grandly were a row of tall cypress trees swaying gently in the morning breeze, their tips reaching up towards the sky like guards standing to attention in a parade. The words on the sign read simply, *Vineyard de Saint Margaux*, in black lettering against a gold plaque.

'Main house or winemaker's building?' Hobbs asked, continuing down a long gravel drive, tyres crunching as they slowed down.

'I would think that an affluent gentleman would keep his safe in the house, don't you think?' Mallery winked sarcastically. 'Pull up over there in the shade, it's going to be a hot day.'

Hubert Vidal was tall, tanned and the epitome of a French wine producer, dressed in red chinos that mirrored his rosy cheeks and a crisp white linen shirt, sleeves rolled up to the elbow. A gold Rolex watch signalled wealth, yet he walked with an easy gait, arms open in a welcoming gesture.

'*Bonjour*,' he said with a nod, striding over to the car. '*Je suis Monsieur Vidal.*'

Mallery shook the man's hand, matching his height and smart casual attire, causing Jack to feel inadequately out of place in his navy trousers and checked shirt. No wonder Angélique had been nagging him to go clothes shopping.

There followed a rapid succession of quick-fire questions and responses in French that Hobbs struggled to follow, but he was soon welcomed into the Vidal's house and spoken to in English. It seemed that Max Mallery had already explained about his new English 'sidekick'.

'So, you're an Englishman.' The winemaker grinned, his accent only tinged slightly with his native tongue. 'Not a Cambridge boy are you, by any chance? I was there in the late nineties, a bit before your time though, I suppose?'

Jack shook his head. 'No, sir. Hendon Police Training College.'

Hubert Vidal seemed unfazed by the response and continued to lead the detectives into a vast study, in the centre of which stood a grand oak desk covered in paperwork. Jack stood taking in the lavish décor. Heavy woven tapestries depicting ancient battles hung on two of the walls and an oriental vase delicately painted with cranes stood on the sideboard. The Vidals were certainly worth a bob or two, he reckoned.

Mallery tugged on Jack's jacket, lowering his voice. 'Get your notebook ready.'

'We haven't touched anything,' Monsieur Vidal was saying, stopping at the edge of a Persian rug and surveying the room as though for the first time. 'As you can see, the safe was open when I came in this morning and the patio doors have been forced from the outside.'

Max Mallery strode over to the window and examined the lock. There were no visible prints on the glass or door handle, but the wooden frame was scratched as though a metal object had prised them open. There was nothing of note on the glass and no footprints on the patio tiles outside.

'Who else lives in the house, Monsieur Vidal?'

'My wife Cecile, of course, and our housekeeper, Madam Paradis. Our children are presently away at university. Ah, here is Cecile now, Inspector.'

Squeaky loafers on the highly polished hall floor signalled the arrival of Madam Vidal, an attractive, petite woman with soft blonde curls and an enigmatic smile. She wore a simple shift dress in a bright shade of coral and wore no jewellery except for a smaller, feminine version of her husband's timepiece and a leaf-shaped gold brooch.

'*Bonjour*,' she said solemnly, looking over at the gaping safe. '*C'est terrible*.'

Hubert quickly introduced the policemen and put an arm around his wife's shoulder to comfort her. She smiled at Hubert and put a hand on top of his.

'Detective Hobbs *est Anglais*,' he murmured, bending slightly to Cecile's ear.

Madam Vidal smiled weakly, acknowledging the young red-haired man, 'You remind me a little of the Royal prince, Harry," she said in English. 'I'll ask Madam Paradis to make us some coffee. Or would you prefer tea?'

'Coffee would be lovely,' Max answered, shooting a glance at his colleague, 'if it's no trouble.'

As the Frenchwoman retreated to the kitchen, Jack blushed. This wasn't the first time that he'd been compared to the Queen's grandson.

'So…' Mallery coughed, trying to steer matters back on track, 'what is missing?'

'Well, that's the strange thing,' Hubert replied, gesturing towards the desk, 'As I told the uniformed officers earlier, not a single thing has been taken as far as I can see.'

'And you say you definitely haven't touched anything?'

'No, not a thing,' Hubert assured him, glancing around the study. 'When the other officers left, I shut the door and haven't opened it again until now.'

Mallery peered closely at the hinged door of the safe and peered inside.

'Let's see what could possibly be of interest to someone else then, shall we?'

Jack Hobbs scribbled quickly, noting every item and document as Monsieur Vidal relayed the information to him, and hoped that he'd be able to read his notes without difficulty later when he came to write up the report.

'So, let me get this straight,' Mallery was saying. 'The alarm wasn't set, you didn't hear the door being forced open and whoever it was that broke in, knew the combination to the safe? On top of that, nothing was taken, *oui*?'

The winemaker rubbed a hand over his tired face and shrugged. 'Yes indeed, Inspector, that sums it up completely. In all the years my family have owned this vineyard, four generations, we have never had so much as a cup stolen. The alarm works but, to be honest, we never feel the need to set it.'

Jack looked over at the papers on the desk and then back at the various letters, passports, money and folders carefully stacked up in the safe.

'Monsieur Vidal,' he probed, pressing the biro to his lips, 'is there anything on the desk now that would have been in the safe last night?'

'What are you getting at?' Max asked, not grasping Hobbs' line of questioning.

'I mean, sir, that perhaps the intruder came to look at something specific.'

Enlightened, Mallery looked to the vineyard owner and raised his eyebrows, causing the red-faced winemaker to look closely at the documents on his desk.

'Well, well,' he said presently, just as Cecile returned with a pot of fresh coffee on a silver tray, 'I do believe there is!'

Mallery and Hobbs leaned closer as Hubert Vidal pointed at a crisp blue folder on top of his 'In' tray.

'May I ask what it is?' Mallery prompted. 'But please do not touch it, Monsieur.'

Cecile, who had been standing slightly back from the men, stepped forward and cleared her throat. 'It's an official document giving my share of my father's house to my brother-in-law.'

Jack waited, pen poised above his notepad.

'And who is your brother-in-law?' Mallery pressed.

'Maurice Fabron. He owns the boulangerie in Saint Margaux and presently lives in my father's 'Maison de Maitre'. Maurice and my sister Valerie moved there when my father died, it was his wish.'

'Is Monsieur Fabron aware of your intentions?' the Inspector asked, suspecting the case could be easily solved in its open simplicity.

'Naturally. Maurice had lunch with us yesterday, together with our *avocat*… erm… lawyer, and the papers were signed afterwards. Hubert locked our copy of the document in the safe straight away, and the *avocat* took the original.'

'Madam Vidal, do you perhaps have a clear plastic bag big enough for the folder?'

Cecile nodded, pushing her hair over one ear before exiting the room.

'We will take it for finger-printing,' Max announced. 'Besides there being no theft, there is still a crime.'

'Hubert Vidal furrowed his brows, pensive and morose.

'Who on earth could possibly want to look at our private papers?'

Over coffee, the detectives asked further questions. It was established that Cecile Vidal's late sister was the boulangerie owner's wife and the two women had been bequeathed the large 'Maison de Maitre' in the village by their father. However, now that the Saint Margaux vineyard was flourishing and with a handsome home of their own, the Vidals had generously decided to sign over the property entirely to Maurice Fabron so that it could eventually belong to his only son, Cecile's nephew.

'And your sister's son?' Mallery probed gently, replacing his empty coffee cup on the tray. 'Would he have any reason to…'

Madam Vidal shook her head. 'Certainly not. Dearest Telo is….'

She turned to her husband, searching his eyes for the correct word in English.

'Autistic,' Hubert supplied, smiling at his wife. 'A lovely young man, very clever in many ways but with certain difficulties in social situations.'

Max Mallery took in the information, his junior also absorbing every detail like a sponge as he continued to write, concluding the interview only when he was satisfied that there were no more details to be had.

'One last thing,' Mallery queried, as the Vidals escorted the officers out to the car, 'how long have you had your housekeeper?'

'Madam Paradis has been with us ever since we married,' Cecile said staunchly, 'and before that, she worked for Hubert's parents.'

Mallery instinctively knew when his line of questioning had hit a brick wall and bid the couple good day.

'I'll be in touch if we have any updates,' he promised, tugging at his shirt cuffs before opening the door of the Mondeo. '*Au revoir.*'

He noticed the couple slipping their hands into each other's automatically as soon as they turned to re-enter the house. He missed that intimate closeness with a woman and momentarily thought of the Commissioner's wife.

Jack Hobbs inserted the key into the ignition and started up the engine.

'Monsieur Fabron's bakery?' he suggested, easing off the handbrake.

'You're quick!' Mallery grinned, pushing the plastic bag containing the folder into the glovebox. 'Turn left at the bottom of the drive.'

'Sir, if you don't mind me asking,' Jack ventured, keeping his eyes on the road, 'How come forensics haven't been to check for fingerprints?'

Mallery shrugged, a noncommittal movement that gave nothing away. 'We simply don't have the resources at the moment. Besides, it's not a burglary unless something is taken, correct?'

'Well, in a way they did. Perhaps they took information,' the younger man said smugly, pleased with his deduction. 'That document could mean a lot of things to different people.'

'I'm sure you're going to explain…'

'Well, sir, perhaps the Vidals' children are unhappy about Maurice Fabron getting the house. After all, if it belonged to their maternal grandparents, surely they're entitled to inherit a percentage?'

Max yawned, stretching his legs down into the deep footwell of the Mondeo, in his opinion the only redeeming factor of the Ford.

'As Monsieur Vidal told us, they're both away at university right now.'

'It's not unthinkable that one or both of them could have come back down on a Sunday afternoon and waited somewhere until their parents had gone to bed.'

Jack was becoming animated as he warmed to his conclusions and earned a steely glare from the wily Inspector.

'You're going to have to come up with something better than that Jacques. Now, do you mind if I smoke?'

'Not in the car, if you don't mind,' Hobbs replied tersely. 'The baby…'

'*Oui, oui, oui*,' Mallery sighed, putting away his cigarettes, 'zee baby.'

Maurice Fabron was just taking a second batch of freshly baked baguettes out of the oven when the boulangerie door opened, causing the brass bell to tinkle. The smell of warm bread lingered and filled the back room with a deliciously mouth-watering aroma.

'I'll go,' said his new assistant, Isobel, 'I've finished icing these cupcakes.'

'*Merci.*' The baker nodded, sliding the red-hot baking tray onto a marble work counter. 'I'll be out in just a moment.'

Isobel wiped her hands on a damp tea towel and wandered through into the shop, expecting to test out her French on the morning's first customers. Instead, she was greeted by two men, one of whom held out a police identity wallet. She read the name *Inspector Max Mallery* and a tingle ran up her spine.

'*Je voudrais parler à Monsieur Fabron,*' he said boldly, while the other man eyed the tasty bakes in the glass display cabinet, '*s'il vous plaît.*'

Izzy turned to see Maurice hurrying out from the back room on hearing his name, a sprinkling of flour still lying like fresh snow on his shirt sleeves.

'*Oui? Je suis Maurice Fabron.*'

Isobel wrangled with the coffee machine while the three men settled themselves at a round table. Telo was out making deliveries and therefore the Englishwoman had to work out the complex piece of equipment by herself while her employer sat looking deeply perplexed as the men introduced themselves.

'Would it be alright if we speak in English?' Inspector Mallery asked politely. 'For the benefit of my new colleague, Jacques?'

'Of course,' the baker replied, turning to point towards Isobel. 'My new assistant is also English.'

Isobel turned on hearing her name and smiled at Maurice.

Max raised both eyebrows and looked inquisitively at the young woman, quite a unique sight in a rural French village with her bleached, cropped hair and multiple ear piercings. He noticed she was dressed in three-quarter length jeans and a gingham shirt under a white apron. Very 1950s, he thought, before turning back to Maurice.

'I'm afraid to tell you that the Vidals' vineyard had an intruder last night,' Mallery explained, as Izzy set espressos out for the group. 'Nothing was taken, fortunately, but the patio door was damaged and it seems that a certain document was taken out of the safe.'

'Oh, that is terrible news!' Monsieur Fabron exclaimed. 'But you say nothing was stolen?'

'No,' Max continued, leaning back in the chair and stretching out his long legs, 'nothing was taken, but it seems the safe was opened and the document looked at.'

'Poor Cecile and Hubert! But I don't see how this has anything to do with me.'

'You dined with the Vidals yesterday, correct?' Max pressed. 'And the document you signed was the very same one that was taken out of the safe.'

Maurice nodded and then frowned, putting the pieces of the puzzle together in his mind before answering.

'Yes, that's right. I had lunch there and we signed an agreement about the house. What is it you're asking of me, Inspector?'

'Well, to be honest with you, it's still a mystery as to why someone would want to read the document… unless, perhaps, the information disclosed in it benefitted them in some way.'

Maurice rubbed his temples. 'But only myself and my son, Telo…'

'The Vidals' children?' Jack interjected. 'Your nephew and niece?'

The baker shook his head. 'They're both at university and haven't been home for weeks. Besides, they were well aware of Cecile's intentions and had no problem with their mother's decision.'

'Perhaps you could get us another coffee while I go over the fundamentals of French Inheritance Law with Monsieur Fabron,' Max asked Hobbs. 'Easier done in our local language.'

'Sure, no problem,' Jack smiled, heading towards the blonde Englishwoman, relinquishing the fact that his boss's conversation would most probably go right over his head anyway. He leaned on the glass counter, eyeing a chocolate cake.

'So, how long have you been in Saint Margaux?' Hobbs casually asked Isobel, as she pressed numerous buttons on the coffee machine once more.

'Erm… all of two days!' Izzy laughed, rolling her eyes in mock embarrassment.

'I've not been here much longer,' Jack confessed. 'Jack Hobbs, from Leeds.'

He put out a hand and shook the young woman's as she told him, 'Isobel Gilyard, also from up north. Manchester.'

'So, what brings you to this little backwater?' the police officer pressed, noticing the absence of a wedding ring on the woman's left hand as she held up a cup to catch the dribbling beverage.

He could have sworn that Izzy's eyes narrowed as she digested the question, perhaps conjuring up a way to avoid a direct response. When she finally answered, Hobbs' gut instinct told him that he was right.

'I could ask you the same question, detective.'

Isobel picked up the fresh coffee cups and marched briskly over to the table where Max was concluding his questioning. She collected the empties and then stacked them noisily in the dishwasher.

Jack watched with interest. There was something odd about Isobel Gilyard; a lack of sincerity in her actions, the need to avoid eye contact, her accent tinged with something other than that of her hometown. He immediately thought of a phrase that his father would have used – 'Never trust a skinny cook'. And Isobel Gilyard didn't exactly look as though she ate a great deal of the sumptuous cakes that she baked, Jack mused. Monsieur Fabron, on the other hand, looked like an open book.

'*Merci, Monsieur Fabron.*' Max smiled as Maurice carefully wrapped up two warm tomato and brie baguettes to go. '*Au revoir.*'

The Englishwoman had returned to the rear kitchen, eager to continue her work, but the woman's absence wasn't lost on Jack who called a farewell through the open doorway.

''Bye Miss. Gilyard.'

''Bye, Detective Hobbs,' the voice shouted, although no face appeared at the door.

Isobel busied herself with mixing a fresh batch of icing, while Maurice stood looking out of the window perplexed. His eyes followed the detectives as they walked over to a blue car.

'Are you alright?' Izzy asked, coming to stand beside him.

'Yes, yes, I'm fine.' The baker nodded, without moving. 'It's just very strange, that is all. We have very little crime in Saint Margaux and when it's family, well… I'm just shocked, that is all. Thanks for your concern.'

'Perhaps you should take a break for a while… go and talk to your sister-in-law, perhaps.'

Maurice considered the suggestion but dismissed it almost immediately, 'I'm sure Cecile has had enough visitors for one day, with both the uniformed police and now the detectives. I will call her later. Hubert is there to sort matters out.'

'If you're sure.' Izzy sighed, looking at the man's tired eyes, 'Try not to worry.'

'So,' Mallery quizzed, as soon as the Ford Mondeo engine had spluttered to life, 'I think Maurice Fabron is sincere, nothing to hide. What do you think?'

Jack gently manoeuvred around the village square, taking in the immaculately planted tubs of flowers, before replying, 'I agree. He seems like a really decent bloke. Besides, if he saw and signed the document yesterday afternoon, why on earth would he break into the safe later on to look at it again?

'Exactly! Now, pull into the station car park and we'll enjoy our baguettes.'

'I'm not arguing with that, sir, I'm absolutely starving!' Jack grinned cheekily.

Back at the station, Thierry had been running a background check on the Vidals' business and their associates. The whole team were eager to get involved in some real detective work, given the currently diminishing caseload, and the room had buzzed with activity all morning.

'The vineyard is clean,' Thierry told Mallery and Hobbs as they entered the air-conditioned Incident Room. 'Not even so much as a late Tax Return. No illegal sales, or dealings with underhand companies. Everything in order, all suppliers paid on time and with legal receipts. No history of any disagreements or court cases, either. They run a tight business.'

'Send this to the lab to check for fingerprints,' Mallery told Gabriella, passing the pretty young detective a plastic bag containing the Vidals' folder. 'Mark it as urgent, please.'

'Yes, sir, right away.'

'This is ridiculous,' Max told the others, as they gathered around for an informal briefing. 'What the hell is going on then?'

'I've checked out the baker's son also, sir,' Thierry told them, his dark eyes gleaming at the thought of an exciting crime to get stuck into. 'Not even a traffic offence. Telo Fabron is mildly autistic and has never left the country.'

'What about that woman at the bakery? Isobel something?' Max asked, turning to Jack. 'Anything unusual? Luc, maybe you could run a check on her.'

'I think that's clutching at straws if you don't mind me saying so, sir,' Hobbs answered honestly, hoping his boss could catch the gist of his meaning, and then turning towards the computer whiz. 'She was a bit stand-offish, but I can't see any reason for her to benefit from looking at that agreement.'

'Stand-offish?' Thierry laughed. 'What is that?'

'Erm, a bit rude, not very forthcoming with answers,' Hobbs informed him.

'Ah!' Thierry and Luc gasped in unison, feeling much enlightened.

'You're right,' Mallery sighed. 'She's only just arrived in Saint Margaux according to Fabron and knows next to nothing of his personal affairs.'

'That's the impression I got, too.' Jack nodded.

'Luc,' Max called over to the technical member of the team, 'forget that for the moment, it could be a total waste of time. We have nothing to go on and no real crime to solve, for now we are at what our English Jacques would call 'a dead end', *oui*?'

CHAPTER FIVE - A TRIP TO BORDEAUX

Sitting in her beloved VW Beetle on Wednesday morning, Isobel Gilyard inhaled the undeniably soapy aroma that lingered in the driver's seat. There was another more fragrant smell, too and, as she followed her nose, she found it was centred around the passenger's side. She quickly wound down both windows to allow fresh air to circulate before backing out of the rear courtyard. As far as Izzy was concerned, the car had stood untouched since Saturday, when Maurice had asked his son to drive it around the back and help unload her suitcases. She didn't dwell on the matter for too long, however, as thoughts of another day in which to explore her new surroundings filled the young woman with excitement.

Having now worked contentedly beside Monsieur Fabron in the bakery for two days, it had been agreed that Isobel should take Wednesday off, as she would be needed in the boulangerie on Saturdays, the busiest day of the week. It seemed that quite a few of the businesses in Saint Margaux chose to close their doors in the middle of the week and Izzy had asked Maurice why he didn't follow suit, to give himself a break.

'Everybody needs bread, every day,' he had said, winking at her. 'Just imagine poor Jean without his evening croissants, or Cecile, Simone and Dominique unable to take their afternoon tea with fondant fancies!'

'If you're sure,' she'd told him, itching to do some shopping. 'See you later.'

As the shops in town would undoubtedly be closed on Sunday, her next day off, Izzy had decided to drive there to stock up on a few essentials.

As it was still early, there were few cars on the road into the village as Isobel steered the Beetle down the winding main street of Saint Margaux, but she feared that traffic might be heavier towards Bordeaux. In a sudden flash of inspiration, Isobel was reminded of Maurice's explanation that Bordeaux now provided a very efficient tram system in order to cut down on congestion, and she pulled into the station car park, deciding to take the train instead.

Saint Margaux railway station was a quaint, antiquated building with red brick walls and ornamental railings running the full perimeter of the platform. A few people milled about, looking at their watches and checking mobile phones, just the way that human nature causes them to when waiting expectantly for a train to arrive. As Isobel stepped out of the car, a dark-coloured estate pulled up at the entrance and the male driver leaned over to kiss the female passenger. Izzy attempted to avert her eyes, but it was difficult, as she needed to pass the car to get to the station entrance, and she immediately recognised the woman as one of Simone Dupuis' friends from the previous Saturday. Was it Dominique or Cecile? She couldn't recall which one of them was the curly-haired blonde.

As Isobel fumbled in her shopping tote for her purse, the blonde lady strode purposely around her to purchase a ticket and then went to stand underneath the station clock, her back stiff, a black designer handbag clutched tightly in both hands. Izzy raised a hand to be polite, but the woman ignored her, instead focussing all her attention on the railway tracks in front of her. The woman was dressed smartly in a polka dot dress and black jacket, looking as though she, too, was off for a day's shopping.

Isobel turned towards the ticket office, where a large middle-aged man was sitting bolt upright in his chair. She instantly recognised him as 'Jean the cold croissant eater.'

'*Bonjour,*' he said, the deep voice steady and serious despite the flicker of recollection in his eyes. '*Ou allez-vous?*'

'*Bordeaux, s'il vous plaît,*' Izzy answered, proud at how easily the unfamiliar French words had fallen from her lips.

'*Sept Euro,*' Jean informed her, putting up seven chubby fingers to ensure that the foreign woman was clear about the price.

Isobel unzipped her purse, counting coins, then huffed loudly when she realised that she didn't have enough change. '*Vous acceptez…*' she began, waving her bank card but not remembering the rest of what she needed to ask in French.

'*Non, le billet est sept Euro, payer en liquid.*'

Izzy counted out her ready cash again, scraping together a mere four Euros and fifty-three cents, cursing herself for not having been to the cashpoint over the weekend, all the while being eyed narrowly by the ticket office clerk. A middle-aged couple stepped up behind her, peering intently, first at the flustered Englishwoman and then at the coins in her hand.

'I'll have to go to the bank,' Izzy muttered, more to herself than the man in the booth. 'Sorry, thank you.'

She stepped away from the platform hurriedly, but just in time to hear the arrival of the eight o'clock train to Bordeaux being announced.

'Damn!' she cursed, heading back towards the car park. 'I guess I'll have to drive, after all.'

Reaching the outskirts of the town, Isobel parked in a side street and headed for the nearest tram stop. As she pulled a one Euro coin out, ready to pay her fare, Izzy almost jumped out of her skin as four police cars with flashing lights tore past at an alarming speed, a red BMW sports following closely behind. Passers-by craned their necks to see where the vehicles were heading, such excitement obviously an uncommon sight in the town. As the sirens faded into the distance, so did people's curiosity and as the tram pulled up, the humdrum bustle of mid-week shoppers continued.

On reaching the town centre, Isobel headed for the nearest bank and then stopped at a small café, ordering coffee with a pain au chocolat for breakfast. She was lucky, having inherited her grandmother's slender figure, and didn't have to concern herself with calorie counting. There were already a fair number of shoppers out and about, buying bread and waiting patiently for the butcher, *la boucherie*, to open his doors. Izzy had selected a table outside in order to enjoy the morning sunshine and sat back with thoughts of Telo still weighing on her mind.

Could Maurice's son have used her car over the weekend? Perhaps he had a girlfriend and had taken her out for a drive. That would certainly explain the sweet smell inside the Beetle. Surely she would have heard the car being driven out of the courtyard, Izzy mused as coffee arrived, but the thought of Telo being in her car without permission grated upon her. He didn't frighten her, exactly, but it was the way in which he conducted himself that spooked Izzy slightly, sometimes just a knowing look here or a gesture there, imparting glances that said he understood far more about the conversations in English between her and Maurice than he let on.

Having set herself up for a stroll around the shops, Izzy left money under her saucer and waved to the waiter before navigating the cobbled pedestrian areas of the busy town.

Bordeaux possessed everything that a woman might desire. There were shoe shops, boutiques, delicatessens, a leather handbag store, dozens of restaurants displaying tasty lunch menus and bookshops selling everything that a literary junkie might ever wish to read. Izzy noticed that a couple of the stores sold foreign reading material, too and she picked up a couple of thick volumes to tide her over the long summer evenings. She then crossed the street and stared longingly in a boutique called 'Etienne's', where her favourite 1950s styles were displayed in an array of modern multi-coloured fabrics, the perfect combination. Isobel pushed open the door and headed to the nearest rail. A pale pink tea dress with shoulder ties instantly grabbed her attention and she lifted the hanger to admire it properly.

'*C'est très chic,*' the sales assistant commented, coming up behind Isobel as she flattened the dress against herself.

'*Oui, très chic,*' she agreed, turning to face the mirror.

It was at that moment that the price tag fluttered into view, almost as though it felt the need to warn Izzy of its hefty cost. Three hundred Euros.

Stifling a cough, Isobel swiftly pushed the garment back onto the rail and casually pretended to peruse a table of silk scarves before thanking the shop assistant and heading for the door. No matter how beautiful the dress, she wouldn't spend even half that amount on such an extravagance.

Time passed fairly quickly that morning and, after treating herself to a lunch of bread, mixed cheeses and a glass of red wine, Isobel Gilyard was ready to make two final stops before heading back to her car. The first was to buy a few boxes of hair dye to cover her protruding dark roots, and then on to the grocery store to stock up on essential food supplies. As she finally reached the Beetle, sitting sadly alone in the deserted street, Isobel noticed that the area seemed unrestricted, as nobody had left a parking ticket on her windscreen, a rare treat in a busy town. This saved her a few Euros and put her in a pleasant mood for the drive back to Saint Margaux.

Feeling relaxed and having enjoyed her day off, Isobel felt it reasonable to enter the boulangerie through the front door in order to speak to Maurice. During the day, she had forgotten about the sweet smell inside her car, but the drive back had set her mind racing again and she was determined to get to the bottom of the mysterious odour. She didn't intend to confront Telo, but perhaps the baker would be able to shed some light on whether or not his son might have taken liberties with her vehicle.

With this in mind, Izzy parked the Beetle underneath the carport at the rear, collected her shopping and headed around the side of the bakery, a smile pasted on her face, ready to greet Monsieur Fabron and any customers who might be inside taking afternoon tea. However, when she got inside, she found that something very odd was taking place.

Ten or twelve people were clustered around the glass counter where Maurice displayed his bakes, all of them silent and staring at a portable television set that was tuned into a local news channel. The volume was turned up and a reporter spoke animatedly. Isobel dropped her shopping next to a table at the rear of the group and strained to make out the foreign words.

'*Le matin… la femme… la voiture…*' she caught, desperately trying to translate the French accurately into English: 'Morning… woman… train carriage.'

The three words alone didn't make any sense and Izzy gently caught the sleeve of an old, wizened man who was at the rear of the group.

'*Excusez-moi?*' Izzy whispered, '*qu'est-ce qu'il y a*? What's the matter?'

The pensioner grunted and put a gnarled finger to his lips, gesturing her to be quiet until the news report had finished. '*Écoute*! Listen.'

Several minutes later, the news item was over, and Maurice Fabron switched off the television set, his eyes downcast and solemn. As he looked up, the baker caught Izzy's eye and beckoned her to join him behind the counter.

'Ah, you are back safely.' Maurice laid a hand on her arm and gave a deep sigh. 'It is such a terrible thing that has happened today.'

'Oh? What is it, Maurice?'

'A woman has been murdered,' he said, in a low, desperate voice. 'On the train this morning, travelling to Bordeaux from Saint Margaux.'

Instinctively Isobel's hand flew up to cover her own mouth. This was shocking news. A murder!

'Did you take the train, Izzy? Or did you drive?'

'No, I, er… I drove,' she mumbled, meeting Monsieur Fabron's startled look.

'Thank goodness.' He sighed again, seeming genuinely relieved.

'Who was it, Maurice? Someone you know? Somebody from Saint Margaux?'

The tall man shrugged, splaying his hands wide. 'We do not know yet, the police have not released a name, but this is such a small place that we are sure it will be somebody with whom we are all familiar.'

Isobel turned to where the baker was nodding, towards the locals who were still talking in hushed tones, checking that each knew the whereabouts of the women in their families. It was some time before the crowd dispersed and, when they did, Maurice Fabron pulled a bottle of brandy from under the counter and poured himself a large measure, one eyebrow lifting enquiringly.

'Will you join me?' he asked. 'I have had quite a shock.'

Isobel nodded in acceptance. 'Just let me drop my shopping upstairs. I'll be two minutes.'

Maurice watched steadily with an ashen face, as his employee gathered up her bags, aware that Isobel could very easily have been a victim on the train that morning, had she chosen not to drive. He carried the small shot glasses to a table and then turned the *Fermé* sign to close the shop.

'Things like this, murder, they never ever happen here,' Monsieur Fabron told Izzy tearfully as the brandy warmed their throats, 'It's just… how to say… unheard of? We are such a tight community.'

Isobel sat holding her glass, wondering if Maurice was going to tell her all that he had learned from the news programme. Patience was one of her better traits.

'It seems the woman boarded the eight o'clock train from here, after buying a ticket to Bordeaux. She must be local, leaving so early in the morning,' he surmised, glancing up at Izzy. 'The reporter said that the poor woman was stabbed to death.'

Isobel sucked in her breath at the thought, and then realised that she was there, at the station, when the train was pulling in, but there was no need to tell Maurice this trivial detail, she thought; he was distressed enough without her wittering on about her own narrow escape.

'Do you have any idea who she might be?' Izzy finally asked, her head a little fuzzy from the strong liquor.

'Not yet,' the boulangerie owner admitted, 'but I don't think it will be long before someone reports a loved one missing.'

Maurice Fabron was right. Twenty minutes later, as Isobel helped him to clear away the remnants of the day's business, the phone rang.

The tall man murmured quietly into the receiver, leaning his head against the cold stone of the shop wall, his lips hardly moving as he took in the information that was being relayed before hanging up.

'What is it?' Isobel cried, taking in the baker's pallid face and tearful eyes.

'That was Madam Paradis, my sister-in-law's housekeeper,' Maurice explained, his voice still no more than a whisper. 'The woman on the train has been identified. It was Cecile.'

Izzy paused for a second, running the name through her head. Cecile Vidal was Maurice's late wife's sister, wasn't she? The one who had been burgled last weekend. That was right.

'Oh, Maurice!' she cried, rushing to put an arm around her boss's shoulder. 'I'm so sorry, that must be such a shock. How dreadful.'

Monsieur Fabron bent at the waist, allowing Isobel to guide him to a chair as he pulled a clean white handkerchief from his trouser pocket.

'I cannot speak,' the baker muttered. 'Oh poor, poor Cecile.'

Izzy fetched a glass of ice-cold water, wishing to make herself useful in the midst of such a desperate situation, and then reality dawned on her. There was a murderer out there on the loose, either living in or around Saint Margaux. Suddenly, her new, idyllic life felt vulnerable and threatened. If whoever had murdered Cecile was still out there, he could kill again. And still, a rational part of her mind was turning over a question. Where was Telo?

'Maurice, perhaps you should go home and check on Telo,' she suggested tactfully, her heavy heart hoping that the young man was employed in some innocent venture. 'He might have seen the news and be concerned.'

Maurice stood, shakily at first, but then, with determination, using both hands to pull himself upright as though the effort took every last ounce of energy.

'You are right, of course, I should go to him. Telo is very fond of Cecile. *Was*. Oh, how am I going to tell him? And of course, then I must go to Hubert, he will need me. Who could do such a terrible thing?'

The baker strode towards the door, allowing Isobel to reassure him that she would take responsibility for locking up the boulangerie. His shoulders were hunched, features taut.

'I am so sorry,' Isobel told him sincerely as they parted company. 'Maybe you should rest tomorrow. I'll look after things here, I'm sure everyone will understand.'

'We will stay closed tomorrow,' Monsieur Fabron announced, suddenly straightening his back and looking Izzy in the eye. 'As a mark of respect to Cecile.'

'Of course. I'm sorry, Maurice, I didn't think.'

As Maurice stepped out into the late afternoon breeze, Isobel looked over to the baker's residence, half expecting Telo Fabron to appear. The young man did just that, although he was not alone. Telo was accompanied by a handsome man of around thirty and they were exiting the front door together, each holding a parcel under their arm.

'Oh, do you have a guest, Maurice?' Izzy blurted out, her eyes following the men as they turned left towards the church.

'That's just Gaston,' the baker informed her. 'He's an artist and stays here with Simone Dupuis each summer. You'll meet him soon enough. I must hurry to catch up with them. Good night.'

Izzy watched her employer stride purposefully across the square, calling out to the men and beckoning them to return to the 'Maison de Maitre,' before closing the bakery door, turning the key in the lock and switching off the lights.

Upstairs, realising that her head was pounding with irrational thoughts and a slight sense of fear, Isobel Gilyard popped two painkillers into her mouth and washed them down with a glass of orange juice. She had triple-checked the boulangerie doors, front and back, before coming upstairs, and Monsieur Fabron was right across the street, but still she knew that she would find it impossible to sleep that night. The knowledge that it could easily have been her on that train to Bordeaux was the most troubling aspect of her anxious thoughts. A local train, travelling just two stops, with passengers who probably encountered each other on a regular basis… It didn't bear thinking about.

She stood at the window, contemplating whether to bolt the shutters, too. It seemed that even the local dogs were too rattled to stay outside that evening and Isobel couldn't blame them. It seemed that Saint Margaux was not quite the crime-free community that she had been led to believe after all.

Rat-a-tat-tat. A sharp knocking on the back door alerted Izzy to a visitor and, quickly putting down the hot cup of instant noodles she was about to start eating, she ventured downstairs. Through the pane of patterned glass in the rear entrance, a man's face was peering in, as though wondering whether the occupant had heard his rapping knuckles. Isobel unlocked the door and pulled it open a fraction, leaving the brass chain secured.

'*Bonsoir,*' a dark-haired hunk said, his voice husky and soft. 'Isobel?'

'Yes.'

Immediately, Izzy recognised the man as the artist that had been with Telo Fabron just an hour earlier. He wore a pair of smart navy shorts and had several leather wristbands on his bare forearms.

'I am Gaston. I'm sorry to disturb you,' the visitor was explaining, his dark eyes peering into the dark corridor behind Isobel, 'but Maurice is preparing a light supper and cannot find his bread knife. Is it possible that we could borrow...'

'Ah, yes, of course, from the bakery...'

The man nodded, gesturing to the boulangerie kitchen. '*Oui, merci.*'

Isobel couldn't help but fix her eyes on the few stray hairs that protruded from the artist's white linen shirt, alluring in their darkness as they curled around an unfastened top button.

'I'll just get it for you,' she told him, turning to leave but still not unlatching the door.

A minute later, Izzy was back, the long, steel-handled bread knife in her hand, its sharp length wrapped carefully in a tea-towel. 'Here you go. I hope everything is alright over there, with Maurice and Telo.'

'Naturally, we are all very upset,' Gaston said, taking the blade through the gap in the door. He sighed deeply. 'Madam Vidal was a wonderful woman. Thank you for this.'

'Please, tell Maurice to let me know if I can help in any way at all,' Izzy said, more of an afterthought than with real conviction.

The young man leaned forward, a whiff of perfumed soap escaping from his warm skin. 'Thank you, I will tell him.'

As Isobel's hand let go of the bread knife, a flicker of red caught her eye. She squinted, wanting to be certain of what she was seeing and then let out a gasp. On the cuff of Gaston's shirt was a thick, dark streak of red that curved upwards and disappeared, almost as though the wearer had folded the cuff up and over the stain in an effort to hide it. Such a dark red mark could only be blood.

'Are you alright?' the man asked, hearing a slight shriek from Izzy's lips.

'Yes, just caught my nail on the door latch. Good night.'

Gaston raised a hand before turning back towards the Fabron's house, seemingly unaware that he'd caused Isobel Gilyard's heartbeat to skip more than one beat. The woman's eyes followed him out of the courtyard, taking in the thick dark hair and confident air with which he walked.

Izzy eventually fell asleep that night, but dreams came erratically, causing her to toss and turn as she struggled for wakefulness. The image of the blonde woman with a black handbag was the clearest of the illusions; for some reason, she was laughing at Isobel, showing perfect teeth and bright red lipstick. The station clerk, Jean, was chuckling loudly too, causing Isobel's ears to ring so loudly that, when she did finally bring herself to the surface, she found her own hands clasped tightly to the sides of her head.

Beads of perspiration trickled down between her breasts as she lay gasping on top of the cotton sheets, the name 'Cecile' foremost in her mind. Had that really been the murdered woman that she'd seen this morning, she asked herself, trying desperately to remember. She wished that she'd taken more notice now, especially of the other people standing waiting for the train. The perpetrator could quite easily have been there, too, she realised, hiding in plain sight without anyone wise to his identity.

At three in the morning, she gulped a glass of water and sat down on the edge of the bed, trying to straighten out fact from fiction in her head. Fact: she had seen Cecile Vidal at the station that morning. Fiction: she hadn't been laughing. Isobel remembered the racing police cars and figured that the time might have coincided with the discovery of the murder. It was strange, too, that she hadn't seen Telo that morning, when on the previous two days he had been loading up the delivery van with orders. Of course she couldn't suspect Telo of

anything untoward, simply based on the fact that he was a little strange –
Maurice had already explained about his son's learning and social difficulties –
but nevertheless, it was an odd coincidence.

Two niggling thoughts came pushing their way to the forefront, things so
damning that Isobel just couldn't ignore the implications. The stranger, Gaston,
had only appeared that afternoon, from where, she had no clue, and the same
soapy smell that had filled her car came from the man's body. Not only that, but
there, as plain as day, was a huge red blob of dried liquid, blemishing an
otherwise spotless shirt.

CHAPTER SIX – A MURDER INVESTIGATION

Paul Theron washed his large rough hands in an industrial-sized sink before pulling off the latex rubber gloves and clinical mask. He breathed deeply through his nose and gestured for the two men to follow him through into a small, cluttered office. Lighting a filtered cigarette, he offered one to Mallery and Hobbs, but only Max accepted.

'As you know, she was stabbed to death, but there are actually seven deep wounds, the most fatal of which punctured her left ventricle,' Theron admitted, speaking in English for the benefit of the younger detective. 'The murder weapon was a knife of some kind, with a serrated edge.'

Max Mallery rubbed his stubbled chin, slightly ashamed that he'd had to forgo his usual pristine appearance that day. 'Serrated… you mean something like a hunter's knife?'

Paul Theron exhaled and shook his head. 'No, nothing quite as wide as that. This was longer in the blade, but thinner, I think more like a domestic bread knife.'

'Poor woman,' Jack Hobbs remarked, looking back to where Cecile Vidal's cold body lay prostrate on the autopsy table. 'Are we looking for a left- or right-handed suspect?'

'Most definitely right-handed, I should say, given the angle of entry and the force with which the weapon was applied. Although the victim put up a good fight. She has lacerations on both hands, no doubt from trying to defend herself.'

Max coughed slightly, trying to rid himself of the nausea that had begun as soon as they'd stepped inside Doctor Theron's workspace. 'Right-handed. That's about three-quarters of the population of France. Great. Are there any other clues at all that you can give us, in particular anything specific to go on?'

'One strange matter is the pastel candy that was stuck in the victim's throat,' the doctor told him, pointing to his own larynx to demonstrate the exact positioning. 'An unusual type, square and striped.'

Theron left the room, immediately returning to the stainless-steel bench where he retrieved a clear plastic bag containing a hard-boiled sweet. 'Here we are.'

'Have either of you seen anything like that before?' Mallery asked the other men, holding the small bag up to the light.

'Not since I was a lad,' Hobbs answered, looking closely at the object, a pink and white square candy. 'Our local sweet shop used to have jars of those when I was a kid. I haven't seen any for years, though.'

'I don't suppose there was…' Max started.

'Nothing to connect it to your killer,' Paul Theron confessed, his bald head shining under the fluorescent office lighting. 'Although no other confectionery was found in the victim's handbag, either. No empty wrapper or paper bag to suggest where it came from. I can only surmise that the murderer gave it to her, perhaps as a way to start a conversation?'

The detectives pondered the theory, admitting that it could easily have been a friendly gesture between two passengers.

Theron gestured to another, larger bag containing the deceased woman's personal effects. A small vial of perfume spray, black purse, set of house keys, a few items of make-up, a small compact mirror and a cigarette lighter made up the entire contents. It didn't give the investigators much to go on at all.

'As you see, just the regular items one would expect to find inside a lady's bag.'

Max lifted the plastic carefully between two fingers, turning it back and forth. 'Do you see that? The lighter?' he asked his colleague, frowning slightly.

'Yes, sir, but why would a Frenchwoman have a Union Jack lighter?'

'Why indeed, Jacques?'

'So, in the carriage,' Jack questioned after completing his notes, 'nobody saw or heard anything? Have we interviewed everyone?'

'I spoke to several passengers myself,' Max said, 'and Gabriella has been through the background of each. Just regular people going about their business. It was a quiet time of day. Most commuters catch the later train at eight-thirty.'

'What about the murder weapon?'

'Still no sign of it. The knife disappeared along with the perpetrator,' his boss answered candidly. 'We've had men out searching the tracks since yesterday morning as you know, in case something was thrown from a window. I've told Thierry to call me immediately if they find anything.'

'Tragic,' Theron commented, slowly rubbing his forehead. 'That's what it is.'

The detectives stood silent for a few moments, desperately seeking inspiration for more questions, yet each wrapped up in their own thoughts.

'If you think of anything else that might be of any relevance, Paul...' Mallery sighed. The slightest clue would be much appreciated.'

'Naturally, Max. I will be in touch.'

Paul Theron shook hands with the detectives, although Max couldn't shrug off the image of the man's huge hands cutting open Cecile Vidal's body just an hour earlier. He'd met Theron a few weeks previously at a conference and the two had instantly hit it off, despite their twenty-year age gap and conflicting interests. The Inspector instinctively knew that Theron would have done a thorough job of examining Cecile Vidal and had no reason to question his findings.

'Where to now, boss?' Jack Hobbs asked, as they left the clinical-looking Coroner's building with its long, dark windows and glass double doors.

'Didn't that bother you at all?' Max scowled, hunching over to quickly light another cigarette. 'That place makes me so… so queasy.'

'Of course it did, sir, but there's a fair bit of knife crime in Leeds. Not that I'm used to it, I just kind of shut off my feelings for a while. I also stick Vicks menthol rub up my nose and then keep my mouth closed.' He proudly produced a round blue and green jar from his jacket pocket.

'Hmm, you'll have to teach me how to do that. I never get used to that smell, it's like iron and blood. Well, I suppose the first place to visit is the vineyard. We need to plot Madam Vidal's movements since we last saw her.'

'Yes, sir. Do you want me to drive?' Jack offered, gesturing towards the practical Ford Mondeo. 'I really don't mind if you're tired.'

'No chance,' Mallery huffed. 'I need at least another three cigarettes on the way, and I take it the 'baby policy' still stands. Leave your car here and we'll take mine. I'll drop you off later.'

'I'm sorry I missed your call this morning, sir,' Hobbs told his boss, as they got out onto the open highway. 'Angélique and I had been up all night with…'

'*Oui, oui*,' Mallery interrupted, 'but don't make a habit of it. When it comes to a murder investigation, the more pairs of eyes, the better, Jacques. Your record is exemplary in this field and I need you to be, how to say, on the ball? Nevertheless, we covered a lot of ground yesterday and have made a good start today, although I can predict a lot of long working days ahead of us.'

'I'm fine with that, sir, it won't happen again, I promise.'

Max inhaled deeply. He wasn't immune to the plight of the new father but, not having any children of his own, didn't completely empathise, either.

'Finding it tough?' Max prompted, realising that perhaps he'd spoken too sharply to his new foreign recruit.

'Not exactly, sir, but with the move and Thomas teething, I'm a bit knackered.'

'Knackered,' Mallery repeated, the word playing on his lips as though it tingled. 'What a great expression.'

Hobbs rubbed his eyes. He hadn't arrived home until well after nine the previous night and Angélique had immediately handed Thomas over to him. Not that Jack minded, but he'd spent the whole day at the murder site and had hardly eaten anything. As Angélique ran herself a hot, bubbly bath, Jack had been left to reheat some soup and deal with his red-gummed child.

'How come there wasn't a single witness?' Jack asked, trying to tactfully steer the conversation back to the investigation.

'Well, as we saw, there were four carriages on that train,' the Inspector explained, 'yet only a handful of passengers. It is quite strange that nobody heard a cry for help, though, but Madam Vidal was seated at the rear of the train so perhaps her screams were muffled.'

Hobbs mulled the information over in his mind for a few minutes.

'Something just doesn't add up. Somebody must have seen something.'

As the duo arrived at the gates of the Saint Margaux vineyard early that afternoon, they noted several other vehicles parked outside the entrance to the main house. A group of workers were huddled together, looking solemn and tired, evidently feeling shocked by their employer's demise.

'*Bonjour*!' Mallery called, waving at the men. '*Je suis Inspecteur Mallery.*'

The oldest of the group rose and pointed towards the expansive and well-tended garden. '*Monsieur Vidal est là-bas.*'

Hobbs followed his boss down a path of neat yellow paving stones flanking low hedges at the rear of the property, to where Hubert Vidal was leaning against a fence, looking skywards. He seemed to be oblivious to the approaching officers.

'*Monsieur Vidal*,' Max called, '*je suis désolé.*'

Hubert reacted to the voice and turned his red-rimmed eyes towards them.

'Ah, the Inspector and the Englishman. *Bonjour.*'

'I'm sorry for your loss and I'm also sorry to have to do this today, under the circumstances,' Mallery told him, 'but the quicker we gather information, the faster we will catch the person responsible for Madam Vidal's murder.'

The winemaker nodded. 'I don't know what I can tell you really. Cecile hadn't left the house since you came here on Monday. Yesterday was her first trip to Bordeaux in a few weeks. I just can't believe anyone would want to hurt her.'

'Was she planning to meet anyone?' Jack pressed, flipping his notebook to a clean page. 'Or did she have any appointments that you know of?'

'I did ask what she had planned,' Hubert shrugged, 'but she just tapped her nose. It's my birthday next week, you see, so I presumed that Cecile was going into town to buy something special for me.'

'How did she get to the train station? Did she walk?' Max asked, figuring that it would take a fit person no more than ten minutes to reach the village.

'No, no. I was driving down to check on the vines in the lower part of the estate fields, so naturally I offered to give her a lift.'

A thought popped into Jack's head and he poised his pen over the paper, thinking. 'Your wife caught the eight o'clock train to Bordeaux, Monsieur Vidal. Isn't that rather early, considering that the shops don't open until nine?'

Hubert feigned a laugh. 'No, not at all. She would occasionally meet up with friends for breakfast before shopping, a habit of most French women.'

Hobbs wrote down the information, thinking about his own wife Angélique and how, in the three years of their marriage, cultural differences between them had often caused some minor arguments, occasionally all-out war.

'It's a difficult question to ask under the circumstances,' Mallery began, looking out across the fields, 'but can anyone corroborate your whereabouts yesterday morning, Monsieur Vidal? I mean, after you dropped your wife off?'

Hubert sniffed and pointed over to the men who were still milling about by the parked cars. 'I was with the workers all morning. We were taking samples and clipping back the top vines. We finished around midday, then came back to the barn to have some lunch. Madam Paradis had prepared it, and that's when two of your officers arrived and broke the news. Ask any of my men, Inspector.'

Max wished he'd been the one to speak to Hubert the previous day and he hoped that the uniformed officers tasked with the difficult job of telling the man about his wife's murder had been considerate. Pain was etched all over the winemaker's face. His cheeks were sallow as he looked at the officers directly, resigned to the fact that it was their duty to ask such personal questions. He took a deep breath and blinked back tears before looking away.

'We'll leave you now,' Max decided suddenly, seeing the sheer exhaustion on the recently widowed man's face. 'But should you think of anything, or perhaps anyone you saw near the station yesterday morning, please…'

He took out a rectangular card with his name and mobile phone number printed in blue ink, which Vidal accepted with shaking hands.

'Inspector,' Hubert Vidal called out, as the detectives began retracing their steps towards the car, 'I did see someone who may have been on the same train. It was Maurice's new bakery assistant, or so Cecile pointed out to me.'

'Are you certain, Monsieur?'

'Yes… well, my wife seemed sure it was her. You see, I haven't met the woman myself, but Cecile said she'd seen her arriving on Saturday. When we pulled up at the station, I suppose it was about five to eight as we were running late, she was getting out of a battered old Volkswagen Beetle and heading towards the ticket office.'

'Thank you, Monsieur, you've been very helpful.'

'Miss Gilyard wasn't amongst the passengers that we interviewed,' Jack pointed out, flicking his notepad.

'Let's go and see what Isobel Gilyard has to say for herself,' Max told his junior officer, as soon as they had made themselves comfortable in the BMW.

'Bit of a coincidence that she was at Saint Margaux station,' Hobbs remarked, tugging at his seatbelt, 'but why the hell wasn't she there at the other end?'

Seeing the doors of the Saint Margaux boulangerie firmly closed and the linen blinds pulled down, Max asked a passer-by where he might find the proprietor and was pointed in the direction of a grand house across the street. Maurice Fabron was sitting at the breakfast bar in his kitchen when Mallery and Hobbs arrived. A cup of coffee had been left to go cold in front of him and the daily newspaper was still folded and unread. A dark-haired stranger was at the counter, carefully laying out slices of bread, tomato and cheese on four side plates, and an elegant woman entered the room from a side door, gliding silently into the room.

'Please take a seat,' Maurice told the policemen, gesturing to the tall stools. 'Officers, these are friends of mine, Simone and Gaston. How can I help you? Have you found the despicable person who murdered poor Cecile?'

'Not yet, Monsieur Fabron,' Max admitted, 'but I promise you we're working on it. Perhaps we could speak to you in private?'

The baker stood to get a drink of water, gripping the sink with clenched fingers as he filled the glass. 'No need. Simone is a close friend and Gaston, too. We are all affected by this. Poor Cecile. I still cannot take it all in.'

The woman lifted a lace handkerchief to her cheeks and dabbed gently at the tears that rolled down. 'She was my best friend.'

'Monsieur Fabron… Maurice,' Max went on, alerted to the apparent anger coursing through the shop owner's veins, but also aware of the man and woman listening intently as he spoke. 'We need to speak to your new assistant, Miss Gilyard. Do you know where we might find her?'

'Izzy? Why yes, she has the little apartment above the boulangerie. What has she to do with my sister-in-law's murder?'

Simone gasped and turned to Gaston, who immediately drew her close.

'It could be nothing,' Jack jumped in, diffusing the accusation in Maurice's voice and the obvious conclusions being settled upon by the couple, 'but apparently she was seen at the station, so we just want to talk to her – see if she noticed anyone else hanging around when Madam Vidal boarded the train.'

'But…' Maurice queried, looking pensive. 'Izzy told me that she drove to Bordeaux. Yes, I saw her in the car, she definitely didn't catch the train.'

The detectives looked at one another, confusion and intrigue on their faces. Why had Isobel Gilyard lied to her boss? Was Maurice just confused?

'Perhaps we should pop over there now,' Max ventured, tugging Jack to his feet, 'just to clear things up. I'm sure it's just a misunderstanding.'

'As you wish.' Monsieur Fabron narrowed his eyes as he followed the men down the cool elegant hallway. 'Knock loudly on the back door, through the courtyard,' he instructed. 'She's probably there. But I'm sure you are mistaken about Izzy being at the station.'

Telo Fabron had heard the detectives arrive and leave. He'd spent the whole morning in his bedroom, inconsolable after hearing the news of his beloved aunt's death, but now he shuffled to the top of the winding staircase, eager to hear what the men were telling his father.

'*Comme c'est interessant*!' he heard Gaston comment as soon as the front door was firmly closed.

Telo peered over the polished banister to see his father's reaction and was just in time to see a look of shock on the man's face. '*Oui. Beaucoup.*'

Simone Dupuis shook her head and touched Maurice on the arm, saying in French, 'You might regret the day you let that strange Englishwoman into your life.'

'So, let's be clear on this,' Max repeated, as he counted off the facts on his fingers one by one. 'You did go to the train station yesterday morning, you did see Cecile Vidal arrive, but you didn't buy a ticket as you didn't have enough change and then you decided to drive to Bordeaux. Is that correct so far?'

'Yes, that's right,' Isobel agreed, wide-eyed at the subtle interrogation. 'Where are you going with this, Inspector?'

'Can anyone verify your movements?' Jack pressed, checking his notes, 'Do you perhaps have a parking ticket from when you arrived in Bordeaux?'

'No, I parked in a quiet side street.'

'So, nobody can corroborate what you've told us?'

'Well, not really, I was on my own. Oh, hang on, maybe, the man in the ticket office. He'll probably remember.'

'I'll make a phone call,' Mallery offered, stepping out of the bright living room where Izzy had her feet tucked underneath her on an over-stuffed sofa.

Jack Hobbs looked around at the obvious lack of personal effects. 'You haven't had time to unpack yet then, Miss Gilyard?'

'I'm not one for ornaments,' she replied tersely. 'Does that matter, Detective?'

'Not at all,' he countered, turning to read the title of a book on the sparse shelf. 'Thought you might have a few family photos, though. It's tough living away from home.'

'Is it? Maybe for you, Detective Hobbs, but I'm perfectly content here.'

The woman deftly unfolded her legs, flashing a glimpse of her thigh as the summer dress lifted with the movement, and padded into the kitchen to light a cigarette on the gas stove. Jack Hobbs watched closely from the doorway.

'Don't you have a lighter, Miss Gilyard?' he asked, trying to keep the excitement out of his voice as pieces of the puzzle slotted themselves together in a jumbled but coincidental manner.

'I seem to have misplaced it,' Izzy snapped, blowing a circle of smoke in Jack's face as she pushed past him on the way back into the sparse living room.

Max Mallery announced his re-entry into the apartment with heavy footsteps on the stairs as he leapt up them two at a time, panting slightly as he reached the top. It had taken him all of three minutes to gather the information needed.

'Well, I'm afraid we're out of luck today. Jean Manon, the stationmaster, was looking after the ticket office yesterday for an hour or so but, unfortunately for us, he's now on his way to Switzerland for two weeks.'

Izzy threw her head back, remembering Maurice mentioning Jean's vacation plans to her a couple of days ago. 'Oh, yes, I'd forgotten about that.'

'You knew he was taking a holiday?'

'Yes. Monsieur Fabron told me about it, after Jean came in late on Saturday afternoon to buy some croissants.'

'How very convenient,' Max replied, curling his lip as a suspect profile began to form inside his head.

'What do you mean, "convenient"?' Izzy spat fiercely. 'I didn't have anything to do with Cecile Vidal's death. I barely knew the woman!'

'Just one more thing,' Jack stated proudly, ready to impress Mallery with his skills of detection. 'Could you describe your lighter, please?'

'What? My lighter? What on earth for?'

'A lighter was found in the victim's possession,' he continued, despite a confused glare from Max, 'and I rather suspect that it didn't belong to her.'

'If you must know, it had a Union Jack on it,' Isobel informed them proudly. 'So, quite unique in these parts but hardly likely to be the same one.'

Mallery indicated with a jerk of the head that Jack should head outside with him; they didn't want to give too much away too soon.

'We'll be in touch,' he called as they descended the stairs. 'Don't go too far, Miss Gilyard.'

Isobel rushed to the window, eager to see the detectives departing before pulling the drapes across. She could just make out Telo across the street, watching the red BMW turn full circle in the square, but he was too far away for her to read the expression on his face.

A shiver went down Izzy's spine. She thought she was immune to the fear that sometimes came with being questioned, but evidently not. What was all that about a lighter? Surely it was a coincidence? On reflection, Isobel wished she'd mentioned the artist to Inspector Mallery, and that strange red stain on his cuff. If Gaston had been involved with Cecile Vidal's murder, he would have had time to wash his shirt, and the evidence, by now. There was a tight knot in Izzy's stomach, one that felt familiar yet hadn't presented itself for almost a decade. She ran to the bathroom just in time to hurl up the contents of her lunch into the sink.

'What do you make of that?' Max inquired, as soon as he and Hobbs had descended the apartment stairs. 'Defensive? Definitely covering something up, and that lighter has to be hers. I'll make sure it's being tested for fingerprints.'

Jack wasn't quite so eager to agree. 'Isobel Gilyard does seem a bit odd, but she's only been in Saint Margaux a few days. Hardly enough time to make enemies and carry out a crime, sir. I agree that it's too much of a coincidence for her to have lost a Union Jack lighter at the same time as one is found in the victim's bag, though.'

'Are you saying you think she's been set up in some way?'

'Not exactly. She's hiding something, but I'm not sure what. She certainly doesn't seem the type to stab someone to death. She's feisty, but not crazy.'

'Who is? Until the right motive comes along, eh, Jacques?' Max conceded.

Jack bristled as his boss put emphasis on the French pronunciation of his name. It seemed the more he asked Max to call him 'Jack', the more he ignored the request.

'There was something that I noticed, though,' the young protégé admitted as the sports engine started up and sped out of the village, feeling smug that he'd been the one to spot the unusual item in Izzy's living room.

Mallery swung round, eyes glimmering like a shark spotting a bather's bare leg. 'Come on then, out with it.'

'Well, there was a brand new book on her shelf. It still had the price sticker on the front. I'd say that, from the perfect spine, it hadn't been read yet.'

'And what about it? For goodness' sake, what relevance does it have to us?'

Jack Hobbs paused for effect, casually looking at his fingernails and then out through the car window at the passing countryside.

'The title was *The Invention of Murder*, by Judith Flanders.'

CHAPTER SEVEN – CONFRONTATION

On Friday morning, Isobel was up early; 'at the crack of dawn' as her father would have commented. Having slept soundly and without the repetitive nightmares that sometimes caused her to wake drenched in a cold sweat, she had woken to the sound of a car being driven around the back of the building. She knew that the only vehicles that should have been there were the Citroën delivery van and her own Volkswagen Beetle, and the distinctive ticking of the engine gave Izzy a fair idea of which one she could hear.

Hurrying to the bathroom window that overlooked the small courtyard, Isobel shrugged on a light dressing-gown as she went. Down below, coming out from underneath the carport, was Telo Fabron. The young man looked around sheepishly as he strode across the cobbled stones but failed to look upwards at the curious woman who was watching him. Izzy did a double-take. Had Telo been using her car without permission? How dare he? In a state of fury, she raced downstairs, catching Telo as he unlocked the back door and entered the boulangerie kitchen.

'Hey!' Izzy yelled, the colour rising in her cheeks, fingers trembling as she pulled her flimsy gown closed. 'What the hell do you think you've been doing?'

'*Comment?*' Telo sneered, raising his brows. 'What?'

'You,' Isobel pointed, making driving motions with her hands, '*mon auto.*'

Telo stared, appearing wide-eyed and confused, as though the accusation was the most ridiculous thing he'd ever heard and pushed past her to enter the shop, where he set about brewing coffee.

Izzy followed, desperate to collect her rudimentary French together in order to make herself perfectly understood. She concluded that the simplest words in short sentences might be best.

'*Telo, où allez-vous?*' she gasped. 'Where have you been?'

Telo Fabron stood with his back to Isobel, clattering cups and spooning ground coffee into the machine, ignoring her question, yet his spine stiffened quite noticeably.

'Don't turn your back on me,' Izzy growled. 'I bloody well saw you. You've been out in my car.'

'Who has been out in your car?' another voice called out in clear English. 'Izzy? Is there something I should know?'

Isobel turned, coming face to face with her puzzled employer.

'Telo has been driving my car without asking,' she explained, her temper reducing to a mild simmer in the hope that Maurice would now take over the interrogation.

Telo turned towards his father and asked simply, 'Papa?'

Isobel stood quietly as the baker put her accusation to his son in plain French, Telo answering clearly and without faltering once.

'Well, that is cleared up,' Maurice shrugged, facing Izzy now. 'A simple explanation. It seems that when you returned on Wednesday, you parked your car behind our van so Telo had to move it this morning in order to get the Citroën out to do the deliveries. I'm not happy about him driving your car without insurance, but no harm done.'

'But…' Isobel faltered, 'how did he get the key?'

'*Où est la clé?*' Maurice asked.

Telo responded by shrugging his shoulders and opening his palms to show that he had nothing to hide. '*Dans l'auto.*'

'Could it be possible that you left the keys in the car when you came back after your shopping trip?' the baker enquired, his demeanour giving no clues as to whether he was annoyed or completely calm.

Izzy thought quickly, retracing her steps. She'd parked up and carried her shopping bags and… 'Oh, gosh, yes, I think I did!'

Maurice sighed. 'So now, we are clear, nothing to be alarmed about, *oui?*'

Half an hour later, Isobel Gilyard was showered, dressed and making her way back down the stairs to the bakery for the second time that morning. It was by now eight o'clock and she looked forward to applying her skills as a baker. If nothing else, it was therapeutic and would take her mind off the embarrassing accusations that she'd made a while earlier. Izzy had to admit to herself that Telo's explanation had been completely plausible, yet she could kick herself now, as a recollection of the soapy smell in the Beetle came to the fore.

Maurice seemed unfazed by the car scenario, although, as he simultaneously kneaded dough and slid golden loaves out of the oven, there was a dark cloud hanging over the bakery as all three co-workers dwelled deeply upon Cecile Vidal's murder and the ongoing investigation.

Within the first two days of her employment at the boulangerie, Izzy had tirelessly toiled over ginger biscuits, cream horns and custard tarts, the enthusiasm to prove herself a worthy baker knowing no bounds. It was effective, too, for Maurice Fabron was delighted with her work and layered on praise after praise. Isobel was unsure whether it was the pastry-rolling, creating delicate icing which required her full concentration, or the whisking of cream for her delectable fillings, that caused her intense feelings of pride. Each process had its own merits.

However, the surprise visit from Mallery and Hobbs was weighing heavily upon her and, as she worked, she could feel an inexplicable growing anxiety. Maurice was naturally morose, but Izzy couldn't work out whether he was taking Cecile's death badly or knew that the detectives had paid her a visit. She didn't have to wait long to find out.

'So, Izzy,' Monsieur Fabron called into the back room where she was carefully piping cream cheese onto a freshly baked carrot cake, 'it must be time for us to take a break, *oui*? If we continue in this way, so busy, I shall have to change the business name from 'Fabron's Boulangerie' to 'Fabron's Patisserie.'

Isobel looked up from her task, a faint smile on her face. 'Just give me two minutes, Maurice, and then I'd love a cup of tea.'

The baker nodded approvingly, as much at the woman's dedication to her cake-making as to the fact that she was willing to sit and talk with him.

As the pair sat with a pot of Earl Grey and a plate of vanilla biscuits between them, Maurice ran a finger around the rim of his cup and carefully considered whether to ask the question that had gathered on the tip of his tongue. Relief washed over him as Isobel took the reins and ploughed right in.

'I had a visit from the police yesterday,' she said openly, taking a sip of the tea. 'They wanted to ask me why I was at the station.'

'I wasn't aware that you were there. Didn't you drive to Bordeaux?'

Maurice looked perplexed, as Isobel's version of events somehow conflicted with those of the officers, but he waited patiently, allowing his assistant to explain what had occurred two days earlier.

'Now it is very clear,' he sighed, when Izzy had supplied every last detail. 'Do you think you might have seen someone following Cecile?'

'I'm so sorry,' she confessed. 'I was only there for a few minutes and was mostly preoccupied with counting out enough coins for the train fare.'

Maurice looked disappointed but had nothing to admonish Isobel for. 'Let's hope that they find this despicable criminal very soon. I still cannot believe there are such evil people in the world. Saint Margaux has always been a peaceful and safe place, until now.'

The bakers were suddenly interrupted by the appearance of Gaston. This time, he was wearing cut-off jeans and a casual plain t-shirt that revealed the curves of taut muscles beneath.

'Bonjour, Maurice, bonjour, Mademoiselle Gilyard.'

'Ah, Gaston!' Maurice enthused, getting up to greet the artist and hugging him warmly. 'We are just taking tea. Will you join us?'

'I can't stay.' The young man smiled weakly. 'I just came in to pick up a loaf for Simone and to ask if there was any news, you know, about the investigation?'

Isobel noticed the artist's impeccable English and promised herself that she would spend an hour every evening practising French from that day onwards.

'Nothing at all,' Maurice told him, continuing in English, in order for Izzy to join if should she so wish. 'Let's hope this Max Mallery is a smart detective. And of course, how is Simone? Has she opened up the shop today?'

'Naturally she is still very upset, so I am working in the shop this morning and I've told her to get some rest. In fact, I was wondering if you could spare Telo for a couple of hours to do a few deliveries. Simone has had lots of extra orders today, as people want to leave tributes at the station for Cecile.'

Maurice rubbed his eyes. 'Of course, he'll be glad to help out. I think he's out back, washing the van. Tell Simone I'll visit later, when we close here.'

The young man bowed his head solemnly. 'Simone will be glad to see you. Having something to keep him busy might keep Telo's mind off his aunt, too. I think he's taking it pretty hard.'

Isobel looked down at Gaston's bare wrists, reminded of the stained shirt he'd been wearing the first time they'd met. It was hard to imagine that there was anything more than an innocent explanation, but the mark had most definitely looked to her like dried blood. Watching the men interact, she wondered how well Maurice really knew the artist. Didn't they always say that most crimes were committed by people you knew?

As a warm loaf was carefully wrapped in brown paper and passed across the counter, Isobel stood up and gathered the empty cups. 'I'd better get the cakes finished. Nice to see you again, Gaston.'

'My pleasure, Miss Gilyard.'

'Take a little longer,' Maurice told her. 'There's no rush for the cakes as we're not busy. Maybe go up and have a proper lunch break today? It's been a difficult couple of days for all of us.'

'Thanks. Do you know, I think I will.'

The artist tilted his head, watching the woman closely, although no smile was present as he saw her disappear into the kitchen.

As soon as Izzy was out of earshot, Gaston leaned over the counter and tugged gently at Maurice's sleeve. 'What did the police say to her? Do they think she is involved?' he asked, in rapid French.

'I'll explain later,' the baker promised, glancing back over his shoulder to where Isobel was now unlatching the door to upstairs. 'It's just a mix-up. It seems she wasn't on the train, after all.'

Gaston accepted the response but was only just warming to the topic. 'That's good to hear, Maurice. But look, if you don't mind me saying, there's something a bit secretive about your new assistant. I feel as though she's hiding something. What do you actually know about her?'

Maurice looked up and frowned. 'Izzy is simply here to help me in the boulangerie, there's nothing more to it. Gaston, you are mistaken. She was just in the wrong place. The police have cleared things up, I'm sure of it.'

'Think about it, Maurice,' the artist pressed on. 'Saint Margaux has been crime-free for centuries and now suddenly we have a murderer in our midst. Is it just a coincidence that Miss Gilyard showed up here, just days before Cecile was murdered?'

The baker rolled his eyes up towards the ceiling where, in the room above, he could hear Izzy's footsteps moving around the little apartment.

'Mere coincidence. Now, stop letting your imagination run away with you.'

Isobel lay back on the soft cotton bedspread, intending only to close her tired eyes for a few minutes, just long enough to gather her torrent of thoughts into some kind of rational perspective. She tried to compartmentalise everything in her head; Cecile Vidal's murder, the strange scent in the Beetle, Telo's behaviour, the red stain on Gaston's sleeve and the visit from the detectives. Out of all these 'anomalies', Izzy knew that it was the surprise appearance of Mallery and Hobbs that had shaken her up the most. Even the fact that they'd been there, in her apartment, full of questions, was almost too much to bear.

And then Hobbs, asking about her cigarette lighter… Why on earth would that be significant? Izzy hadn't missed the lack of subtlety in Mallery's pulling the junior detective away, just at the point where he was going to explain, either. A flashback to a scenario that happened over a decade before caused her to give an involuntary shudder. She prayed that history wasn't just about to repeat itself…

A cold grey room, cups of lukewarm coffee that tasted like dishwater, hours of sleep deprivation and then questions, so many endless questions. She'd been allowed just one phone call and had spoken to her father, who in turn had waited until almost the end of his working day before ringing the family solicitor. Isobel had waited for hours, knowing that her family would treat the incident as yet another of their daughter's misdemeanours. How right she had been.

Isobel had sat still facing a barrage of enquiries, her mind drifting to the house in Greater Manchester where she imagined her parents sitting down to a dinner of shepherd's pie or bangers and mash before even remotely considering that their daughter might need some moral support. In the windowless room, she'd been left alone to consider why she was there, a kind of mental torture dished out by the local police who had deemed her guilty before she could pause to draw breath. There was an empty chair in the room next to her, supposedly reserved for an appropriate adult. Whether that was her mother, a psychiatrist or a legal representative she never did find out…

Back in the present, Izzy gulped down a tumbler of ice-cold mineral water, tears pricking at her eyes, before getting down on her hands and knees in front of the huge bedroom closet. Delving to the back, behind sensible loafers and strappy sandals, she reached for the familiar shoe box, pausing before lifting the lid and looking inside. Staring back at her was the photograph of a man who looked around twenty-five years old. His mousy-coloured hair was trimmed neatly, in fact it was almost too perfect, while a smattering of freckles covered a smallish nose.

Isobel continued to take in the face, the curves of his shoulders, the prominent Adam's apple. Yet she was afraid, too scared to pick up the picture, almost as if the photo-paper would burn her fingers if she dared to lift it. Perhaps she had been foolish to keep this constant reminder, but it served a greater purpose in Izzy's mind. It ensured that she remained vigilant and didn't get too comfortable. She lifted the box onto the bed and lay down, thinking about her past and fearful for the future.

Martin Freeman had been the most attentive man she'd ever met. Sensitive, kind, sober, but in a way slightly boring compared to Isobel's numerous previous boyfriends. Izzy's friends had often commented on Martin's clothes, the smart blazers that were years out of fashion, the trousers that were just that little bit too short so you could see his white socks, and his unwavering obsession with ties.

Their tastes couldn't have been more different, either. Martin played the trombone, took part in amateur dramatics and collected stamps, whilst Izzy listened to heavy rock, was obsessed with black eye make-up and revolved her weekends around getting drunk. Nobody would have put them together as a couple, but something, a strong magnetism, attracted the two and they had started dating just a few weeks after they first met.

Martin would arrange to meet her from a friend's house so that she didn't have to walk home alone after dark, a gesture she took to be caring and cute. He would text throughout the day – if she counted, it could actually have been as often as every hour – just to see how she was doing. Isobel was a natural rebel and, despite her gothic clothing and alternative outlook on life, she relished the fact that her new boyfriend broke the mould. He didn't fit in. He stood out in a crowd and bored the hell out of her best friend. Still, the sex had been great. Martin was a naturally gifted lover and Izzy told herself that if that was his only prevailing positive factor, so be it. Who needed conversation, anyway?

Martin worked as a clerk for a distribution centre in the city and was able to afford to rent a flat, which at first was great. Instead of sneaking around and having sex in the back of his car, Martin would invite his girlfriend round for dinner, playing the perfect host and always taking her home by midnight. Clueless as to their evenings of lust, Isobel's parents had immediately warmed to the idea of Martin Freeman becoming their son-in-law. His ability to talk about politics with a fair degree of intellect won Mr Gilyard over at once, and by the time he'd brought numerous bunches of flowers for Isobel's mother, it was almost a given that the couple would eventually be married. Izzy's parents gave up lecturing their daughter about her choice of black clothing and back-combed hair, instead hoping that lovely, sensible Martin would tame her into a state of domestic submission.

However, it wasn't long before the alarm bells started ringing. Isobel felt suffocated, controlled, uncomfortable with Martin's constant presence and need to track her movements. He would always be there, just happening to drive by when she'd arranged to meet friends, offering lifts to the pub and back even though Martin was himself teetotal. At first, she'd thought his actions were caring and natural, the throes of first love, giddy and warm-hearted, normal for a lover obsessed, but after just a few short months together, panic set in and things began to change.

Having left work at the town library one Monday afternoon to attend a dental appointment, Isobel had caught sight of a red Ford Cortina with a black vinyl roof, exactly like Martin's, parked across the road. Due to the distance, she was unable to make out the registration number and presumed that it was sheer coincidence that a similar car was in the area. However, after exiting the dental surgery an hour later, she noticed the same car crawling down the street towards her. This time, she was in no doubt that it was Martin.

'Hey, thought you were at work all day,' she said with a grin, as he pulled up alongside the kerb and revved the engine.

'Never mind me, why aren't you at the library?' he'd bawled through the open window, wagging an index finger. 'Get in!'

Isobel had obeyed, not wanting to cause a scene in the middle of town where so many residents knew her parents and oblivious to the reason for Martin's short temper.

'I had to have a filling,' she'd told him innocently, turning to put her bag on the back seat of the car. 'It really hurts.'

That's when it happened.

Martin Freeman drew back a balled fist and punched his girlfriend so hard that she felt her jaw crack instantaneously with a loud splintering sound. Tears immediately welled up in her eyes from the pain.

Isobel's reactions had been too slow to get out of the car, the shock of his knuckles connecting with the side of her already swollen face a harsh distraction, and seconds later, Martin sped away, taking her out of town and down a country lane, miles from home.

Eventually, his rage dissipating, but with clenched fists still gripping the steering wheel, Martin had slowed down, pulling the car off the road and into a densely wooded area.

'Where are we?' Isobel had ventured, her words muffled from the inability to shape her mouth where it needed to be. 'Please, Martin. I'm scared.'

He rounded on her, teeth snarling like a rabid dog, spitting harsh words in her direction and grabbing a handful of her soft dark hair. 'Don't you ever, ever lie to me again, do you hear?'

Isobel kept one hand on her throbbing face as she nodded her head. The dental anaesthetic was beginning to wear off and pain seared through her cheekbone with an unbearable intensity.

'I didn't lie to you.'

Smack. Izzy's head connected with the car window as Martin pushed her backwards.

'You told me you were working all day,' he hissed, spittle frothing on his lips.

'I was. I forgot I had a dentist's appointment. Mum rang to remind me.'

'A likely story! You were meeting someone, weren't you? You lying bitch. Tell me who he is? How long has it been going on?'

'I haven't… there's nobody…'

A wave of nausea forced Isobel to close her eyes for a second, praying that this was all just a bad dream, but when she opened them again Martin's face was pressed close up against hers.

'I'm going to make sure you never lie to me again.' He laughed, reaching down to grab something from under the car seat. 'Look what we have here.'

Isobel Gilyard woke, her scream only slightly muffled by the pillow on which she lay. The cotton dress and bedsheets underneath her were drenched with perspiration as her eyes tried to focus on the unfamiliar surroundings. Spying the flimsy lilac drapes of the French apartment, she struggled to sit up, desperate to regulate her erratic breathing, anxiety causing Izzy's heart to thump in her chest. She blinked, fighting against the memories, grasping to cling onto the present day as though it were her only lifeline.

She was still clutching the box of memories and hastily replaced the battered lid, wanting to lock away the scenes from the past before they could jump out of their hiding place and cause mischief. The image of Martin Freeman's features, inches away from hers in a vile moment of jealous anger, still floated in her mind. Despite the years that had passed, despite the miles she had travelled to get away from the ghastly memories, still they had followed her here, to France. Isobel wondered whether she should let go, burn the papers and photos, truly put everything where it belonged, in the past. Letting go would mean never going back, so for now she would keep them as a reminder that she now had a new life.

Reaching into the closet, Izzy pushed the shoebox as far back as it would go, pulling a few pairs of shoes and bags over the top like a pirate covering treasure. If she kept Martin Freeman in here, locked away, he couldn't get at her. Yet she needed the constant reminder like an alcoholic sometimes needs to see a full bottle of vodka, to prove that she was over him and that from now on, things would be different.

Izzy staggered to the kitchen, desperate for a drink before her throat closed up on itself. The mineral water was finished but she spied the quarter bottle of wine in the fridge door and took a long swig, not bothering with a glass. Slowly, the nightmare clouded over, yet the experience still caused her to clutch at the work surface to steady herself. Would she ever be able to forget what had happened, she asked herself silently. Would that ordeal haunt her forever? Mum, Dad, Vivien, none of them had believed her. They'd simply decided on their own version of events, choosing to pity Martin over her.

She could still hear her father tutting, 'Look what our Isobel's gone and done now.'

Her mother had been practical, bringing clean clothes, eventually. Vivien had steered clear, disgusted at her sister's behaviour and terrified that she might become tarnished by association.

'Isobel!' a voice called from the bottom of the stairs. 'Are you alright up there?'

Izzy looked at her watch and saw to her surprise that she'd been gone for over an hour. 'Sorry, Maurice, I'm fine. I'm coming down now.'

But of course she would brush her teeth first, disguising the fact that she'd needed to resort to alcohol to steady her nerves, in the face of everything being far from fine.

CHAPTER EIGHT – THE MURDER WEAPON

While a heavy atmosphere hung over the boulangerie in Saint Margaux, the incident room in Bordeaux's police station was buzzing with chatter as Inspector Max Mallery gathered his team.

'Luc,' he called, splaying arms to quieten the rest of the group to a dull hum, 'what do we have from the CCTV cameras at the train station?'

The young techie brought up an image on the projector screen and began running the tape, stopping it at a point where a woman could clearly be seen entering the rear train carriage.

'Here, we have Cecile Vidal getting on the train,' he explained in English for Jack Hobbs' benefit, using a ruler to point to the passenger, 'but the most interesting part is next.'

He ran the footage in slow motion, stopping when another figure appeared, carrying a large shoulder bag. 'As you can see, another person got into the same carriage.'

There was an intake of breath as the group leaned forward, straining to make out the dark, grainy image.

'Damn,' Mallery muttered. 'He or she is wearing very plain dark clothes and a cap of some sort.'

'Excuse me, sir,' Gabriella interjected, 'that's a woman. Look at the shoes.'

Luc zoomed in on the person's feet and Mallery nodded when a pair of high-heeled stilettoes came into view.

'Well spotted.'

'Luc, do we have an image of this person getting off at the terminal in Bordeaux?' Jack asked, feeling that very slight headway was being made.

The computer whiz shook his head. 'No, sorry, I've checked through several times. There weren't many passengers arriving on this train and certainly no-one who matches this picture.'

Mallery looked at Hobbs and raised his eyebrows. 'Jacques, what are you thinking?'

'That this is our murderer. How many other stations are there between Saint Margaux and Bordeaux? Maybe she got off somewhere else.'

Luc rubbed a hand through his hair, 'There's only one, at Salbec. Unfortunately, it seems that the CCTV system there hasn't been working for several weeks.'

Jack exhaled loudly, the frustration evident on his face. 'Can you zoom out again please, Luc? Let's see if we can get some idea of this woman's proportions.'

The screen skipped back several clicks until they could see the back of the person as they ran towards the train carriage.'

'It looks as though she was waiting until the last minute to enter the train,' Thierry commented. 'I'd say she's quite skinny and not much over five feet two.'

'Gabriella?' Mallery asked, turning to the only female detective in the stuffy room. 'Do you agree?'

The petite blonde nodded. 'Yes, I'd say she was about my size.'

Mallery returned to his position at the front of the room. 'Okay, Luc, shut it down,' he said, pointing to the screen and holding up a large plastic bag containing Madam Vidal's handbag and its contents. 'The only other clue we have so far, is this.'

Eyes scrutinised the tri-coloured Union Jack lighter that had slid to the corner of the evidence bag.

'This points us to Isobel Gilyard.' The Inspector shrugged. 'Especially as she told Jacques that she'd lost her lighter, and I would say her stature fits the suspect at the train station perfectly.'

'I have to agree with you,' Hobbs added, turning in his seat to retrieve a notepad from the desk. 'I also noticed a pair of black stilettos in her hallway. But something just doesn't feel right. What motive would she have to murder Cecile Vidal?'

'It looks like we need to head back out to Saint Margaux,' Max stated, his face stern yet solemn. 'With no other suspect, we have little choice.'

After giving instructions to the rest of the team, Mallery held up five fingers to Jack and pointed to the staircase. He then returned to his office to retrieve his jacket and to try the Paris telephone number one more time. It still rang out, an endless trill that went unanswered, causing him to press the 'end call' button with more force than necessary. It seemed that Vanessa really had been serious when she'd told him it was all over.

'We'd better take your car, in case we need to bring Miss Gilyard in,' Max told Jack, as he stood waiting on the police station steps. 'Unless you have enough room in the trunk?'

The joke was lost on Hobbs as he pulled out a set of keys. 'We call it a boot. "Trunk" is American.'

Mallery shook his head, confused. 'One language, but so many different words for the same thing. Let's get going.'

'Any thoughts on a motive, sir?' Jack ventured, as he took the Mondeo steadily out of town, stirring his boss from troubling thoughts about his personal life.

'Well, it certainly wasn't for money. There were over two hundred Euros in the victim's purse and Monsieur Vidal has confirmed that no credit cards are missing.'

'I'm wondering if Isobel Gilyard might have met Cecile previously,' Hobbs pondered, jabbing the horn as a van pulled out in front of them. 'Perhaps there was a grudge between the two.'

Max shook his head, certain that his colleague was speculating. 'I very much doubt it. Thierry has interviewed most of Madame Vidal's friends and has found nothing to suggest that she knew anyone at all from England. Cecile is local to the area and has barely been overseas, except for holidays.'

'So, where did she meet the highly educated Hubert?'

'As he told us, his parents owned the vineyard, so I guess the couple grew up together. Still, I'll ask Gabriella to check, just to be sure.'

Jack Hobbs turned his full attention to the drive ahead, trying to remember how far off the highway he needed to turn, while Mallery pulled out his phone to ask Gabriella to check out the Vidals' younger days.

Telo Fabron was busy sweeping the front step of the boulangerie with a great deal of concentration when his eyes caught a glimpse of the Ford Mondeo cruising down the main street. He carefully leaned the broom up against the shop door and stepped inside, his face flustered as he called to Maurice.

'*Papa, la Police.*'

Monsieur Fabron finished cutting the ribbon on a box of macaroons before placing the parcel on top of the glass cabinet and taking the proffered five Euro note.

'*Trois Euros cinquante, Dominique,*' he told the customer, a rather plump lady with large, doleful eyes. '*Merci.*'

'*La Police,*' the woman repeated, looking quizzically from father to son.

Maurice moved from behind the counter and ushered Dominique out, while at the same time laying a hand on Telo's arm to pacify him. As they reached the door, Mallery and Hobbs were just entering.

'*Bonjour, Monsieur Fabron.*' The Inspector smiled, waiting for Dominique to leave. '*Je voudrais parler à Mademoiselle Gilyard.*'

Dominique's eyes widened further as she shuffled out through the entrance, clutching the box of macaroons to her chest. Maurice noted that instead of making her way back to the gift shop, where Dominique had closed up only a few minutes ago to collect her afternoon treats, she made a dash for the flower shop. The baker rolled his eyes at the thought of what gossip might be imparted within the next few minutes.

'Inspector, Detective Hobbs,' he said simply, gesturing for them to come inside. 'I'll fetch Isobel.'

The men stood looking at the delicious array of goods displayed on silver trays and in wicker bread baskets as Maurice went through the rear kitchen and opened the door at the bottom of the staircase.

'Isobel, are you alright up there?' they heard him call.

The response was muffled but the baker continued, 'Please come down, the detectives would like to speak with you again.'

'Is Miss Gilyard not working today?' Jack ventured, gesturing towards the empty back room.

'She is just having a break,' Maurice explained. 'We were very busy this morning.'

Mallery craned his neck as a woman's footsteps clattered down the stairs, culminating in the appearance of a tired-looking Isobel Gilyard.

'Inspector Mallery, Detective Hobbs,' she sighed, bristling slightly at the sight of the men. 'What can I do for you?'

'We have a few more questions regarding your whereabouts on Wednesday morning,' Max told her openly, hoping that Maurice Fabron might add his own thoughts should the woman be unable to give the required information.

'I've already told you. I drove to Bordeaux, did some shopping and drove back.'

'In the VW?' Jack queried.

'Yes, of course,' Izzy tutted. 'How else would I get there?'

'Has anyone else driven the car?'

Isobel shot a look at Telo, who had visibly reddened and dropped his gaze, 'Not unless…'

'Telo?' Maurice grumbled, able to sense his son's guilt.

The detectives swung around to look at the young man who was whispering in his father's ear.

'My apologies, Izzy,' the baker sighed. 'It seems Telo used your car to collect Gaston from the airport on Wednesday evening.'

Isobel was flabbergasted. After the earlier scenario of Telo insisting that he had only moved her car, she could hardly believe her ears.

'But he did fill up the tank with petrol,' Maurice added, as if it were at least some consolation. 'Don't worry, Telo and I will be having a conversation regarding this later, I promise.'

'Perhaps we could take a look at the car?' Jack suggested, before Izzy could fly off the handle at the baker's son. 'Just for the record.'

'I don't see why,' the woman snapped. 'There's nothing to see. Oh, good grief, I'll fetch the keys then.'

Outside, in the glare of the afternoon sun, Max Mallery put a hand up to shade his eyes as the group stood around the carport at the rear of the boulangerie. It was a makeshift building, antiquated in its design and build, but serving a purpose, nevertheless. Isobel had pulled open the driver's door and stood with her arms folded tightly across her bosom, scowling at Jack Hobbs as he peered inside.

'Can you open the passenger door please, Jacques?' Mallery instructed, stepping around the opposite side of the battered old Beetle.

He lifted the catch and swung the door wide before leaning over into the back seat. With Isobel having emptied the car of her belongings on arrival, there wasn't much to see, and Max soon stood back up and flexed his shoulders.

'The trunk,' he told Jack, 'erm… boot?'

Hobbs pulled a lever, allowing the senior detective to pull up the front-facing cavity. Mallery moved a few items, a spare oil can, some cleaning cloths and a basic tool kit.

'Sir!' Hobbs shouted from inside the vehicle. 'Here!'

Max banged his head on the underside of the bonnet-boot as he straightened up. 'Urrghh.' He rubbed the painful spot.

Jack Hobbs was pointing to something inside the glove box and was blocking the passenger's door of the VW with his body.

'In there, sir,' he said quietly, glancing over at the trio standing at the rear of the car. 'I think it's a knife wrapped in an item of clothing. You can just make out the handle sticking out.'

'Fetch an evidence bag from the car,' Max instructed, swapping places with his junior. 'Let's see what we have.'

'What are you doing?' Isobel called, preparing to move towards the front of her beloved vehicle. 'Inspector?'

'Stay there, Madamemoiselle Gilyard,' Mallery shouted, in a firm voice. 'Do not move.'

Less than a minute later, Hobbs was back, pulling on latex gloves.

'Carefully, Jacques,' Max told him, allowing Hobbs to take control of bagging his precious find. 'Make sure you keep the cloth around the weapon.'

The young detective knelt down close to the footwell and used both gloved hands to lift the object into the plastic evidence bag being held by his boss.

Mallery looked down at what his colleague had so deftly retrieved. Inside the bag lay a rolled-up denim shirt with the wooden handle of a long knife protruding out from the edge of the cloth.

Maurice Fabron stood open-mouthed, his face ashen, a hand on his son's arm. Next to him, Isobel made a strange squeaking sound, as though a mouse had got stuck in her throat. Telo looked confused, frantically switching his gaze back and forth between the detectives and the evidence bag.

'Can you explain this, Madamemoiselle Gilyard?' Inspector Mallery queried, holding up the evidence bag for the woman to see clearly.

'No… I… it's not possible…' she gasped.

'We are going to need you to accompany us to the station now,' Jack stated. 'In accordance with French law, Inspector Mallery will now read you your rights.'

In a flurry of French, Max recited the caution and then nodded to his colleague to repeat the English version.

Izzy stood rooted to the spot, visibly shaking and on the verge of tears.

'Monsieur Fabron, it might be an idea if you follow us down in a short while,' Mallery requested, rubbing his chin. 'Given the nature of the weapon here, we may need you to take a look and see if it belongs to the boulangerie.'

Maurice nodded, unable to utter a word.

'Telo can you drive your father?' Jack asked, not pausing to think whether the young man could speak English or not.

'Yes, no problem,' came the reply.

Isobel did a double-take. Not only did Telo Fabron understand English, he evidently spoke it, too. What else had he lied about, she thought in her moment of panic. Could Maurice's son have set her up for murder?

'Please, I'm innocent! I had nothing to do with Cecile's death. I have no idea where that knife came from.'

Isobel Gilyard's protests were wearing thin on Max Mallery's patience as he sat in the rear of the Ford Mondeo at her side.

'Please, don't say anything else until we interview you formally,' he warned.

'You have to believe me,' she wailed, twisting in the seat, the handcuffs loose on her slender wrists. 'I've been set up!'

Jack Hobbs glanced in the rear-view mirror and caught the woman's eye. 'Please be quiet now. You'll have chance to explain your side of things at the station.'

Isobel settled back against the seat, hoping that, with a native British detective there, she might have an easier time during the interview.

Mallery shot her a warning glare and pulled a packet of cigarettes out of his jacket, tapping it against his knee before tilting the lid.

'Sir, if you don't mind...' Hobbs began, frowning slightly.

'*Oui, oui*, Jacques... I know.'

Isobel Gilyard had been sitting in a cold grey-walled interview room for the best part of an hour. This was part of Max Mallery's strategy to stress her into a confession, or at the very least to trip herself up over any supposed alibi. She'd been given a glass of tepid water and told that someone would be with her soon, but the clock on the wall ticked away the minutes, causing her temper to rise.

'Bloody hell,' Izzy muttered, standing up to look out of the one small window. 'What's going on?'

'*Asseyez-vous, je vous en prie*,' the uniformed constable grunted. 'Sit down.'

Regarding the man's large stature and serious expression, Isobel thought better of arguing and pulled out the uncomfortable chair on which she'd spent every minute since her arrival in Bordeaux. She brought the glass of water to her parched lips and took a sip before replacing it on the table and putting her head in her hands.

'Oh God, I just want this to be over.'

Inspector Mallery had decided to wait for Maurice Fabron to arrive before conducting a formal interview with the baker's employee. He figured that if the boulangerie owner could identify the knife as one of his, it would add to the evidence that was quickly stacking up against Isobel Gilyard. Jack Hobbs had been a great asset so far in his first case, the senior detective conceded, and he wanted him right by his side while conducting the investigation, although he didn't share Hobbs' view that Isobel Gilyard was not their prime suspect.

'Sir, she has no motive whatsoever and no connection to the Vidal family,' Jack explained over a cup of cappuccino straight from his boss's machine. 'There's a lot more to this case than we're seeing, I'm sure of it.'

Mallery eyed his colleague over the desk while running a finger around the rim of his mug. 'You're wrong, Jacques. I think it's an open and shut case.'

'So, how do you want to do this when we go through to interview her? I take it you want to play your cards close to your chest?'

Max looked confused. 'Do I want to do what?'

'Sorry, an English expression, sir. It means not to give away too much of what we know.'

'*Oui*, that's exactly how I want it to go.'

A knock on the door caused both men to turn their attention to Gabriella, who was standing with one foot in the office. 'Sir, Monsieur Fabron is here. I've put him in Interview Room Two. I'll take his son down to the café to get a drink.'

'I do apologise,' Maurice gabbled, his words rapid and disjointed as the detectives entered the room. 'We had a customer, needed to lock up the boulangerie and then we had to stop for Telo to use the toilet.'

'It's no problem.' Jack smiled, taking a seat on the opposite side of the table while Mallery held the evidence bag aloft. 'Can you just tell us if this knife might be one from your bakery?'

Maurice Fabron shook his head and splayed both hands in a dramatic manner, 'Certainly not. All of the boulangerie knives have steel handles, not wood. But it does look like the one that went missing from my house.'

Mallery and Hobbs looked at each other, a flicker of confusion passing between them.

'Are you sure?' Max pressed, pulling out a chair to sit down. 'When was the last time you saw it?'

The baker rolled his eyes upwards. 'Well, I know I used it on Sunday, as we had bread with our evening meal, but on Monday and Tuesday Telo and I had croissants for breakfast, so I probably wouldn't have noticed if it were missing. However, Gaston and Simone came for a little supper on Wednesday, after the terrible… well, after Cecile… and I had to ask Gaston to go to the boulangerie to tell Isobel to get a bread knife from the kitchen there, as mine had gone.'

Jack held his breath for a couple of seconds, letting the information sink in. 'But you definitely had it on Sunday?'

Maurice thought for a moment and nodded. 'Yes, we had fish, vegetables and a full bread-basket. Isobel will confirm it.'

'Madam Gilyard had dinner with you on Sunday?' Max asked excitedly, seeing that an opportunity to seize the knife had fallen straight into their suspect's arms.

'Well, yes, I thought it polite to invite her, as the shops were closed on Sunday and Izzy hadn't had chance to go grocery shopping.'

Mallery pulled a pair of latex gloves from his pocket and slid the knife from its place within the denim shirt. 'For the record, Monsieur Fabron, does this bread knife belong to you?'

'*Oui*, Inspector,' Maurice replied without hesitation, 'it is mine.'

'And have you ever seen this denim shirt before?' Jack quickly jumped in. 'Have you noticed anyone wearing it?'

The baker shook his head with surety. 'I've never seen it before in my life.'

Outside in the corridor, Max Mallery leaned against the cool brick of the wall and pushed his hands deep into the pockets of his jeans. 'Fabron's knife,' he told Jack. 'Gilyard had the opportunity to take it, too.'

'Hang on a minute, sir, what about the son, Telo?'

'The boy's a little soft in the head,' Max retorted, 'but not a murderer. I'm not prepared to keep the Fabrons here for any longer than necessary and, with the business being local, they're unlikely to do a midnight flight.'

'Flit, sir, midnight flit.'

Mallery fixed Hobbs with a steely glare before putting a cigarette to his lips. 'How are your French lessons coming along, Jacques?'

In Interview Room One, Isobel Gilyard felt the beginnings of a deep and nauseous sensation building inside the pit of her stomach. It had now been an hour and a half since her arrival at the police headquarters in Bordeaux and, despite telling herself umpteen times to stay calm, panic was setting in. It didn't help that she'd skipped lunch, instead imbibing only a mouthful of wine after falling asleep on her bed.

The grey walls and stark surroundings, with sparse functional furniture, reminded Izzy all too well of the hours she had spent being questioned ten years previously. At that time, too, she'd had to sit awaiting information, as though the powers in charge relished her agonising situation. She desperately needed to know what was being discussed, and how the hell that knife had got into the glove compartment of her Beetle… unless someone was trying to frame her? Her instinct led Isobel to believe that Telo Fabron had put it there. After all, he'd just confessed to his father that he'd been out in the VW without asking permission. How dare he? And to pick up that artist from the airport, too? What cheek!

Isobel's eye twitched involuntarily as a flash of recollection triggered her memory. The artist, Gaston; the night he'd come for the knife, there was that red patch on his shirt, something resembling dried blood. What night had it been? Slowly retracing the days and nights, Isobel found herself recalling that it had been Wednesday, the same day that Cecile Vidal had been murdered.

'I need to speak to Inspector Mallery,' Izzy told the uniformed officer, who was now leaning against the windowsill watching the traffic outside. 'Please fetch him.'

The policeman pretended not to hear, instead tilting his head back to smooth down his carefully oiled hair.

'I said –'

The door was suddenly flung open, causing the officer to quickly straighten up.

'Mademoiselle Gilyard,' Max Mallery murmured. 'Sorry to have kept you.'

'An hour and a half, I've been sitting here,' the Englishwoman told him, stiffly.

'I'm sorry, did you need to be somewhere else?' Max asked sarcastically. 'Now, I need to ask if you would like a solicitor? Some legal representation?'

'No, there's no need. I haven't done anything. I've been stitched up, framed,' Isobel announced, pressing her palms against the formica tabletop. 'And I think I know who the murderer is!'

Jack Hobbs sauntered over to the chair next to his superior and folded his arms, watching the woman with intrigue. He'd had a keen interest in body language from an early age and noticed that Isobel Gilyard's movements were defensive but not closed, telling him that she believed what she was saying.

'Would you mind sharing that information with us?' Max asked, somewhat amused, while checking that the tape recorder was switched on.

'Gaston, the artist staying in the village,' Izzy replied eagerly. 'I even saw blood on his shirt last Wednesday.'

'Really? Very interesting, I'm sure,' the Inspector continued. 'We will speak to that gentleman in due course. Jacques, please make a note of his name.'

Hobbs pulled out his scribbling pad and let the pen hover over the page, 'Gaston? And his surname, Miss Gilyard?'

'I... I don't know,' Isobel confessed. 'He didn't tell me.'

Mallery smiled a satisfied grin, as though he were a fox having just caught the fattest chicken in the coup. 'How very convenient. Jacques, please bring both evidence bags.'

'Miss Gilyard, is this your shirt?' Jack asked, holding up the plastic bag for Isobel to see.

'Yes, it looks like it. I wore it last Saturday when I drove over from England.'

'And could you explain what it's doing in the glove-box of your car with a bloodied bread knife wrapped inside it?'

Izzy faltered. Her head was starting to hurt as she searched her memories of the past few days. 'It was really hot, I was sweating, so I changed into a t-shirt.'

'Did you stop somewhere along the route?' Max inquired casually.

'On the side of the road,' came the whisper.

'And is this your cigarette lighter?' Jack went on, holding up the second bag.

Izzy nodded, tears streaming down both cheeks, 'Yes, I lost it. But I…'

'Isobel Gilyard I am charging you with the murder of Cecile Vidal,' Mallery announced stiffly. 'I will call the duty solicitor.'

CHAPTER NINE – SUSPICIONS

Isobel sat with both knees pressed against her chest on the flimsy grey mattress. A cup of pale, milky tea had been thrust through the grill in the holding cell several hours before, but it remained untouched and cold.

Stark walls gave the illusion of bricks and mortar closing in on the lone occupant, yet outside, the station buzzed as word of a murderer in their midst filled the Bordeaux constabulary. It had been three hours since Inspector Maxime Mallery had cautioned Isobel Gilyard, yet still no word of a defence lawyer or legal aid was forthcoming. Izzy could feel the familiar acidic build-up in her throat, a combination of the earlier wine and hours of starvation taking their toll.

'Hey, is anyone out there?' she croaked, desperate for information. 'Can you tell me what's happening?'

The cell shutter opened, and a tray of unidentifiable food sat on the slim shelf at eye level. It looked like cold mushroom stroganoff, but the origins of its contents could have been from any part of the universe as far as Izzy was concerned.

'Please, let me speak to the Inspector!' she cried, desperate for attention.

Max Mallery stubbed out his third cigarette and swivelled his chair around to face the station's newest recruit. 'What's troubling you, Jacques?' he asked tentatively. 'Is it Madamemoiselle Gilyard?'

Jack Hobbs glanced at his watch, fully aware that his wife would be expecting him home within the hour and gave a noncommittal shrug.

'Sorry, sir, there's something not quite right about all this. I know that Isobel Gilyard's not the full ticket, but I really can't see her being a murder suspect.'

Max smiled, lifting an espresso to his lips before speaking. 'Jacques, your record for detection is indeed exemplary but we have no other suspect. Let's go through what we have…'

Mallery lifted his fingers from the cup and ticked them off one by one. 'A woman at the station in heels similar to those worn by Madam Gilyard. A cigarette lighter exactly the same as the one lost by her. Sightings at Saint Margaux station confirming that Isobel Gilyard was there on Wednesday morning. And now, most damning of all, a murder weapon found in her car and wrapped in the woman's shirt. Am I missing something, Jacques?'

Hobbs sat silent for a couple of seconds, allowing his superior to calm down, before taking a deep breath and preparing his speech.

'Sir, there is no motive, on that we both agree. It's hard to identify the woman on the CCTV footage, therefore we cannot prosecute without a formal identification. The admission by Telo Fabron that he used Miss Gilyard's car tells us that evidence might have been planted, and… I just don't…'

'Ah, Jacques,' Max interrupted, lighting yet another filtered cigarette, 'your instincts, eh? Sometimes you have to let things lie… go with what the circumstances show us, *oui*?'

'Sir,' Jack ventured, 'would you at least let me contact some of my former colleagues back in the Manchester force? See what they can dig up?'

'Manchester? I thought you worked in Leeds?'

'Yes, I did, but a lot of the lads I went to police training college with are now working detectives in Manchester. If that's where Isobel Gilyard hails from, they'll be able to do a background check in no time at all.'

Mallery blew a swirl of smoke out through parted lips whilst considering the young man's suggestion. 'Very well, contact them. It can certainly do no harm to our case.'

Isobel instinctively lifted her head as the cell door opened.

'*Bonsoir*,' Max Mallery smiled, regarding the unkempt and dishevelled woman with evident distaste.

'Why are you still holding me here?' Izzy snarled aggressively, curling her lips and clenching both fists. 'You do actually realise you've made a huge mistake, don't you?'

'*Non.*' Max shrugged. 'I cannot find a reason to let you go just yet, Mademoiselle Gilyard. However, I need to ask if there is someone who can bring you a few necessities – nightwear, toiletries, that kind of thing.'

Isobel was astounded. She had never contemplated spending more than a few hours being questioned, let alone a night or more. She bit her lip and tried to show an outward semblance of control.

'Maurice,' she said finally, wondering whether it might be prudent to go along with the detective for now. 'Maurice Fabron.'

Mallery raked a hand through his thick dark hair and nodded. 'Very well, I will ask him to come.'

At eight o'clock that evening, Maurice Fabron pulled up outside the police station in Bordeaux for the second time that day. He was tired and distressed, having witnessed the arrest of his new employee that very afternoon. Maurice was accompanied by Gaston, one of his dearest friends and the artist who had met Miss Gilyard just a few days before.

'Monsieur Fabron.' Max nodded to the men, ushering both of them into the reception area. 'Thank you for coming. Mademoiselle Gilyard asked for you specifically.'

Jack Hobbs stood back from the trio, hands in his pockets, eyes fixed upon the station clock that ticked away every minute that the young man was missing his wife's supper.

'I have brought some sleepwear and a few toiletries,' Maurice was saying, showing Max a canvas tote bag. 'A friend of mine gathered a few things as we didn't want to pry into Izzy's apartment.'

Mallery's instincts were on high alert as he noted the boulangerie owner's words. 'I'm sure, under the circumstances...'

The baker shook his head. 'Simone, my neighbour and dear friend, was able to provide the necessary overnight comforts.'

'And Telo?' Jack asked, concerned for Maurice's autistic son.

'He is having supper with Simone tonight.'

A heavy key being turned in the lock of the cell door alerted Izzy to her visitors.

'Perhaps just Monsieur Fabron,' Mallery advised, putting a hand on Gaston's arm. 'For now.'

The artist acquiesced, slinking back against the cool, stark wall of the corridor. 'Of course, no problem.'

Maurice stepped forward, regarding the stark grey walls before focussing his gaze on Isobel Gilyard, his skin prickling from the contrasting coolness of the cell.

'Maurice,' Izzy cried from her bunk, 'please tell me you've come to help sort out this mess.'

The baker stiffened, his instincts completely split between condemning his employee and hatching an escape plan.

'I've brought you some things,' he said eventually, placing the bag on the bed. 'Simone thought you may need some pyjamas.'

Isobel stared at the neatly packed items, floral nightwear and an assortment of cleansing gels. 'I shouldn't be here, Maurice, I didn't do it.'

The boulangerie owner looked down at his fingernails as if inspecting them for the very first time. 'They found a knife in your car, Izzy. A knife covered in blood.'

Isobel's throat clogged, filling with every word she needed to say yet unable to spit out a single utterance.

Maurice lifted his head, a fatherly gesture, as if awaiting a confession. 'If there was a good reason… if you need to tell us...'

'Maurice, please!' Isobel cried, tears falling down her pale cheeks. 'I promise you I did not kill Cecile.'

'Okay, okay,' the baker conceded, as his employee gripped both of his hands in hers. 'Is there someone in England that you need me to call?'

The words came like the heavy blow from a shovel on the side of the head. 'What?' she whispered.

'Izzy, do you want me to call your father, or perhaps your mother?'

Isobel shuffled backwards on the makeshift bed, clutching her knees once again as if protecting her body from harm.

'No, I… I don't have anyone.'

Maurice Fabron was less than convinced and placed a warm hand upon his employee's head. 'Have a think, Isobel. Is there anyone that can help?'

Isobel sobbed silently, desperately racking her brains for inspiration. She couldn't possibly phone her father. He'd judge the situation before even getting on a plane. Her mother would be a nervous wreck, going along with whatever her dominant husband decided, and Vivien… God forbid, not Viv! She would be about as much use as a chocolate teapot.

Outside in the corridor, Max Mallery watched the interaction with interest. It intrigued him how the boulangerie owner and his English assistant had seemed to gel, despite the short time of their professional life together. He supposed that in some ways, it was similar to his liaison with Jack Hobbs, although he would never admit out loud how much he admired the lateral thinking of his newest team member.

A buzz on the Inspector's phone alerted him to an incoming message. Just as he had hoped, it was an unfamiliar number. Max typed in his passcode.

MAX, VA T'EN. JE NE PEUX PAS TE REVOIR. VANESSA.

He swallowed hard, reading once again the message that she never wanted to see him again and that he should go away.

Resting the back of his thumping head against the stone police station wall, Mallery breathed deeply, then rested both hands on his knees before standing upright again. Fuck, this really was it. Out of all the women he'd ever made a play for, the one he really wanted was going to get away.

'*Inspecteur.*' Maurice Fabron rapped on the cell door, his features tired and vacant.

Max nodded to the guard to unlock the steel door, allowing the baker to step out into the narrow corridor. 'This way. Let's get a coffee,' he said, speaking French to his fellow countryman.

Maurice followed the tall policeman up the stairs and through into a large office, where an antique desk took up a prominent position. His legs were weary and his mind jumbled with theories and postulations.

'Café au lait?' Max offered, holding up a spotless china cup.

Maurice nodded gratefully, turning slightly as Jack Hobbs entered the room.

'Don't you need to go home, Jacques?' Max suggested kindly, switching back to English for the sake of his young deputy.

'Not yet, sir. Let's see if we can find out any more about Miss Gilyard.'

Mallery smiled, grateful for the spark that had ignited itself within his new recruit. He could see a good deal of himself in Hobbs and knew instinctively that the young Yorkshireman was top class material, if only he could let his head rule over his heart. A good track record was only as good as its commanding officer would allow it to be, Max thought inwardly. Being overconfident or too flippant could also lead to mistakes. He was also concerned that, with their one and only suspect being English, Jack Hobbs would be overly sympathetic towards her.

Max pressed various buttons, dispensing hot cups of white coffee to the two men seated at his desk.

'Well,' he finally asked, leaning forward to better hear Maurice, 'is there anyone she wants you to call?'

Monsieur Fabron sipped the fresh coffee, grateful for the caffeine hit but well aware of Gaston waiting downstairs and Telo at home with Simone Dupuis.

'*Non.*' He shrugged and sighed. 'She says there is nobody.'

Mallery glanced up at Jack, trying to telepathically convey that this might be one of the areas that they would need to check. Family. Background. Friends.

He turned his gaze to Maurice. 'Anything you can bring from her apartment?'

'Oh no,' the baker said adamantly. 'Izzy said she doesn't want me to go up to the apartment. The things that Simone sent are enough.'

'*Merci, Monsieur Fabron,*' Max told the baker. 'You have been very helpful. I understand that Cecile Vidal was your sister-in-law and we are very sorry for your loss.'

Maurice drained his cup and then stood up, a soft white handkerchief knotted between his fingers. 'Inspector Mallery, Detective Hobbs, please find the person who did this. I am sure that Isobel Gilyard is not a murderer. I pride myself on being… how to say?… a good judge of character, and she really seems a sincere young lady.'

Jack escorted the baker downstairs to the reception area, where Gaston sat with his head in his hands underneath a continuous ticking clock.

Maurice shook hands with the English detective, before resigning himself to leaving the station. *'Je reviens demain.* Sorry, I mean, I'll come back tomorrow.'

'Merci, Monsieur Fabron.' Jack nodded sympathetically. 'Thank you.'

Hobbs watched as the artist slid behind the wheel of the boulangerie delivery van, leaving Maurice Fabron to get into the passenger's side. The evening was late and heavy thunderclouds gathered overhead, mingling together like a witch's brew. He watched as Gaston made a U-turn in the police station car park before swinging the Citroën into westbound traffic. So engrossed was Hobbs in the men's departure that he didn't notice his boss sidling up behind him.

'Well?' Max whispered, making Jack jump out of his skin. 'Did she do it?'

Hobbs rubbed the ginger stubble on his chin, conscious that he must go home and shave before beginning another shift, let alone find something to eat.

'I'm still not convinced. Although the fact that Isobel won't let Fabron call her family is a bit concerning.'

'It certainly is,' Mallery agreed, lighting up a cigarette. 'Get on to your colleagues in Manchester first thing tomorrow.'

'Are you going home now, sir?'

Max shrugged, the tip of his cigarette dangling limply from his lips. 'Don't worry about me, Jacques, just go home before Angélique puts your dog in the dinner.'

Jack smiled at the erroneous analogy. At least his boss was having a go at the English language, which meant he needed to make more of an effort to brush up his French.

'Thanks. I'll see you tomorrow then.'

Mallery watched the Ford Mondeo spring to life as its driver turned the key. He envied the ease with which Jack Hobbs had integrated himself into life in rural France and wished that things could be as simple for him. He detested the daily grind of Bordeaux, where life plodded rather than buzzed as it had in Paris. Imagine being a young detective with a gorgeous French wife, he mused. Life had no limitations for such circumstances. The world was their oyster.

'Sir,' a soft female voice called from behind him. 'Mademoiselle Gilyard is very restless.'

Max turned, eyeing up the young detective with lustful eyes before reprimanding himself. It was circumstances such as this that had brought him to this back of beyond town in the first place.

'I'll deal with her, Gabriella,' he stated, looking over and beyond the petite blonde's head. 'Go home and get some rest, there will be lots to do tomorrow.'

'*Merci.*' The young detective blushed, shrugging on a flimsy navy raincoat just as the first wet spots dripped down onto her shoulders. '*Bonsoir.*'

The cell peephole flipped open for the third time that evening, allowing Inspector Max Mallery to cast a wary gaze over the single occupant. He could see a prone body lying on its side, knees hunched up and head tucked in, but Max was wise to the helpless foetal pose of Isobel Gilyard and rapped on the steel shutter to announce his arrival.

'Good evening, I hope you are comfortable.'

Izzy rolled over, her stomach lurching as she swung her legs over the side of the cot. 'Can I go yet?'

Max feigned a laugh and placed a solid tab of gum on his tongue. 'Not until we know the truth, Mademoiselle Gilyard.'

'I promise you,' she pleaded, 'I've told you all that I know. I have no idea how that knife got into my car, I wasn't on the train to Bordeaux last Wednesday and I didn't murder Cecile Vidal.'

Mallery used his usual delay tactic as he considered a response and studied the back of his hands carefully. 'And your cigarette lighter, Mademoiselle Gilyard? How do you suppose it got into the purse of the murder victim?'

Izzy faltered, gathering her thoughts then dropping them, as a basket weaver might stumble with an armful of twigs. 'I have no idea, honestly. I lost it… what, Monday, maybe even Sunday. Besides, a Union Jack lighter isn't exactly uncommon.'

'Maybe in Britain, but in France…' Max grimaced. He then decided upon a different tack and swivelled around to rest against the bedstead next to Isobel.

'Why didn't you want Maurice Fabron to contact your family?'

Izzy swallowed hard. 'I… er… we're not close.'

'Surely, in a situation such as this, one would turn to their family for some kind of… assistance?'

Isobel leaned back against the cold bricks and exhaled loudly. Maybe she should have asked Maurice to call her father, but what then? He'd presume, not incorrectly, that she'd got herself into 'a spot of bother' and would consider a few days in a cell the perfect punishment for a minor misdemeanour. Except this time, it wasn't. This time she was innocent. This time she needed her family's support more than anything in the world.

Max ran a slim finger over the green-lit message on his mobile phone. Anger welled up inside him until he thought better of it and reached down into the bottom drawer for a bottle of finest Cognac.

'Damn you, Commissioner Chirac. Damn you, Vanessa,' he cursed, pouring a large measure.

Mallery bit his lip, fighting back the tears of frustration that threatened to burst forth from his cat-like eyes.

'*Inspecteur,*' an unexpected voice boomed into the darkness. '*Voilà.*'

The senior detective brushed a hand across his cheek and swung both legs off the desk where he'd been resting them.

'Luc? *Bonsoir.*'

The techy hopped nervously from one foot to the other, eager to impart his findings to the superior officer. The conversation continued in French, now that Hobbs had gone home.

'You asked me to check the motorway cameras from last Saturday?'

Max nodded, eager to find another piece of the so far evasive puzzle. 'And?'

'On my computer.' Luc smiled, proud that his attention to detail was paying off. 'I have something you need to see. It's from last Saturday.'

Hunched over the grainy screen of Luc's police computer, Max Mallery couldn't believe his eyes. He wound a finger backwards, motioning the computer whiz to rewind the tape to the beginning.

Unlike the Saint Margaux train station footage, this time the images were clear and easily decipherable.

'Isobel Gilyard.' He grinned, peering at the picture of a woman leaning back against the bonnet of a 1970s Volkswagen Beetle. 'Well, well, well.'

Luc, encouraged by his new boss's enthusiasm, zoomed in on the woman's face, leaving no doubt whatsoever that it was the Englishwoman at the side of the highway heading towards Bordeaux.

The pair watched in silence as the film continued in slow motion, eventually showing the arrival of a middle-aged man in a battered van.

'Ah, so who do we have here?' Max murmured, regarding the newcomer with interest. 'Did you run the plate?'

Luc pushed his shoulders back, proud of his own initiative. 'Yes, Inspector. The driver is Louis Perant, a known drug dealer from Toulouse.'

Mallery rubbed his hands together without realising the exaggerated action. 'Superb! Now we can connect Mademoiselle Gilyard with a criminal and perhaps, behind that, lies a motive for murder. What do you think, Luc?'

Luc nodded. This was the first time he'd seen his new boss visibly enthused by anything since his arrival in Bordeaux.

'Well done, Luc,' the Inspector continued. 'This is great work. Perfect!'

Isobel Gilyard lay on the lumpy mattress, a scratchy blanket pulled half-heartedly around her cold shoulders as the evening wore on.

'Why the hell don't they let me go?' she mumbled. 'This is ridiculous.'

She closed her eyes, knowing that sleep would be evasive tonight, yet eager for any slight sound to keep her from drifting into the dark, emotional pool that beckoned. Izzy's eyelids were heavy both from tiredness and crying, threatening to pull her down into the abyss of nightmares.

The first face she saw was Vivien's. A smiling, domesticated grin that wielded a feather duster just as a Samurai might hold his sword. Isobel tried to hold the image, afraid of what might follow, but it wasn't long before Viv was swept along on the tidal wave of dreams, laughing loudly, ignorant to her sister's plight.

Mrs Gilyard shook her head, hands held tightly over both ears, unwilling to hear about the atrocities that her eldest daughter had committed. Undoubtedly, it was the shame of what the neighbours, the vicar and fellow members of the Women's Institute would think that halted her tiny steps as she toddled towards Izzy with outstretched arms. Oh no, that wouldn't do, whatever would other people think?

Isobel's father pulled at the braces on his trousers. It was that very stretching motion that had alerted Izzy to his errant temper. Partial to a brown ale on a Friday night, Mr Gilyard was a pillar of the community, union representative at the tileworks where he toiled for twelve hours, five days a week, and a church warden on Sundays. Nobody could want for a better role model. Or so they said. Nobody had warned of their father's leather belt, removed only for purposes untold. Yet Izzy had felt its wrath on many an occasion and she still bore the scars to prove it.

'Mademoiselle Gilyard,' a voice was calling, although it seemed far away and echoing, as though it were being filtered through a tunnel.

Izzy stirred, gently pushing herself up on one elbow before blinking into the harsh white light of the bright overhead bulb.

'What is it?' she whispered hoarsely.

'I've brought you some tea, and some biscuits,' Mallery offered, pushing the snacks onto a small side table. 'Can we talk?'

'What time is it?'

'Around midnight,' Max admitted, rolling his eyes upwards. 'Not too late.'

Isobel flopped back down onto the mattress, exhausted. 'Don't you ever sleep?'

'Rarely. I need to ask you about your connection to Louis Perant.'

'Who?'

The Inspector pulled up a stool and sat, stretching his long lean legs out towards the bed on which Isobel Gilyard lay.

'Now, now. Don't try to be smart. We have seen you on the highway, obviously meeting up with Louis Perant.'

Isobel pushed herself upright, rubbing the bottom of her spine where the mattress springs had been digging in. 'I have no idea what you're talking about.'

Max folded his arms, appearing amused and unwilling to accept Isobel's replies.

'*Louis Perant,*' he emphasised, glancing towards the door to ensure that the uniformed guard outside was alert and listening, should he require a witness.

'Inspector, I've never heard of anyone called Louis Perant, let alone met him.'

'Did you stop on the side of the southbound carriageway entering Bordeaux? Did you step out of your car at that location? Did you or did you not interact with a man driving a dark-coloured Citroen van?'

Isobel Gilyard's walls of defence came crashing down around her as the scenes from Saturday's overheated engine episode fast-forwarded in her mind like a children's cartoon show. Was Mallery talking about the dirty man that had pulled up and spoken to her for a few minutes? Surely not! She rubbed a hand over her eyes, desperately trying to summon up a clear image of their interaction. They'd hardly spoken, he hadn't even understood her properly. Then suddenly he was gone, the man, and that's when she'd changed her sweat-stained top. She'd been wearing that denim shirt, the one that they'd found in the glove compartment of her Beetle, wrapped around the bread knife. The weapon that supposedly killed Cecile Vidal.

Isobel Gilyard wept. For the first time in years, thick, wet tears rolled down her cheeks uncontrollably, her shoulders shuddering with grief.

Max Mallery stood, satisfied that he now had the evidence to close his very first murder case for the Bordeaux Municipality.

CHAPTER TEN – PAST CRIMES

Jack Hobbs stretched silently and tiptoed out of the bedroom as quietly as he could, which wasn't quietly enough as, three steps later, his bare foot landed upon a baby's soft toy which emitted a high-pitched squeak.

'Jack, what are you doing? Come back to bed.' Angélique yawned, patting a hand on the sheet next to her.

'I'm sorry, sweetheart, I have to go to work. You get some more rest.'

'It's Saturday,' his wife moaned, her sleek long hair fanned out across the pillow like a peacock's plume. 'Surely you don't need to go in today?'

The young man padded back to the bed and kissed his wife's lips tenderly. 'Until we have a prosecution, the murder investigation is still ongoing, I'm sorry.'

Angélique glanced over at the pretty white crib, checking that their newborn son was still sleeping contentedly, before pulling the duvet up around her ears. 'Fine,' her muffled voice huffed, 'Do what you need to do.'

In a sleek modern apartment across town, Max Mallery had slept for four hours before rising and draining a carton of orange juice. His body ached from lack of exercise and he promised himself an hour or two at the gym later that day. The Inspector also yearned for a female to warm the vacant side of his bed, but last night's text messages remained unanswered and he was becoming resigned to a life of bachelorhood.

Max stood in the doorway of his built-in wardrobe, proud of the neat rows of perfectly pressed shirts and trousers, before stepping inside and selecting a navy polo shirt and designer jeans. During his previous post in Paris, Max had openly encouraged his team to dress casually yet smartly and tried to lead by example. A quick glance in the mirror told him that standards were being maintained.

'Team, well done so far,' Mallery told the group as they gathered in the Incident Room, 'yet we still have much to do.'

There was a murmur of agreement as he raised a hand and continued.

'Gabriella, any news from forensics?'

The young woman shook her head. 'Not yet, sir, we probably won't get anything back until Monday now.'

The Inspector sighed. Relying on other teams to work weekends was not something that he tolerated well, especially when he knew that the lead scientist spent his Saturdays on the golf course.

'Very well, keep on it. Now, as I've explained, Luc has found footage of Isobel Gilyard interacting with a known drug dealer, Louis Perant. I suggest that you two, Thierry and Gabriella, take a drive down to Toulouse and question the vermin. Okay with you?'

The pair nodded. 'Any chance we can take your car, sir?' Thierry asked cheekily

Max smiled and raised his eyebrows. 'What do you think?'

'That'll be no, then,' Gabriella remarked, tying back her hair into a long, soft ponytail.

'Luc, see if you can locate Madam Gilyard's car in Bordeaux on Wednesday. Try the side streets and lanes. She claims not to have used a main car park.'

'On it now,' the techie replied, giving a thumbs-up sign.

'Now, Jacques, that leaves you to contact those Manchester colleagues of yours.'

By the time his boss strode in with a lunch invitation at mid-day, Jack Hobbs was still struggling to bring forth information. He quickly closed down the computer and followed Max out into the street, where they headed for a local café. It was a typically busy weekend lunchtime, with both shoppers and tourists stopping to eat, but the proprietor instantly recognised Bordeaux's newest police inspector and ushered the pair to a quiet table at the back of the room.

'*Deux eaux pétillantes, salade composée et poulet, s'il vous plaît,*' Max requested, waving away the offer of menus. 'Okay, Jacques?'

'Salad and chicken?' Hobbs ventured, his face quizzical as they sat at the small corner table.

'And fizzy water,' Mallery confirmed. 'Your French is improving.'

Jack Hobbs blushed, a pink tinge that rose upwards from his neck and skimmed the ginger-coloured fringe at his hairline.

'Thanks. Anyway, sir, the lads in Manchester haven't come up with anything. No Isobel Gilyard on any election records, either. It's looking bleak.'

'Bleak?'

'It's almost as though she doesn't exist.'

Mallery looked up, startled. This wasn't the news that he'd been expecting but, in regard to the case, it was extremely disappointing.

'We can't be sure that the date of birth she gave us is correct,' he pointed out, trying to remain calm, yet feeling positively niggled.

'Since first meeting Miss Gilyard, I've had the feeling that she's not quite been telling the truth. But I reckon there will be clues somewhere...'

'Go on.'

'Well, in my experience people don't just evade documentation. There are usually credit card records, passports, utility bills.'

'How about finger-printing?' Mallery smiled. 'If she has a police record, your ex-colleagues could match fingerprints, *oui*?'

'Yes, sir, that's one possibility. I'll arrange it this afternoon.'

There was a sudden vibration and Mallery snatched up his phone, eyes quickly scanning the message.

'In the meantime,' Max grinned, 'we have a search warrant being sent over. First, we will look over Isobel Gilyard's apartment.'

'Excellent, sir. That's good news. And for the record, I have to apologise. It seems your instincts were right, and I was way off the mark. There's something wrong with this whole set-up. Isobel Gilyard can't be all that innocent, after all.'

The Inspector pressed his fingers onto Jack's shoulder. 'It's not a competition, Jacques. Your contacts will prove very useful, I'm sure of it and now we have plenty to do to help us move forward with a prosecution.'

Hobbs was silent as the café owner brought sparkling water and two tall glasses filled with ice and lemon.

'It's frustrating that we haven't made more progress since Wednesday,' he said, as soon as the man had departed to fetch their food.

Once it had been put on the table, Max dug a fork into his meal and sighed. 'Sometimes, to do a job properly it is necessary to look under every rock…'

'Leave no stone unturned,' Jack supplied. 'And you're right.'

Having consumed their chicken salads in relative silence, Mallery and Hobbs returned to the police headquarters with heavy thoughts.

'I'll contact the Prosecutor,' Max announced. 'See if we now have enough to detain Gilyard until forensics come back with something. You pick up the warrant to search her apartment. It should have arrived at the front desk by now.'

'Is it worth getting a psychiatric evaluation, too?' Jack ventured, biting his lip.

'What makes you ask that?' his senior officer replied.

'Just a hunch, sir. Never mind.'

In Saint Margeux, Maurice Fabron was trying his best to continue running the boulangerie as normal, yet a lack of sleep and the predicament of his new employee weighed heavily upon him. At least Telo had seemed in better spirits since Isobel's arrest, talking excitedly about the steak that Simone Dupuis had prepared for supper the night before, followed by lashings of vanilla ice-cream. Maurice felt indebted to Simone. Her hospitality was so generous, despite this being a difficult time for her, having lost her best friend. The chic, slender woman now sat across from Monsieur Fabron's rather empty-looking patisserie counter, her slim hands around a hot cup of black coffee. The pair had chatted quietly in between customers, Simone asking the baker's advice on whether she should resume normal opening times at the flower shop. Maurice had told her gently that life must go on, sadly, even though it was without Cecile Vidal.

The air changed between the pair as a strip of red flashed across the mirrored ceiling light, both heads turning to witness Max Mallery pulling up across the square in his flashy sports car. Maurice said nothing, but visibly tensed as both the Inspector and his English colleague began their stroll across the street.

Simone finished her coffee and rose, intending to leave her friend to speak with the detectives alone.

'Monsieur Fabron,' Max said solemnly, pulling out a piece of paper from his back pocket. 'We have a warrant to search Isobel Gilyard's apartment.'

Simone Dupuis laid a hand on her heart as though greatly shocked and used the other to grip the back of the chair.

'Detectives.' The boulangerie owner nodded. 'This is Madame Dupuis, a good friend. It was she who kindly provided Izzy with the nightwear yesterday.'

The men gave a slight bow, acknowledging the attractive female for the first time. Mallery couldn't help thinking how much she reminded him of the Commissioner's wife and had to hold himself in check when his mouth began to fall open.

'*Bonjour*,' Simone replied sweetly, a half-smile appearing on her pink lips. 'Is there any news? Why are you searching Isobel's apartment?'

'You'll excuse us if we can't discuss the case, Madame Dupuis,' Hobbs stepped in, before his boss could answer. 'The investigation is on-going.'

'Of course, I understand perfectly. I am just eager to see Cecile's killer put away as soon as possible. It hardly bears thinking about.'

'Naturally,' Jack conceded, 'I'm very sorry for your loss.'

'Well, perhaps I should now get back to work.' Simone sighed, turning her attention to Maurice and kissing both his cheeks. 'Thank you. You know where I am should you need anything.'

Monsieur Fabron touched hands with Simone as she brushed his face with her lips, lingering a few seconds longer than necessary as he inhaled the heady scent of her signature Chanel No.5 perfume.

'Merci, Simone.'

Three heads turned as the men watched the flower shop owner make her way next door, slender legs walking carefully on the cobbled pavement in kitten heels. Mallery wished that this was a normal Saturday, in which case he might be inclined to purchase a bunch of sunflowers to brighten up his apartment and then perhaps extend an invitation to take Simone Dupuis to dinner.

'Gentlemen.' Maurice cleared his throat. 'You need to go upstairs?'

Max unfolded the search warrant and held it out.

'We're here to look through Isobel Gilyard's belongings. If you wouldn't mind unlocking the door, please, Monsieur Fabron.'

'Really? Inspector, I cannot believe that Izzy has committed this terrible crime.' The baker frowned. 'Surely there is some mistake?'

'I'm afraid we can't go into details with you at the moment,' Hobbs explained, 'but let's just say that we need to find out more about Miss Gilyard's past.'

Maurice stood dumbfounded, wondering what on earth the Englishman was hinting at, until Telo walked in with an empty delivery basket.

'This way, please,' he suddenly answered, patting his son on the arm as he passed. 'I'll get the spare key.'

Telo turned to the fresh juice machine to quench his thirst, unaware that the woman he despised was just about to have all her darkest secrets laid bare.

With Maurice Fabron back downstairs and out of earshot, Max pointed Jack towards the living room. 'You look in there, I'll take the bedroom.'

'No problem. Let's see what we can find.'

As Mallery entered Isobel's bedroom, he was firstly struck by the lack of personal effects. There were the usual bits of jewellery and a make-up bag on the dressing-table, but very few items that would give clues to the occupant's identity, such as photographs or a diary. He noted that the bed was neatly made, with the sheets tucked into 'hospital corners'. Just one painting hung on the wall, a copy of Claude Monet's *Water Lilies* but, as the artist was French, Max presumed that it was probably purchased some time before by Monsieur Fabron.

He crouched down to look under the bed, but only an empty void stared back and Mallery quickly turned his attention to the vast built-in cupboard that took up most of the shortest wall.

A continuous row of pastel-coloured dresses, jeans and floral tops were neatly hung from the rail, portraying Isobel's penchant for 1950s fashion and pretty patterns. Running a hand along the clothing, the Inspector looked closely at the items, waiting for a clue to drop out from a pocket or sleeve. As he neared the end of the rail, he glanced down to where Miss Gilyard's shoes were neatly lined up and it was then that he saw the space behind them.

Hunkering down on all fours, Max reached into the depths of the cupboard all the way to the back. It was several seconds before his hand touched upon something other than footwear and he found himself grasping a long, rectangular box.

'Jacques,' Mallery called, 'I think I've found something.'

Hobbs strode down the short corridor and arrived just as his boss lifted the box onto Isobel's bed and pulled off the lid.

'*Merci*, Monsieur Fabron.' Mallery lit a cigarette outside the boulangerie as the duo prepared to leave.

'And now?' Maurice enquired. 'What will happen to Izzy?'

Mallery shrugged. 'We don't yet have enough to prosecute her for Cecile Vidal's murder, but she is certainly not the innocent woman you think she is.'

'If Isobel had anything to do with Cecile's murder, I think I have a right to know,' the baker confessed. 'After all, she has been living and working here for a week. What is inside the box?'

'Monsieur, you know we can't divulge that,' Hobbs answered, 'but as soon as we're able to tell you something, I promise we will.'

Max's expression told Maurice that the young man was being as honest as he could be, and the conversation drew to a close.

'It won't be long before we have news.' Mallery winked. 'I am sure of it.'

Back in the incident room, Gabriella and Thierry had just returned from Toulouse.

'Besides having witnesses that put Louis Perant in Bordeaux half an hour before the CCTV caught him talking to Gilyard, there's nothing. He swears he never met her before, and it was just a chance meeting as he saw that her car had broken down,' Thierry explained. 'Perant's employer has also confirmed that he hasn't been outside of Toulouse at any other time this week.'

Max nodded, wondering what their next step should be and if it was worth bringing the drug dealer in for more formal questioning.

'Well, we've had a more productive afternoon,' Jack announced, sliding Isobel's battered shoebox across the table with gloved hands. 'In here are photographs of a man we presume to be Gilyard's murdered boyfriend, a wristband from the high security psychiatric unit where she was held, a passport in the name of 'Isobel Green', showing her with long dark hair, a discharge letter recommending her release and several photocopies of documents from her trial.'

Gabriella looked at the contents, her eyes wide and startled, 'Seriously? This woman has murdered before?'

'Apparently so,' Max muttered, lifting out a file from the box. 'Isobel Green served ten years for murder. She's a very dangerous young lady.'

Hobbs swung around to face the Inspector. 'Now that we have her real name, I'll get back on to the lads in Manchester.'

Mallery sighed and waved a hand at his team. 'Go home, all of you, but be sure to get here early in the morning. And tomorrow, I want to hear your ideas on how we are going to convict Mademoiselle Gilyard. As Jacques might say in English, a tiger never changes its spots.'

The word 'leopard' was on the tip of Hobbs' tongue but he thought better of it. Max had shown him a great deal of respect in letting him take the lead on this case and he wasn't going to start rocking the boat now.

Jack Hobbs sat alone in the incident room, a large mug of Yorkshire tea on the cluttered desk next to him. He had refused to return home until detectives in Manchester had returned his call requesting information and he didn't have to wait long. Max Mallery was close by, rewriting parts of the information on the whiteboard, straining his ears with excitement to hear what news his colleague was gathering.

'Wow!' Jack dropped the telephone back into its cradle and stared down at his notepad. 'They're sending over the full records now,' he explained, leaning back in the chair, 'but basically, Isobel Green served ten years in a high security psychiatric unit for the murder of her boyfriend, Martin Freeman, in 2007. She was released in November last year after several positive evaluations. Her record inside was exemplary, and she even took a course in…'

'Don't tell me, it was patisserie,' Mallery supplied, coming over to lean on Jack's desk.

'Exactly.'

'Mmm, hence the position at Fabron's boulangerie,' Max tutted.

Hobbs nodded, appreciating how switched on the Inspector's mind was.

After a few moments' contemplation, Jack pressed a pen to his lips and pondered, 'There's still no motive for the murder of Cecile Vidal, though. Stabbing a man that you know and murdering a practical stranger in cold blood are two very different things, aren't they? But we can't hold her much longer without evidence. It's either charge her on Monday or let her go.'

'Do we know why she was sent to a psychiatric unit rather than prison?'

'Hold on, I'll see if the file's here yet,' Jack replied, his fingers flitting deftly over the keyboard. 'Yes, here it is.'

He skimmed the document quickly before hitting upon the information.

'Apparently Mr. Green used his life-savings to hire a top solicitor who got the plea reduced to 'diminished responsibility'. Otherwise she would have ended up serving thirty years or more. Nasty case, too. Martin Freeman was stabbed seven times in the stomach and according to the Coroner's report would have bled to death within minutes.'

'Stabbed seven times in the stomach,' Max repeated, leaning forward to look at the screen. 'Exactly the same as Cecile Vidal!'

Mallery and Hobbs looked at each other, a combination of shock and revelation pasted across their faces. It was time to question Isobel Green.

As soon as the cell key turned clockwise in its lock, Isobel was on her feet desperate for the news that she was about to be released. Her usually neat blonde hair was flattened at the back where she'd been leaning against the wall, and dark purple ridges were emerging from underneath her eyes.

'*Suivez-moi*,' the policeman grunted, holding open the door. 'Come with me,' he added, in heavily accented English.

'Where to?' Isobel urged, moving across the room. 'Am I free to go?'

The uniformed officer curled his upper lip and regarded her with distaste but didn't respond, merely pointing to the corridor where a second guard joined them. Isobel was ushered along with one man in front and one behind, until they arrived at the all too familiar interview room.

'*Merci*, Paul.' Max nodded to his colleague. 'Mademoiselle, please sit down.'

He flipped on the tape-recorder and spoke clearly. 'For the record, interview with Isobel Green commencing at 16:10 pm with Inspector Mallery and Detective Hobbs.'

As soon as the name 'Isobel Green' dropped from the Inspector's lips, Isobel let out a cry and put both hands up to her face in horror.

'Please answer only the questions that we put to you,' Max continued, unfazed by the woman's obvious shock. 'Are you Isobel Green?'

Jack Hobbs pushed Isobel's British passport across the table, the photo identity page open for her to see.

'No... I... yes,' Izzy sobbed, collapsing inwardly on the plastic chair. 'Please, I can explain.'

'Then please do.'

'I wanted a fresh start. Away from everything. A new life,' she began, feeling like a cornered mouse. 'The last few years have been difficult.'

'Since being found guilty of murdering Martin Freeman, you mean?' Mallery ventured, watching the woman's reaction closely.

Isobel was aghast. At first, she'd had no clue how the detectives had discovered her real name, but with the passport in their hands it was obvious that they'd searched her belongings. She cursed under her breath, regretting bringing her box of secrets with her to France, but there was a greater underlying fear, that the things she had done back in England were now coming back to haunt her.

Isobel bit her lip, searching for the words needed to explain. 'I know you think I murdered Cecile Vidal, but I promise you, I had nothing to do with her death.'

Max Mallery tapped his wristwatch. 'Perhaps you can tell us how a convicted murderer happens to arrive in Saint Margaux just a few days before one of its residents dies in a horrific attack. We would also like to know about your links to known drug dealer Louis Perant. Finally, the most damning piece of information against you, Mademoiselle Green, after all your time in the cell, all those hours with the chance to tell the truth, why did you not reveal your true name?'

'Please, you have to believe me. I simply wanted a new start. I'm not a murderer.'

'I think Martin Freeman might disagree with you, were he still here to speak out.'

Max delivered the punchline slowly and steadily, causing Jack Hobbs to flinch slightly. Even for him, that was a low blow.

Mallery and Hobbs stood on the police station steps watching the thunderous clouds gathering overhead. It had been a hot and sweltering day, leaving both men ready to head home for a much-needed cool shower.

'Angélique is going to be mad at you,' Max commented, reaching into his jeans for the customary departure cigarette.

'Yep,' Jack confirmed, glancing at his watch, 'but it's been a productive day.'

'When this is over, I owe you a long weekend with your family,' his boss promised, 'but it might be best to warn your wife that there will probably be a few more long days over the next few weeks.'

The younger man nodded, picturing Angélique's image growing horns as her temper swelled. He'd have a lot of making-up to do to compensate for today, let alone the arduous toil of an ongoing murder investigation.

'And tomorrow?' Jack asked, 'What's your plan for Miss Green-slash-Gilyard?'

'Hopefully, she'll do plenty of thinking overnight and have some answers for us tomorrow. Sitting alone in a cell usually has the desired effect on criminals.'

'You're sure she did it then, sir?'

Mallery lifted his chin, contemplating the question. '*Oui*, I think so. Don't you?'

'Everything points that way,' Jack admitted, pulling out his car keys, 'but I have no idea how we're going to get a conviction at this rate. All the evidence so far is purely circumstantial.'

'Don't worry. I think forensics will give us exactly what we need,' Max countered.

The two men headed down the steps and towards their respective cars. Any onlooker might have thought them unlikely friends, yet the comradeship between the two detectives was building, as was their mutual respect for one another.

'See you tomorrow. *Bonsoir*,' Jack called, wrangling with the Mondeo lock.

'*Bonsoir*, Jacques. I don't want to see you before ten in the morning, okay?'

Hobbs nodded enthusiastically.

'Let the others do some work and make sure you get a good rest.'

Fat chance of that, with a new baby that thought it was fun to test out his lung capacity every two hours, the young detective mused, yet he appreciated the sentiment. It proved that Maxime Mallery wasn't immune to the difficulties of family life.

'Thanks.'

Max turned and flipped the fob to unlock his BMW. It was so new that the interior still reeked of polished leather, a reminder of the leaving present he'd treated himself to after being shown his transfer cards from Paris. Taking out his phone, the Inspector set the device on the dashboard clip in front of him. If Vanessa suddenly decided to call, he didn't want to miss the opportunity to talk her around to coming down to Bordeaux.

He closed the door and fastened his seatbelt, watching Jack reverse carefully out of the police compound. He admired the young newcomer very much and wondered if he might be able to secure Hobbs a permanent position on Team Mallery. For now, he was just glad to have the Englishman's help.

CHAPTER ELEVEN – AN OPPRESSIVE SUNDAY

As the congregation of Saint Margaux residents prepared to leave church, Hubert Vidal, Simone Dupuis, Maurice Fabron and young Telo stayed behind to light individual candles for their dearly departed wife, sister-in-law and friend, Cecile Vidal. Flames sparked to life as each took their turn to say a silent prayer, all hoping that Cecile was resting in peace and that her killer would be brought to justice soon.

'Hubert, will you join us for lunch?' Simone whispered to the vineyard owner as the group made their way outside, each smiling and thanking the parish priest as they did so.

'Thank you, Simone but, as this is the last Sunday before Cecile's funeral, I plan to take the children out somewhere special. They were too upset to accompany me today and I feel a change of scenery will do them good.'

Madam Dupuis lowered her thick lashes. 'Of course.'

The woman quickly turned, linking arms with Maurice and Telo. 'Let's go and see what Gaston has prepared for us. Hubert, please call if you need me.'

'Thank you, Simone, and you too, Maurice, I couldn't have got through the past few days without you.'

Hubert hugged Telo tightly to him and whispered, 'Take care of your father, there's a good boy.'

In the kitchen of Simone's pretty stone cottage, Gaston Lauder was sprinkling herbs over a pan of roast potatoes just as the trio entered, a red apron tied around his waist and a large glass of claret on the work-top at his side.

'Gaston,' Madam Dupuis reprimanded him, 'you have started the wine without us.'

The artist shrugged, popping the pan back into the oven. 'I needed to open it for the jus, Simone, so I thought it best to test it.'

Maurice smiled at the handsome young man. His cheek and easy-going manner was a great comfort to them all, and he knew that Simone secretly loved having her regular summer house-guest to stay.

'Sit, have a glass,' Gaston ordered. 'Lunch will be about half an hour. Just time for me to show Telo the painting that I'm working on.'

'Fantastic!' Telo grinned, trudging out of the room behind Gaston.

Simone seized the wine bottle and began filling two glasses. 'So, Maurice, what are you going to do about Isobel?'

The boulangerie owner clasped his hands together and took a deep breath, 'Honestly, I really don't know what to do, Simone.'

'If she was innocent, the police would have let her go by now, don't you think?' Simone raised her eyebrows and took a sip of the claret.

Monsieur Fabron nodded. 'Very true. I think they found something in her apartment, too. The detectives took an old shoebox with them.'

Simone leaned in closer. 'Really? How interesting. Something incriminating, perhaps?'

'I really couldn't say, but whatever it was, I don't think it's looking good for Izzy.'

Simone brushed the back of her hand across her friend's cheek. 'Come on, maybe it's time to admit that maybe Mademoiselle Gilyard did have something to do with Cecile's murder.'

'She just seemed so, bubbly, so normal. You met her, Simone. Surely you can't believe she could kill a woman in cold blood?'

Madam Dupuis made a noncommittal sound and looked into Maurice's eyes. 'I really can't say. I have only spoken to the woman for a few minutes.'

'I feel responsible,' the baker admitted, sliding a finger up and down the stem of his wineglass. 'I brought Isobel Gilyard here, to Saint Margaux. Besides, whatever she's done, I really don't think that Izzy has any family to turn to. I am a compassionate man, Simone. I cannot simply turn my back on her.'

Madame Dupuis regarded her friend's sincere face and then bent forward to kiss him gently on the forehead. 'You are getting soft, Maurice, too soft. If anyone needs to go to take things, or speak to Isobel, I will go. She will manipulate you. Besides, you need to think about Telo. Agreed?'

The man nodded, grateful for Simone's friendship and laid his hand upon hers.

'Now, let's see how our roast pork is coming along,' Gaston interrupted, bouncing into the room with Telo close on his heels. 'It smells wonderful.'

The fact that Maurice's hand slid away from Simone's at that point didn't escape the artist's notice and he smiled inwardly at the oddly matched pair.

Isobel Green nibbled at the tuna baguette, neither tasting its contents nor really focussed on her task. Ever since Inspector Mallery had mentioned Martin Freeman's name, the young woman had been living as though inside a tunnel with sounds echoing around her and thoughts disjointed and bleak.

She felt as though her whole new life, albeit a short one, was about to come crashing down in a swift and brutal motion. Everything she had attempted to build for herself here in France, a job, new lifestyle and home, was threatened by all the events that had come before. There was so much that Isobel regretted about the past, but that had been the purpose of putting every scrap of memories into a single box, in the hope that one day she would have the courage to burn it all.

Izzy had spent the previous night tossing and turning restlessly on her bunk, afraid to close her eyes in case the nightmares came back. She couldn't bear the thought of reliving Martin's last few minutes again and therapy had taught her how to compartmentalise the events in her head, to lock them away and turn the key. Only now, with terrifying conviction that she had might actually go to prison for Cecile Vidal's murder, did Isobel open up that door a fraction and peek inside,

On that fatal afternoon, all those years before, parked in the woods far from home, Isobel's heart had been in her mouth when her so-called boyfriend had revealed his plan. He was fed up, he told her, of his woman flirting with other men and not being where she was supposed to be. How could he trust her, he'd asked. Panic had pushed its way up into Izzy's throat, preventing her from screaming as Freeman pulled out a knife from under the driver's seat. She remembered the weapon all too well, a gleaming hunter's knife, sharp and curved with a strong leather hilt. It belonged in a Viking history museum rather than in the Ford Cortina of a geeky young man, but Isobel knew that this was

Martin's pride and joy, one of a collection of artefacts that he'd purchased from an antiques website.

At first, she had been afraid to move, stunned into silence by the sight of the sharp blade. She remembered pushing herself against the passenger's door as far as she could, with Freeman leering at her and raising the knife to her hair.

'Let's start with this, shall we?' he'd growled, slicing through a chunk of Isobel's long shiny black hair, 'and then we'll get you to show me a bit of respect.'

Isobel closed her eyes, remembering how cold she'd suddenly felt as Martin tore through her skirt with the knife and ripped off her underwear, forcing himself inside her while gripping her neck with his free hand, the other holding tight to the weapon. She had lain as still as she possibly could, afraid that any sudden movement would cause the man to slice through her jugular and it was then, as Freeman jolted and pressed inside her, that Izzy remembered her mother's dress-making scissors.

Careful not to move an inch of her body, yet sliding a silent hand downwards, Isobel Green touched upon the zipper of her bag and pulled gently. It took several long-drawn-out moments before she felt the rounded curves of the silver shears that she'd borrowed that morning to lend to her friend. Her fingers shook as she gripped the scissors tightly, ensuring that the tip was pointing away from her. Isobel waited, for an agonising two more minutes.

As Martin Freeman spent his seed, giving one last thrust to the limp body of his girlfriend, he lifted his torso upwards. Sweat patches splattered his white shirt and a trickle of perspiration ran down his gleaming forehead like a raindrop.

'Maybe that will teach you,' he gasped, 'I bet you'll never... *aarrgghhh*!'

Isobel pushed the sharp scissors into the man's stomach with all the strength she could muster, deftly pulling them out for a second, third and fourth time and repeating the action over and over. She never did count just how many times she had stabbed Martin, but it didn't matter. Now, he would never be able to violate her again.

For a short time, Freeman struggled to comprehend what had happened as he gripped his side in agony, watching the blood ooze through a gash in his abdomen. But as Isobel stabbed again, and again, his face turned white as he suddenly realised the enormity of his fate.

As soon as she was certain that her boyfriend was incapable of chasing after her, Izzy pushed with all her might, forcing the man's body back over into the driver's seat of the car. She grabbed what pieces of fabric were left of her skirt and fled the scene.

It was more than an hour later that a poacher had pulled up in his Land Rover, having seen a blood-covered woman hunched in the hedgerow at the side of the road. He'd immediately called the police and put an old army jacket around Isobel's shoulders while he reluctantly disposed of the buck deer that he'd shot on private land just an hour before. There was no way he was going to play Good Samaritan and then get charged with trespassing and goodness knows what else.

Max Mallery looked proudly around the Incident Room. His team were all present as expected and heads were bowed at their respective computer screens. He hadn't slept well but, judging by the intermittent yawns coming from Jack Hobbs' direction, better than the younger detective.

'Jacques,' he said softly, tossing a twenty Euro note onto the man's desk, 'I'm going down to talk to Mademoiselle Green. I'll take Gabriella with me. Maybe a woman's presence might be able to crack Isobel's tough exterior. Why don't you and Luc go fetch some coffee and pain au chocolat?'

'No problem,' Hobbs replied. 'The fresh air will do me good. Fingers crossed that you can get Miss Green to confess.'

Mallery wasn't hopeful, but he did believe that a different tactic was needed if he were to trip up the Englishwoman about her movements.

'Mademoiselle Green,' the uniformed officer called, 'Inspector Mallery is here to see you.'

The bolts clattered open and Isobel shifted from the bed to the wall, standing rigidly with her back against the cold stone.

'Inspector.'

'This is Detective DuPont,' he introduced, gesturing to the blonde at his side.

'Have you got rid of Hobbs then?' Izzy asked sarcastically before she could stop the words.

Mallery ignored the comment and continued regardless. 'Are you ready to tell us anything, Miss Green?'

Isobel sniffed and pulled her cardigan tighter. 'I have two things to tell you, Inspector. It depends if you want to listen.'

Gabriella looked at her boss hopefully, but Max was unresponsive.

'Go on, we're listening.'

The smell of freshly brewed coffee filled the room and Max inhaled deeply, grateful for the aroma that was in vast contrast to the odour of Isobel Green's cell that he'd just left. The woman's stale body odour, uneaten food and the acidic urine stench from the cell toilet had insulted his senses.

'Pain au chocolat?' Luc offered, pushing a large box forward.

'*Non*.' The Inspector couldn't face food until he'd filled up on caffeine.

'Any luck, sir?' Jack asked hopefully. 'Did she talk?'

It was Gabriella who took the reins, noticing that Max was preoccupied with selecting the hottest mug of coffee.

'She didn't confess, but she did offer up two interesting pieces of information about other residents of Saint Margaux.'

'Trying to put the blame on someone else, eh?' Thierry sighed. 'Typical guilty suspect.'

'I think it might be relevant, though,' the young woman continued, 'if by some chance Green's not guilty. She mentioned that the baker's son, Telo Fabron, had been using her car without permission. As the bread knife belonged to Maurice, isn't it possible that Telo might actually be the perpetrator?'

Max shook his head. 'The lad's a bit simple but I can't see him murdering his own aunt, they were really close.'

'What was the second thing?' Jack pressed, taking a large bite of the warm, flaky pastry.

'Madam Green insists that she saw blood on the artist's shirt last week. What was his name…?' She flipped open her notes. 'Gaston Lauder.'

'The man who rents a room from Simone Dupuis every summer,' Jack clarified. 'What do we know about him?'

Thierry moved across to the whiteboard and read out the profile notes. 'He's been spending every summer in Saint Margaux for the past five years. Lives in Paris the rest of the year, no previous record, quite successful with his artwork.'

Max turned to face the group, inhaling the coffee with relish. 'We have to follow up on Green's accusations, even if just to dismiss these two men and tighten the case around her. Isobel Green has convinced herself that she's been set up. It's our job to prove that she hasn't been.'

Hobbs felt the stirrings of another yawn threatening to descend upon him and clamped his lips shut to prevent it escaping.

'Anything to add?' Mallery queried, looking from face to face. 'Anyone?'

Tiredness was etched on every countenance, but underneath, a bubbling determination to catch a killer was desperate to shine through.

At three o'clock that afternoon, Mallery and Hobbs pulled up outside Maurice Fabron's impressive home and marched up to the front door.

It was several minutes before a voice called to them from across the street.

'Detectives, Maurice is here.'

The men turned to see Simone Dupuis waving at them, her slender form dressed in a cream blouse and green floral skirt.

'*Bonjour, Madame*,' Max replied, gesturing to Jack to follow him across the square. '*Merci.*'

'I saw you from the window just now,' the woman explained, her English perfect yet heavily accented. 'We are all in the garden playing boules.'

'We are sorry to disturb you on a Sunday,' the Inspector said with a smile, as Simone opened the front door of her cottage, 'but there are questions that cannot wait.'

Madam Dupuis did not answer but led the men through a long passageway and out into a well-kept garden full of pink flowers and shrubs.

'*Ah, bonjour*,' Maurice said, looking up from his bent position on the grass before tossing a ball towards its marker. 'There must be an important reason for you to be here on a Sunday.'

'Indeed,' Max replied. 'And we are sorry to interrupt your afternoon.'

'No matter,' Simone added. 'What can we do for you?'

Jack looked at his boss, who nodded for the younger man to step in, 'We've had a couple of accusations from Miss Green and need to check a few things with Telo and Monsieur Lauder.'

As soon as the name fell from his lips, all four residents stopped in their tracks, one question on all of their minds. It was Maurice who spoke first.

'Monsieur, who is Miss Green?'

Mallery rolled his eyes, realising that they would now have to satisfy these inquisitive minds, yet he believed it only fair that the baker find out who he'd really employed. He made a slight grimace at Jack and began to explain.

'Isobel Gilyard's real family name is Green. She has her own reasons for using a different identity, but we are not obliged to go into the details at the moment. Now, if we could just ask a couple of questions, we'll soon be on our way, leaving you to enjoy your activity.'

Maurice frowned. 'I'm very confused, Inspector. Gilyard is not her real name?'

'No Monsieur Fabron.' Max sighed. 'In time, we may be able to explain properly but for now, I'm afraid that's all we can say.'

'But you need to question Telo and Gaston because of something she has said?' Simone clarified, her startlingly beautiful eyes wide and alert.

Mallery paused for a second, drinking in the dark pools that looked his way. God, he thought, Simone Dupuis was an elegant and enticing creature.

Jack Hobbs stepped into the deathly silence that hung in the air, wondering why his senior hadn't responded.

'Yes, just two things. Monsieur Lauder, there has been mention of you wearing a white shirt with red stains on it…'

Gaston shrugged. 'When? Which day, detective?'

Hobbs was unsure. 'Around Wednesday?'

The artist looked blankly back at him. 'I might have been, but all of my shirts have been washed since then.'

He looked at Simone for confirmation, a genuine bewilderment on his face.

'Yes, yes.' The woman nodded. 'Your linen shirt, Gaston. It had red paint on the cuffs, so I soaked it before putting into the machine.'

'Would you mind us looking at it?' Max ventured, his manner calm and non-intrusive, 'Just to confirm.'

'Of course,' Gaston replied curtly. 'I will get it from my room.'

Mallery turned to Telo and said in clear French, 'Now, you're not in any trouble but I need to ask if you again if you have used Isobel's car without her permission.'

The young man was unfazed by the question and answered honestly, only stopping for a moment to glance at his father.

'As Telo told you, he used it to fetch Gaston from the airport late on Wednesday afternoon,' Max translated for Jack. 'But only because it was parked behind the delivery van. Convenience, I suppose.'

Hobbs nodded, trying to gage the degree of sincerity in Telo Fabron's face.

Maurice faced his son and muttered a few stern words.

'We also need to know if Telo opened the glove compartment, or if he saw either the shirt or the knife while in the car,' Jack added.

Maurice squeezed Telo's shoulders with the palms of his hands, urging the youngster to tell the truth.

'*Non*,' Telo replied, shaking his head, '*Non, Papa*.'

Fabron looked up at the detectives. 'There is your answer, and I believe my son. Although we will be having a conversation later about him using Izzy's car.'

Just then, Gaston Lauder returned to the garden holding a neatly folded white shirt.

'Here you go,' he announced, passing the garment to Max. 'I think this is the one, there's a slight trace of something dark on the sleeve that hasn't quite washed out. I'm always getting paint on my clothes, hazard of my work.'

Mallery held the shirt up to the sunlight and regarded the brownish-red tinge. Having washed several of his own shirts after kitchen mishaps in the past, he knew that if the substance were blood, it might have left a stain such as that being shown to him, but it also could easily be paint.

'*Merci*,' he said, handing back the shirt. 'I'm sorry, it was just a line of enquiry.'

'So, is Isobel Gilyard, Green, or whatever her name is, trying to set me up, Inspector?' Gaston laughed, trying to make light of the situation.

'Nothing like that at all,' Mallery lied, 'it was just something said in passing.'

'And now?' Simone asked, clasping her hands together. 'Is she going to be charged with murder?'

Max felt cornered, yet also acknowledged that he owed these good people the truth as they had been incredibly honest with him.

'We have only circumstantial evidence,' he told the group. 'As far as we are concerned, there are still questions to be asked of Mademoiselle Green, but she will not be charged unless further proof of any misdemeanour is forthcoming.'

There was a murmur of disapproval from the French residents as they took in the Inspector's words. His statement was obviously not what they expected.

'We'll let you know of any further developments,' Jack promised, wondering to himself how long they would be running around in circles. 'Thank you all for your time and patience.'

Mallery added that he was grateful for their assistance, before allowing Simone Dupuis to lead them back out through the cottage.

'Your type, sir?' Hobbs grinned as they made their way back to the car.

'I don't know what you mean.'

'Aw, come on. Your tongue was almost hanging out back there.'

Max grunted but couldn't help expelling the laughter that was welling up inside.

'Jacques, you're not afraid to say what you think, are you?' he gasped, punching the detective on the arm.

'Well, just a bit of fun, sir,' Hobbs returned. 'She's got a bit of old-style Hollywood glamour about her, hasn't she?'

'Less of the "old",' Mallery retorted, glancing back towards Simone's cottage. 'I think just a few years older than me and very chic indeed.'

Hobbs shook his head. 'You rascal.'

As the BMW raced forward on the main highway back into Bordeaux, Max took the opportunity to go over the day's revelations with his junior.

'Do you think Green is just playing for time? Sending us on a… what do you say, Jacques, a goose chase?'

'A wild goose chase, sir. I'm not so sure. Telo Fabron *had* used her car without asking and Gaston Lauder *had* got reddish stains on his shirt. Just as she described to us. It's a bit far-fetched to think Isobel Green made that up. Too much of a coincidence.'

'I agree,' Max conceded, 'I tell you, there will be some harsh words in the morning if forensics haven't got anything for us. We've literally got until lunchtime or we'll have to let Miss Green go.'

'There is one thing that I find strange about her, though,' Jack ventured, gripping the side of his seat as Mallery overtook a lorry at breakneck speed. 'She's still refusing legal help.'

'Well, we haven't charged her, so unless she's going to confess, there's no need.'

'Do you think she will?' Jack asked, shutting his eyes as the car swerved back into the middle lane.

'No,' Mallery sighed, easing off the accelerator with a smile pulling at his lips. 'I don't think she will.'

In her cell, Isobel Green was frustrated. The lack of mental stimulation was causing her mind to go into overdrive and every minute that she was left alone was another step closer to a backwards slide in her mental wellbeing.

It was almost as though the French police were coercing her into admitting a crime by making her confinement as uncomfortable as possible. The room lacked ventilation and natural light and, as Izzy hadn't been wearing a watch when she was brought into the station, she had no clue what hour of the day it was. Every meal that had been brought lacked taste and, with closed eyes, was as bland and nondescript as the next plate.

Isobel wrestled with her conscience, wondering if and when the time would come when she no longer had a choice but to contact her parents. It was an unbearable thought, the tutting and shouting all over again, and the very possible eventuality that she might need someone to pay for decent legal representation. She had no idea whether her father would even consider taking out a loan to cover the fees, or whether he'd been able to start putting a bit of cash away after her trial in 2007 had depleted the family's savings. Every corner of her mind filled with desperation and the dread that her past was coming back at her with a vengeance. Martin Freeman might as well have been there in the flesh, she told herself, as the ways things were heading, he was going to get retribution in the form of Isobel going to jail for the murder of Cecile Vidal.

The Englishwoman curled up in a ball on the iron bedstead, knees tucked up in her familiar foetal position. Had those detectives actually gone out to Saint Margaux to question Gaston and Telo? she wondered. Did they believe what she'd told them? But more importantly, did Isobel believe herself?

CHAPTER TWELVE – MONDAY BLUES

By eleven o'clock on Monday morning, Inspector Mallery had already disposed of three espresso coffees and was contemplating a caramel latte when Gabriella Dupont knocked on his office door. The sound echoed off the high ceiling, causing Max to look up in surprise.

'*Oui?*'

'*Médecine légale,*' she said simply, turning to leave and knowing instinctively that her boss's curiosity would cause him to follow.

The news that forensics had been in touch both excited and worried Mallery. This would determine the team's success or failure in prosecuting Isobel Green. He pushed out of his swivel chair, leaving it spinning in his wake, and strode quickly down to the Incident Room.

Immediately on entering, he could tell by the group's faces that it wasn't the news they'd been hoping for.

'Well?'

'Nothing to incriminate Green,' Gabriella told him. 'No fingerprints whatsoever.'

'Damn! Anything else?'

The young detective read carefully from the notes she'd taken during her phone call to the lab, carefully translating from French to English for Hobbs' benefit.

'The blood on the knife is a match for Cecile Vidal, but apparently it would have dried completely before being wrapped in the denim shirt. They only found small traces, dried flecks, on the fabric.'

'Looks like Isobel Green could have been telling the truth after all, sir,' Thierry commented, looking at the clock on the wall. 'We've only got an hour before she'll have to be charged formally, or released.'

Max grunted, noting the despondency in his detectives. He felt their frustration too, yet could do little to ease the negative tension.

'You're right there, Thierry. With no solid evidence, we're going to have to release her. Although…'

'What are you thinking?' Gabriella asked, noting the wily grin on Max's face.

'Let's put a tail on her. I'll get a couple of uniformed officers to take the night shifts and then, Thierry, you can take the day shift. Green hasn't seen you before.'

The team nodded in agreement, warming to the plan.

'I can help out, too,' Gabriella offered eagerly. 'I've got a dark wig and lots of hats.'

Mallery laughed. 'In this weather? I hope they're sun hats! Go on then, go with Thierry to Saint Margaux and use the pool cars to vary things.'

'What do you want me to do?' Jack questioned, beginning to feel the familiar buzz of joining a stake-out.

'Green knows you too well, as do the other villagers. We'll spend the rest of the day going over what we know so far and then tomorrow, Jacques, you and I will attend Cecile Vidal's funeral. It's widely reported that killers get a thrill out of attending their victim's burial, so we need to be vigilant in case anyone unexpected shows up.'

Hobbs nodded eagerly. It was encouraging that Mallery's thoughts were running along the same lines as his own.

In her lonely cell, Isobel Green was sitting cross-legged on the bunk, desperate for news from outside. She'd spent yet another sleepless night at the police station, but this time her thoughts hadn't been directed towards Martin Freeman. Throughout the long, dark hours, she'd been pondering whether the detectives had bothered to follow up on the information she'd given them about Telo and Gaston.

Despite her intention of getting to know Maurice's son better and healing the rift between them, Izzy knew that he was the only one who had been anywhere near her car and, by his own admission, had used it without asking. It stood to reason that the young man could have hidden the murder weapon inside the glove box. She had doubts as to whether Telo could actually have murdered Cecile. She realised that he was different to her in the way that he thought and acted, but, despite their differences, she could never believe that he could kill someone.

It was obvious to see, from their interaction at Monsieur Fabron's house and at the boulangerie, too, that Telo was very close to the artist. Isobel reasoned that, if it had actually been blood that she'd spotted on his shirt, Gaston could easily have manipulated Telo into covering up his tracks. She wondered whether there had been some ill-feeling between Cecile and Gaston, perhaps a love affair gone wrong? There was plenty to speculate about, sitting there in the lonely hours.

The familiar sound of footsteps coming down the corridor caused Izzy to strain her ears, just in case they were coming for her. She was aware that the police could not hold her much longer without solid evidence and it was impossible, in her opinion, that they would find any.

The steel toe-capped boots plodded on, unlocking a door further down the passage. She'd heard a lot of commotion the night before, when a drunken youth had been incarcerated for making a public nuisance of himself. There had been singing into the early hours as the man serenaded his custodians and then a flurry of feet running to the cell as officers fetched buckets to swill out the contents of the man's stomach after he'd deposited them on the floor.

Half an hour ticked by, although Isobel was unable to count the minutes and it felt like an hour. More clicking on tiles, coming closer, arriving outside her door.

'Mademoiselle Green,' Inspector Mallery called, 'please come with me.'

Izzy groaned. She couldn't handle any more questions, the torture of reliving her past crime, the detective's incessant droning about her guilt.

'What for?' she asked, slowly getting to her feet.

'Please, you will see.'

Max led her to reception where she was asked to sign for her belongings. Isobel did so with an air of disbelief, finding it incredulous that her ordeal could really be over.

'Isobel Green,' Mallery stated, watching her scribble on the record book, 'you are free to go, but please stay available in case we need to question you further.'

Izzy looked at the clear plastic bag containing her few items of jewellery and the watch that her parents had bought for her twenty-first birthday. 'What? That's it, Inspector?' She frowned. 'No apology?'

Max drew himself up to his full height and stared down at the petite blonde, noting that dark roots were now pushing their way through her peroxide bob. 'As I said,' he retorted, choosing his words carefully, 'we may need to question you again, but for now, you may leave.'

Isobel didn't need to be told twice. She picked up her personal items but then stopped in her tracks. 'I don't have any money with me.'

'Please, feel free to use the telephone here at reception, or perhaps you would like me to call someone to collect you?'

Isobel thought for a moment. All she really wanted to do was get the first flight out of France.

'What about my passport?' she demanded hoarsely.

'The rest of your effects will be returned to you at some point, but we still need to keep hold of your passport. Don't forget that the passport you entered our country with is a false document, as Gilyard turns out not to be your real name, Mademoiselle. I suggest you remember that, and the French Government may also have something to say on the matter.'

Isobel dropped her head to her chest. Shit, she was still in deep trouble.

'So,' the Inspector continued, beginning to lose patience, 'a phone call?'

'Maurice Fabron,' Izzy whispered, realising that the baker was her last hope.

'I understand this may be very difficult for you in the circumstances,' Max explained, holding the telephone receiver close to his ear whilst simultaneously lighting a cigarette, 'but we consider it imperative that Mademoiselle Green stays in France until the case is closed.'

Maurice Fabron held the boulangerie phone tightly as several inquisitive customers looked his way, eager to catch any snippets of gossip relating to the baker's new employee.

'Of course, Inspector. I am unable to leave the shop today but will arrange for someone to fetch Izzy within the next hour or so. She can stay here until you have resolved…'

The man's voice trailed off, leaving Mallery to thank him before dropping the line. He loathed the idea of Monsieur Fabron having the burden of accommodating Isobel Green, but there was simply no other choice. Besides, the baker seemed unfazed.

Isobel Green sat in the reception area of the Municipal Police Station of Bordeaux Town, the small bag of personal belongings sitting in her lap as she awaited news. She felt so wretched and unclean that, even if she had been in a position to pay her fare back to Saint Margaux, she would have felt like a vagrant with such unkempt hair and dishevelled clothing.

Mallery stepped into view, his tall frame momentarily blocking the sunlight from the building's open doorway.

'Monsieur Fabron is sending someone to fetch you shortly,' he explained, taking a seat on the bench next to Izzy.

She was taken aback, feeling slightly betrayed. 'He isn't coming himself?'

Max opened his hands and feigned knowledge of the details. 'He must be busy.'

Isobel nodded, accepting that the boulangerie owner would of course be preoccupied with filling the shelves on this first day of his working week.

'Do you know who is coming?'

'*Non*, Mademoiselle, I have no idea.'

Izzy bit her bottom lip, hoping that it wouldn't be Gaston coming to face her after her recent accusation. Or, worse still, Telo with his angry eyes and habitual silence. But who else could there be?

'Mademoiselle Green, if you need to speak to me, if you have anything that I should hear, please will you call?'

Max held out his personal card between two fingers, which Isobel accepted reluctantly. She glanced at the name before pushing it into her pocket.

'Did you follow up on what I told you, Inspector? About the blood and the car?'

Mallery held her gaze, trying to decide whether the tiny female could lie through her teeth while still looking at him so openly.

'Yes, but there was a reasonable explanation for both. Why are you insistent on pinning this murder on someone else, Mademoiselle Green?'

He'd taken a chance, stepped beyond Isobel's comfort zone and prayed that the question would catch her off guard, lull her into a false sense of security.

'Because I didn't do it!' she spat. 'Now, if that's all…'

Max got to his feet, pushing upwards with both hands on his knees. 'As I said, you have my number. *Au revoir.*'

Isobel watched the well-dressed policeman head towards the staircase, stepping lightly as though it required no physical effort at all. He was handsome, she had to concede, with dark, rugged looks and an expensive taste in clothes. Unusually for a man on a hot summer's day, Mallery smelled good, too, the cedar tones of his cologne lingering well after the Inspector's departure.

In Saint Margaux, Maurice Fabron finished serving a customer with bread and fondants before reaching for the telephone. Telo was due back from his deliveries shortly but, as the weather was so fine, the baker expected his son to have stopped near the river for a while before heading back. It was a possibility that Gaston was also down by the water with his easel and paints that morning, as the thickly wooded area and fast flowing water were a subject that the artist had captured on canvas many times before.

The baker dialled quickly and waited just three rings for a response.

'*Oui, Simone Dupuis,*' the silky voice answered.

Maurice took a deep breath, annoyed that he should have to ask such a huge favour of his friend. 'Simone, do you remember how you said if I needed anything I should just ask?' he said in French. 'Well, I think today is that day.'

Madam Dupuis listened carefully as the boulangerie owner explained that he was unable to collect Isobel from the police station in Bordeaux. It was a big ask, he told her, but, it being Monday, he would be tied up with baking and such.

'Maurice, it is not a problem,' the female voice trilled. 'Let me close the shop and come around to speak to you. We can settle the details face to face.'

'*Merci beaucoup, Simone.*'

Despite her conversation with Monsieur Fabron being short, Simone Dupuis was in no hurry to collect the Englishwoman. It was in Isobel's best interest, the florist had told Maurice, that she first gather together some fresh clothing and cosmetics before heading out to the police station. As a woman, Simone knew that the residents would mark the accused's arrival with sideward glances and whispered comments, and for that reason alone she would help Izzy to look presentable for her return to Saint Margaux. Therefore, half an hour later Simone started up her black Renault and left the village. She had no idea what situation to expect upon arrival, but she was doing this for Maurice, nobody else, and she harboured her own doubts about Isobel's return.

'Jacques,' Mallery sighed, taking a seat in Gabriella's empty chair. 'Have you anything new from the detectives in Manchester?'

Hobbs bit the top of his biro, a habit that he had failed to abandon since his student days. 'A few bits and pieces, but nothing too alarming, sir.'

'Oh, like what?'

Max scooted over to Jack's side, peering at the information on the computer screen. He squinted at the small-print, as the machine whirred to life.

'Isobel Green was arrested for shoplifting as a teenager, really went off the rails at one point, and then she served community service for spray-painting a school building after leaving college,' Hobbs summarised, turning the data for his boss to read properly. 'No other grievous bodily harm or assault charges, though.'

Mallery tutted, having expected more. 'Seems she was a very difficult young woman. What do we know of her parents? Anything to suggest they were...?'

'Father works in a ceramic tile factory, he's shop steward. Mother is a housewife. She's got a sister, though, Vivien. Married and works in a bank.'

'Really? So, one normal daughter and one crazy one?' Max shrugged. 'I suppose that happens in more families than would actually admit it.'

Jack agreed. 'I bet it does. I've got a copy of the whole trial transcript if you fancy a read, although there's nothing much in there that we don't already know.'

The Inspector rubbed a hand over his face. 'I'll take it home with me tonight. Have Gabriella and Thierry gone out to Saint Margaux already, Jacques?'

'Yes, they're planning to visit a few of the shops, see if there's any local gossip that might shed light on how the villagers feel about having a murder suspect in their midst. And to see if Miss Green made any friends or enemies on arrival.'

'I doubt that very much,' Max told him. 'She hasn't been in France long enough to get to know people, although I'm intrigued by Maurice Fabron's position. He seems to believe Isobel implicitly.'

Hobbs was confused by that fact, too. 'Perhaps there's more than a working relationship between the two of them? Do you think they might be…?'

Mallery laughed out loud. 'Fabron and Green, in bed together? Ah Jacques, what an imagination you have!'

Pulling up in the police compound, Simone Dupuis checked her lipstick in the mirror before getting out of the car. This was the first time she'd had occasion to visit the building, though she had passed it many times on shopping trips to the town.

Her smart, high-heeled shoes clicked softly on the concrete steps as she climbed them, aware of the appreciative glances she was getting from officers leaving the premises. Simone had always taken pride in her appearance and it was that single fact that had been foremost in her mind when Maurice had phoned. Isobel should look at least presentable on her return to Saint Margaux.

'Madame Dupuis?' Isobel was startled by the sudden appearance of Maurice's friend and at first felt confused as to whether Simone was there by some coincidence, or had actually been asked to collect her.

'*Bonjour.*' The older woman smiled, her perfect teeth as white as marble. 'Monsieur Fabron is very busy so I have come to take you back to the village.'

'I don't know what to say,' Izzy began. 'Thank you so much.'

'Now, where is the ladies room?' Simone asked, looking around at the numerous closed doors. 'We need to get you changed and somehow looking decent.'

Isobel nodded, feeling slightly more encouraged as the seconds passed. 'It's over there. Thank you again.'

'That's much better!' Simone smiled, her heavily accented French sounding exotic and dramatized. 'Now you are ready to go.'

Isobel Green looked at herself in the bathroom mirror, her slim body now clothed in one of Madam Dupuis' simple linen shift dresses, the colour a pale lilac, just like the lavender fields that lined the Bordeaux highway. With a few brushstrokes to her face, Simone had added colour to Izzy's cheeks and hidden her red-rimmed eyes with dark mascara and a touch of concealer.

'I feel almost human again,' Isobel told her. 'It's been hell in here.'

Simone nodded, looking closely at Isobel's reflection next to her own. 'Here, put your dirty clothes in this bag.'

She handed over a paper bag with the logo of a boutique on the side, obviously somewhere trendy and chic that provided the Frenchwoman's amazing wardrobe. Izzy thought it looked vaguely familiar but quickly dismissed the thought.

'I'm so grateful,' Izzy told her, folding the crumpled jeans and musty cardigan into the empty bag. 'Grateful to both you and Maurice. You've both been very kind.'

'Well, hopefully the detectives will sort out this tragic affair soon and we can all get on with our lives. Now, let's go.'

Maurice sat at a table in the boulangerie, a glass of water untouched by his hand, with a feeling of déjà-vu coming over him as he waited for his employee to arrive. It had been just over a week since Isobel 'Gilyard', as she'd called herself, had come into their lives, but since that very first day everything he considered to be normal had been turned on its head.

He sipped the fresh coffee, eager to catch Telo on his return before Simone pulled up. He wanted to be the one to tell his son of Izzy's return. The young man had been so tense over the past few days, and Maurice could pinpoint it to the moment that the detectives had retrieved the murder weapon from the Beetle. It was a difficult decision on his part, bringing a murder suspect back here, but Cecile had been a part of their family and if Isobel had anything to hide, Maurice would soon find out. He was proud of his natural instincts and, although still not convinced of the Englishwoman's part in Cecile's death, he felt that something was amiss. There was surely no better way to keep an eye on Izzy than to have her under his own roof. The hard part would be explaining that to Telo.

There was a hum as the Citroën van skirted the square and disappeared around the back of the bakery, windows open and the radio tuned to Sixties music. Telo had always been musically gifted, just like his talented mother, and Maurice imagined that the young man had been singing in perfect pitch on his rounds, no doubt to the amusement of the residents on his delivery circuit.

Maurice heaved himself back out of the chair and began whipping up a chocolate milkshake for his son. Today, it would be loaded with marshmallows and fresh cream, the coward's way of breaking unpleasant news but the easiest way, he was sure. One look at the sweet creation and Telo would trust his father, although no doubt there would be a good deal of resentment, too.

'Are you alright?' Simone asked, glancing at Isobel as she watched the fields passing in a multi-coloured blur on her right.

Izzy nodded, gulping back the harsh lump in her throat that threatened to bring her to tears. 'Yes, I'm fine. Just feeling a bit sick, that's all.'

'Well, with a good meal inside you tonight, you'll be feeling better in no time.'

Isobel wanted to tell the other woman that some meat and vegetables couldn't take away the fact that she'd been held as part of an ongoing murder investigation, but thought better of it, instead staying silent and allowing the journey to swallow up her thoughts.

'If you need someone to talk to…' Simone ventured again a short time later, 'Sometimes it's easier, you know, woman to woman…'

Isobel wanted to kick herself. No, she didn't want to talk, not to a stranger, not to anyone, except maybe her counsellor. But this kind woman was trying her best to make things easier, so she should at least appear to be grateful for the concern. Unsure of Madam Dupuis' feelings towards her, Izzy tried to explain.

'I'm sorry. It's just that the past few days have been really... tiring. There have been so many questions and I haven't slept much.'

Simone felt the beginnings of an opportunity opening up and decided to tread carefully. 'I cannot begin to imagine what you have been through. Being blamed for such a terrible crime…'

She let the words hang for a while, willing Isobel to fill in the void with an admission of guilt, or at least a hint of doubt as to her own innocence.

'But I really wasn't on that train,' Izzy murmured, blinking back tears. 'I'm innocent. You have to believe me.'

'But of course you are.' The Frenchwoman smiled, fixing her sparkling eyes on the busy main road ahead. 'But we all make mistakes, don't we?'

Izzy repeated the words in head, unable to fathom whether the comment was made innocently or held some underlying disregard for her plight. Simone's demeanour hadn't altered. She sat relaxed in the driver's seat and not a muscle twitched in her elegant features. Izzy sighed, so quietly that not a breath of air could be heard between the two women. It looked as though she might actually have an ally besides Maurice Fabron.

As the car turned off towards Saint Margaux, Izzy began to feel that there might be light at the end of the tunnel. With two people willing to come to her aid, it shouldn't be long before detectives Mallery and Hobbs realised the dreadful mistake they'd made in arresting her.

As Isobel Green made her way back to the village with the florist, Gabriella Dupont stood choosing candies in Dominique Fabre's sweet shop with her colleague, Thierry. The couple were making a great show of pretending to argue lovingly over their selection, while also aware that the shopkeeper had one eye on the door.

'Madam, are we keeping you from something?' Thierry asked casually in French, following the woman's gaze out to the square beyond.

'No, not at all.' Dominique blushed, embarrassed that she might not be attending to her customers as she should be. 'It's just that…'

Gabriella smiled warmly, tilting her head on one side. 'Yes?'

'Well, I shouldn't really gossip,' Madam Fabre went on, obviously warming to her topic, 'but we're expecting an Englishwoman to return here today. She's been held at the police station over the recent murder…'

'Really?' Thierry countered, urging the woman to continue. 'Are you sure?'

'Oh, yes, my dear friend Simone has gone to fetch her. The woman, Isobel has been questioned over in Bordeaux for the past forty-eight hours.'

Gabriella turned, pretending to inspect a tall jar of hard-boiled strawberry sherbets. 'How interesting. Can I have some of these, please?'

'Certainly,' Dominique replied, lifting the candies yet unable to avert her chatter from the topic she was warming to. 'Such a terrible crime. You'd think the police would have charged her by now. Most of the village is convinced that Isobel Gilyard did it. She's just devious, that's all.'

CHAPTER THIRTEEN – ISOBEL'S RETURN

'*Maurice, où est la clé, s'il vous plaît?*' Simone called sweetly through the back door of the boulangerie, as Izzy stood forlornly in the doorway.

'*Un moment,*' the response came, amidst a prattle of voices, as customers chose their goods at the counter.

Madam Dupuis smiled at the Englishwoman, translating the reply in case she hadn't heard. 'He won't be long.'

Isobel nodded but made no sound, instead remaining in the warm sunshine with the bag of washing clasped tightly between her fingers.

Presently, Maurice appeared, the faint shadow of a smile on his tired face as he bent forward and kissed his employee on both cheeks. 'Welcome home.'

A single tear pricked at Izzy's right eye but was effectively wiped away before anyone noticed. The magnitude of her recent ordeal was beginning to overwhelm her. She felt like an outcast, no matter how kind the people around her were.

Monsieur Fabron produced the apartment key and ushered the women upstairs. 'Go, settle in. I will bring you coffee and cake. We can talk properly later.'

'Would you like to be left alone?' Simone asked, quickly darting forward to open the living room shutters in order to allow the daylight to filter inside.

Isobel nodded, her voice catching in the dryness of her throat. 'Yes, if you don't mind. Thank you so much for everything, Madame Dupuis. I'll wash your dress and return it tomorrow.'

The florist flicked her sleek black hair and shook her head. 'No need. Keep it if you like. Besides, the colour really suits you.'

'No, really, I couldn't…'

'Please, I insist,' Simone went on, checking the window-ledge for dust, 'And when you're ready, we can talk over a glass of wine. I'm here for you.'

Izzy nodded, grateful for the kind words and invitation, although deep down she truly doubted whether she would ever want to talk about the events of the past few days. She was caught between the Devil and the deep blue sea in some ways, unable to decide who was friend or foe, yet Madam Dupuis had been so kind, and she was obviously trusted implicitly by Maurice.

Simone left shortly afterwards, allowing Izzy the time and space to get herself sorted out. The Englishwoman felt strange being back in the small French apartment, yet it was the closest thing to a real home that she'd had in years.

It was half an hour before Monsieur Fabron appeared with a cafetière and a slice of chocolate torte and Izzy wondered whether the baker had simply been busy, or was plucking up the nerve to face her alone after the terrible accusations. She considered both scenarios and found it amazing that Maurice was even willing to allow her to return to Saint Margaux after witnessing the discovery of the murder weapon in her car.

'Are you alright?' the baker asked nervously, tapping at the door, 'Perhaps we should sit and talk when I close up the boulangerie later, *oui*?'

Izzy nodded, fearful of how much Maurice might have discovered about her past from the two detectives, yet grateful that she still might have a chance to make a fresh start in Saint Margaux.

'You do believe I'm innocent, don't you?' she whispered, just as the man turned to leave, and then, a little louder, she added, 'I swear to you, I had nothing to do with Cecile's murder. I have no idea how that knife got into my car, but I promise you I didn't put it there.'

Monsieur Fabron bowed his head, unable or unwilling to catch Isobel's eye. 'Yes, so you have told us, but somebody, somewhere, must know the truth.'

The door closed and Izzy was left alone to relax, a rare pleasure that had eluded her for the past three days.

'This coffee is cold,' Gaston commented, pointing at the cup of coffee that he'd prepared for Simone on her return to the flower shop. 'Shall I make you another?'

'What? Oh, I'm sorry, Gaston, my mind was elsewhere. Thank you but no, I might close early today and have something stronger.'

'Are you sure?' he fussed, reaching to put his muscular arms around the tiny woman's shoulders, to comfort her. 'A hard day?'

'Oh, it's just Isobel.' She sighed. 'I can't make out whether that woman is very stupid or incredibly clever.'

'What do you mean?' The artist stood back, a frown appearing on his forehead.

'She's telling everyone how innocent she is, yet Inspector Mallery hinted to Maurice that there's something she's been keeping from him. Perhaps a dark past, and I know that doesn't make her a murderer, but we have to face facts. The knife that was used to kill Cecile was found in Isobel's car.'

Gaston remained thoughtful, before confessing his own instincts. 'I don't trust the woman. After all, she was the one that told the police about the stains on my shirt. I mean how far-fetched is that? I think she was trying to frame me?'

'You know, Gaston, you could be right,' Simone gasped, bringing a hand to her mouth as she contemplated his words.

'Well, in any case, I think we should tread carefully.'

'I agree. Gaston, thank you for being here, I don't know what I'd do without you.'

The handsome young man shrugged, planting a kiss on his landlady's cheek. 'Well, you will have to do without me for the rest of the afternoon as I need to finish my painting. See you later.'

As Simone watched the artist duck out through the low doorway and head next-door to her cottage, where he would work for the remainder of the day, thoughts of Isobel's accusation were at the forefront of her mind.

Alone in her apartment above the boulangerie, Isobel Green stepped into the hot shower, hoping that the teeming water and rising steam could wash away the sensation of dirt and sweat that she'd constantly felt since the day of her arrest.

The small cubicle also gave her time for contemplation, on how much she should confess to Monsieur Fabron and which fragments of her past to keep under wraps. She had no idea how much detectives Mallery and Hobbs had told him about who she really was, but she felt certain that it wouldn't have been part of their protocol to reveal much, unless she was formally charged. Izzy closed her eyes, incredulous at how far removed she felt from the Isobel Gilyard that had arrived in Saint Margaux just ten days earlier.

Fresher, more awake and with a slight renewal of determination, Izzy wrapped herself in a fluffy towelling dressing-gown and switched on the television set. Local news reported a herd of errant cows blocking a country lane into one of the small hamlets nearby, a postmaster retiring after forty years of service and then, unsurprisingly, a few words about the Bordeaux police's inability to capture the killer of Cecile Vidal yet. Isobel felt a shudder run up her spine as she strained to make out the few words she could translate from French; something to do with the release of a suspect?

Later, having slightly recovered her composure and a willingness to talk to Maurice, Izzy styled her hair, put a layer of foundation on her pale skin and pulled out some clothes. A pair of cropped jeans and a white blouse suited her purpose, as she wanted to seem neither over-confident nor boastful about her return, then Isobel descended the stairs just as Maurice Fabron pushed the last bolt across on the bakery door.

'Is Telo still here?' Izzy ventured, looking around the empty café area, half expecting the youngster to pop up from behind the counter.

'No, Telo has gone home already,' Maurice confirmed, sensing that the woman wanted to avoid his son. 'Please, sit down.'

Isobel pulled out a chair and let her palms fall upon the table-top, remembering the way in which the psychiatric unit counsellor had showed her how to mimic gestures of openness and honesty, although she was unsure whether the baker had actually noticed.

'I've made a pot of English Breakfast tea,' Monsieur Fabron was saying, 'Gaston brought it from a shop he sometimes visits in Paris. We thought it might be a nice treat for you. And custard cream biscuits, too.'

'That's very kind. Please thank… Gaston… for me.'

Maurice noticed how difficult it was for Isobel to say the artist's name. He was wondering whether she now felt some guilt at trying to place Gaston at the scene of Cecile's death with her errant belief that his shirt bore smudges of blood.

'You can tell him yourself, Izzy. We are a small community and must therefore bear each other's faults with tolerance.'

Isobel was not sure if he was hinting at her faults or someone else's but dared not ask for fear of a disagreeable response.

The tall baker busied himself with pouring tea, head down and focussed on the task, as though waiting for something... some word or apology.

Izzy took the bait and began her prepared speech.

'Maurice, I'm very grateful to you for allowing me to come back here, and for believing in me. It means such a lot.'

The baker's eyes twinkled mischievously. 'Believing in you? You think I do?'

'Oh, I just presumed...' Isobel was taken aback, the cup in her hand beginning to shake slightly.

'Detective Mallery gave me very little choice,' Maurice explained, holding the woman's gaze. 'As you cannot leave France without your passport, which he needs to hold for now, it was natural that you should stay here. Besides, I am still in need of an assistant and your skills are such to be proud of.'

Izzy sat mystified, unsure of where the conversation was heading.

'However,' Maurice continued, getting into his stride with renewed vigour, 'There are many questions that remain unanswered. I would prefer that, if you have anything to tell me, you do so now, so that we can begin, how do you say, a clean page?'

Isobel carefully put down the cup, spilling a little tea in the china saucer, swallowed hard and wondered how on earth to begin.

'My name is not Gilyard, it's Isobel Green.'

'Go on,' the baker urged, clasping his hands over his stomach and leaning back in the chair, 'I'm listening.'

And so, for the next half hour, the story came tumbling out. Tears mingled with anger and dissolved into grief as Izzy spoke frankly about the events in her life that had led her to change her identity. Maurice listened intently, uttering not one single sound until the tale was spent, only then lifting his eyes to the ceiling and exhaling loudly.

'*Merci*,' he said automatically, the French foremost on his lips. 'Thank you.'

'And now?' Isobel asked, feeling her soul laid bare to the man in front of her. 'Do you want me to leave?'

'Leave? No. You have shared your darkest moments with me,' Maurice said, sighing. 'For that, I am grateful. It is a lot to take in, everything you have told me is quite a shock, but I am inclined to believe that you did what you did in order to save yourself. It doesn't mean that you were involved in Cecile's murder.'

Isobel traced every line on the baker's face with her eyes, wanting to reach out and take his hand in hers, so grateful was she for the words he offered.

'Now, get some rest.' Maurice ordered, collecting up the cups, 'On Wednesday you may resume your work here. Okay? But for the moment, it may be better that you work in the back kitchen preparing the cakes, as the residents of Saint Margaux are still a little overwhelmed by your arrest.'

With a sigh of relief, Izzy ventured, 'That's fair enough. I completely understand how they might feel about me. Why don't I start tomorrow?'

The boulangerie owner lowered his eyes and replied with a heavy heart, 'Because tomorrow we are closed. The village will say farewell to Cecile at her funeral service.'

Feeling that once again she had ended the conversation on a negative thought, Izzy rose to leave, uttering only a last word of thanks as she retreated upstairs.

A knocking on the front door aroused Simone Dupuis from her kitchen where she sat listening to a classical radio channel and sipping a glass of cognac.

'*Bonsoir, Maurice*,' she said with a smile, kissing the man tenderly on his cheek.

The baker entered the cosy cottage eagerly, keen to share his knowledge of Isobel's past with his oldest friend. They sat opposite each other at the circular table, Simone listening intently as Maurice explained, careful not to miss a single detail.

'Well,' Madam Dupuis gasped as soon as the retelling was over, 'no wonder Isobel was coy. Who would ever have guessed that she'd murdered someone?'

'Now, let's not get carried away,' Maurice countered, placing a hand on his dear friend's arm, 'This revelation does not mean that Izzy was involved in Cecile's death. I can fully understand how she acted in self-defence, and it's not something to be proud of, so I can see why she'd create a new identity.'

Simone clucked her tongue, incredulous at Maurice's forgiving nature. 'What about the way she has tried to implicate Telo and Gaston? You seem to have forgotten the trouble and stress that woman has caused.'

'I know, Simone,' the baker acknowledged. 'But now that we know the truth, can we not show her a little compassion?'

'Maurice, you know me better than anyone,' Madam Dupuis replied, getting up to refill their empty glasses, 'I am willing to give everyone a chance, but we have to be careful of those around us, our families and friends.'

Monsieur Fabron contemplated a reply, leaving his cognac untouched. 'Believe me, if there is any hint of Isobel trying to pin this on our loved ones, I will be the first to call Inspector Mallery. However, it is better to have Izzy where we can see her, don't you agree?'

Simone saw sense in her friend's statement and chinked her glass with his. 'Yes, I do. You're a clever man, Maurice Fabron.'

In the tiny art studio adjoining Madam Dupuis' cottage, Gaston was chatting with Telo. The pair had a unique bond, enjoying similar tastes in music and electronic games, despite the nearly ten-year age gap between them. A game of chess sat untouched on the board between them. They conversed in French, keeping their voices low in order to hide opinions from their host in the kitchen next-door.

'Isobel Gilyard is back,' Telo stated, his arms folded defensively across a bony chest.

'Yes, Simone collected her from the police station.'

'Simone? Why would she do that?'

Gaston nudged the younger man with his elbow, prompting a faint smile. 'Because someone had to, and your father was busy.'

'I don't see why she has to come back here at all. She doesn't belong here.'

'Well, she can't go back to England until the police return her passport. Besides, if they have released her it means she didn't… you know… do that terrible thing to your Aunt Cecile.'

'Murder.' Telo scowled. 'Murder.'

Gaston rose, prepared to appease the baker's son should he get over-anxious. 'That's right, it was murder. But they'll find who did it soon, I'm sure of that.'

'I don't like her, Gaston.'

The artist shrugged. 'I'm not sure that I do, either, but we have to say nothing about it. You understand that, don't you, Telo?'

'But the knife was in her car!' the youngster cried, raising his voice. 'I saw it!'

Gaston had to agree. 'I know, but that still doesn't prove anything. You remember reading about Inspector Poirot don't you, Telo?'

A look of recognition crossed Telo's face. 'The detective stories?'

'That's right. Well, just like Poirot, Inspector Mallery has to find evidence that a person is guilty before he can arrest them. Like fingerprints, for example.'

Telo frowned, his forehead lined with doubt. 'But Poirot always catches the bad guy, so that means Inspector Mallery isn't as clever. Right?'

Gaston held up his hands, unable to argue with the lad's reasoning. 'I suppose so, Telo. You could be right.'

The pair laughed, settling down to begin their board-game.

If only real-life was as easy to predict as a whodunnit, Gaston mused.

Maurice Fabron tapped at the door of the art studio to tell Telo to be home for supper at eight, before crossing the square to his home.

'*Bonsoir*, Maurice,' a voice called, followed by the appearance of a jolly-faced woman wearing a bright orange dress that hugged her voluptuous curves.

'*Bonsoir, Dominique*,' he replied. 'How is business at the gift shop?'

The woman smiled widely, 'Very good today actually, a lot of new customers. Are you alright, Maurice?'

'Just a little tired, that's all. Why do you ask?'

Dominique wrung her hands together as though squeezing water from a cloth. 'Well, it's with Madam Gilyard returning. It must be a strain on you.'

So, now we get to the truth of the matter, Maurice thought silently, cursing that he'd chosen that exact moment to return home.

'Well, Dominique, the police did not charge Isobel and so yes, she is back.'

The woman's eyes fluttered across to the boulangerie and then back to the man in front of her. 'But do you think she did it?'

'Dominique, if you don't mind, I really need to go home. I still have to finish my eulogy for Cecile tomorrow.'

'Oh, of course!' the shop owner gasped, moving to one side. 'I'm sorry to have kept you. See you in church.'

Pushing the front door closed, Maurice looked up at the rectangle of light illuminating the window above his boulangerie. The woman inside was nowhere to be seen, a beneficial fact Maurice thought as he retreated inside. Once behind the façade of his house, the baker paused to reflect upon his brief conversation with Dominique Fabre.

Why had he not defended Izzy when the woman had asked his opinion? Maurice knew that Dominique was probably the source of most of Saint Margaux's rumours and leaked secrets, yet he'd been unable to give a definitive answer about his English employee. There was so much he still didn't know about Isobel Gilyard, or Green. She was such a complex woman with an even more complicated past.

Izzy's revelation about her ten-year imprisonment had come as a complete and utter shock to Monsieur Fabron, a man who had lived a pure and simple life, and he was unsure what to do with such a weighted burden. The knowledge of his employee's sentence was starting to cause him a great deal of stress. Maurice could already feel the tension inside him, stretching like a piece of elastic, taut and ready to snap.

Isobel Green felt incomplete without her shoebox of secrets, yet promised herself that every paper document, photograph and folder would be used to start Saint Margaux's biggest bonfire as soon as they were returned to her. There was no point in keeping those reminders now. The past was as startlingly real as if the events had happened yesterday.

Izzy wondered if there was an option of retreating to somewhere new; of doing exactly as she had here and venturing to another country in search of employment and a fresh start at life. But where would she go?

Although relieved that Maurice Fabron appeared to be on her side, the great fear of being arrested again weighed heavily on her that night as she busied herself in the apartment. Izzy was afraid to just sit, alone with her thoughts, and had found a noisy war film to fill the silent hours as she flitted around dusting and polishing. It was as though she needed to scrub her home and rid it of the evil that she felt was looming in every corner. It didn't matter how many hours it took. She was prepared to stay up all night, as long as the place was cleansed. In every object, she saw Inspector Mallery's invasive searching, his overturning of her personal possessions, the thumbing of her books.

Had the men known what they were looking for, she pondered, or had it been pure chance that they'd stumbled across her box of treasures? If only she'd had the foresight to get rid of everything, instead of dragging it here to France, where her misdemeanours had been laid bare for all to see. Isobel needed to get her box back, for her own sanity. The contents had to be destroyed before the whole village found out what was inside.

After half an hour of cleaning the living room, Isobel moved through into her bedroom, gathering clothes from the laundry basket and putting shoes back into the closet. Straightening the bed, she spied a bag of dirty clothes leaning against the bedside cabinet, the ones that had been hurriedly pushed in there at the police station earlier. As she tipped the bundle out onto the bed, a paper receipt came fluttering out of the bag. Izzy picked it up with interest. The heading showed the words, *ETIENNE BOUTIQUE, BORDEAUX.*

Isobel screwed it up, presuming that it belonged to Simone and had simply been left in the bag. But then she stopped, remembering her own visit to the chic store the previous week and, with curiosity, she unfolded the receipt and looked closely at the amount. After all, what if Madam Dupuis changed her mind about the item and decided to change it? She would need some proof of purchase.

It was for ninety Euros for a linen dress. An expensive item by Izzy's standards.

Isobel looked over to the padded chair by the window. The lilac shift that Simone had kindly lent her earlier lay folded neatly over the seat-cushion, ready for laundering. Surely Simone wouldn't have given her a brand-new dress that she'd only just purchased?

Izzy was puzzled. Something wasn't right, yet she couldn't quite put her finger on it. Staring at the flimsy piece of paper in her hand, the Englishwoman searched for something to trigger a response in her brain – anything to give her a clue as to why Madam Dupuis would want to get rid of that beautiful new lilac dress.

And then she saw it. The receipt was dated last Wednesday.

Isobel raced to check the kitchen calendar to be sure, running her thumb over the numbers, but she was right; the garment had been purchased on the day of Cecile Vidal's murder.

Izzy rubbed her head, trying to make sense of the irrational thoughts that were pounding in her mind, thumping noisily like a herd of elephants.

So Simone Dupuis had also gone to Bordeaux on that fateful day. What did that mean? Had Madam Dupuis also driven to the town for shopping, or had she been on the same morning train as her friend, Cecile Vidal?

Izzy sat down heavily on the bed and placed her head in her hands as thoughts whirled around and blurred her vision. She felt very sick, as though she'd spent ten minutes on an out-of-control carousel at high speed. What on earth was she going to do with this wretched receipt? To accuse yet another of the villagers would arouse even more suspicion about her own motives, surely? The detectives wouldn't believe that Madam Dupuis could possibly be involved, especially not after her recent acts of kindness to Isobel. They might think that the receipt belonged to Izzy; after all, both the bag and dress were now in her possession.

Rational thinking was needed and at that moment, Isobel was incapable of making the right decision. There was only one thing for it, she decided; she must watch and wait. If Simone really was somehow involved in her best friend's murder, then her true colours would eventually show and she would slip up, somehow, somewhere. Izzy just prayed that the whole truth would emerge before she became the target of yet more of Inspector Mallery's misguided speculation.

CHAPTER FOURTEEN – GOODBYE TO CECILE

White roses adorned the small wooden casket as it was carried into the Gothic-inspired village church. Father Claude walked solemnly ahead of the procession with his shoulders stooped in silent prayer, a string of rosary beads hanging limply between his fingers. Heads turned, eager to catch a glimpse of Cecile Vidal's coffin as it made the final journey to her resting place. Murmurs of respect hummed through the stone building, echoing off the walls and gathering in volume as they came to rest in the vaulted roof.

Maurice and Telo Fabron stood silently in the front pew, side by side with Hubert Vidal and his mourning children. Madam Paradis, the Vidal's housekeeper, dabbed her face with a lace handkerchief as her employer's body went past, her husband standing stiffly beside her, holding his wife's hand. A row behind, Simone Dupuis, Gaston Lauder and Dominique Fabre linked arms in unity, faces ashen and black clothes stark against pale skin.

Soft leather shoes clicked upon the stone floor as six men from the Saint Margaux vineyard bore the weight of their beloved employer, each pallbearer still unable to come to terms with the loss of a woman who had been so dear to them all. The workers had begged Hubert to allow them to carry his wife into the church, every one of them believing that it would show their utmost respect to Madam Vidal and ease the pain of losing such a revered member of the community, a woman who had gone out of her way to welcome the staff as though they were part of the family.

Arriving just as the last of the mourners entered the church, Inspector Mallery and Detective Hobbs slipped into the back of the church, noting the sheer volume of people packed into the house of worship.

'Any sign of Isobel Green?' Mallery whispered, straining his neck to look through the crowded benches and spotting Madam Dupuis' slender neck adorned in creamy white pearls.

'I can't see her,' Jack replied, looking furtively around, 'but it seems as though every other Saint Margaux resident is here. There must be nearly three hundred people.'

Max shuddered. Despite the intense summer heat outside, the church itself was as cool as a refrigerator, causing him to rub the sleeves of his thin cotton shirt.

A couple of people turned to look sharply at the detectives, wondering whether they had shown up in a professional capacity, or as a mark of respect to the victim whose killer they had, as yet, failed to catch.

Eyes fell upon the intricately carved casket, on top of which a coloured photograph of its occupant was standing upright for all to see. Cecile Vidal looked happy and carefree in the picture, a woman without anxiety, young for her years in both looks and health. There was a sob as one of the children gasped in grief, unable to accept the enormity of losing their mother in such horrific circumstances.

Father Claude coughed politely, an indication that the service would start.

Isobel Green stood looking at her thin figure and gaunt face in the bedroom mirror. She was clothed in black trousers and a short-sleeved black blouse, despite Maurice's insistence that it would be best if she didn't show her face at Cecile's funeral. It would be 'insensitive', he'd told her, given the current circumstances.

The village residents were still on edge, he had explained, not ready to forgive until Madam Vidal's murderer was brought to justice. Izzy had conceded that her boss was probably right, yet the longer she thought about it, the more she was convinced that her absence at the service would reflect her guilt. If she had nothing to hide, surely the villagers would expect her to be there.

Maurice Fabron hadn't stayed long that morning, as he'd been in a rush to assist Simone with the floral tributes and ensure that preparations were perfect for the wake afterwards. He had, however, stipulated that Isobel should rest, a comment so sincere that she felt grateful for it. Yet, how could she rest until her name had been cleared?

The previous night, Isobel's horrific nightmares had returned. This time, Martin Freeman taunted her with the threat of life imprisonment. He wielded the hunting knife wildly before slipping it into his girlfriend's hand, urging Izzy to stab him. Freeman's laughter rang so loudly in her ears that Isobel had woken up drenched in sweat and full of belief that the dead man had returned to haunt her. There had been long hours of silent reflection and unleashed tears, until finally, daylight had broken in through the cracks in the shutters.

As a melodic sound floated across the square from the direction of the church, confirmation that the congregation were giving praise and sending Cecile's soul on its way, Isobel Green slipped out through the back door of the boulangerie.

Max Mallery gently edged out of his seat, gesturing for Hobbs to stay put. He desperately needed a cigarette and also wanted to see if there was anyone else hanging around the graveyard. He closed the enormous oak door and leaned against it to light up, causing a cloud of smoke to drift up towards the stained-glass windows. As a child, Mallery had been so fascinated with the inscriptions etched upon each tombstone, especially the ancient ones that were now almost illegible and grey with age, that he'd kept a notebook for the purpose of writing down the names of the dead. A morbid pastime, his mother had complained, yet it kept him from under her feet and she allowed the boy's strange obsession to continue.

Stepping carefully around a newer plot, Max edged towards the perimeter where large epitaphs leaned like fallen soldiers, shoulder to shoulder against the thick stone wall. Crouching down, he read the inscription, calculating that the occupant of the grave had lived for over ninety years.

'Inspector,' a woman's voice said quietly, scaring the life out of the detective as he bent over the grave. Max straightened up and looked hastily around.

'Mademoiselle Green.' He frowned. 'You are the last person I expected to see today.'

The Inspector noticed the woman's black attire and wondered if he should advise her against going inside the church.

Almost as though she had read his thoughts, Isobel said stiffly, 'Don't worry, I'm not here to attend the service. I just wanted to pay my respects from out here.'

'And what if someone should see you?'

The woman stooped to pick a dandelion from the grass, twirling the stem between slender fingers. 'I won't stay long. I promise.'

Max watched the Englishwoman plucking at the petals and noticed a faraway gaze in her eyes. She looked exhausted, as though she hadn't slept a wink.

'Mademoiselle Green,' he urged, 'go home. The mourners will soon be coming out and I fear your presence may stir up some heated emotions.'

Izzy nodded. 'Okay. You're right, I shouldn't have come.'

'Before you go,' Mallery added, curious as to what Isobel had planned, 'when you leave Saint Margaux, where will you go?'

There was a grin, wide and almost cat-like. 'Leave, Inspector? Why I have absolutely no intention of leaving.'

Isobel turned on her heel, the soft leather pumps making no sound as she walked quickly back down the street to the boulangerie.

Mallery watched, confused. A trickle of perspiration ran down the back of his shirt and disappeared into the fold of his waistband. The policeman was unsure if the sudden wetness had been sweat from the warmth of the summer sun, or the fear that he felt on seeing Isobel Green's sardonic smile.

Maurice delivered the eulogy with a hard lump in his throat, eyes straying towards the two motherless children who sobbed uncontrollably. The words had been chosen to reflect the baker's own personal feelings towards his sister-in-law and the hole that her demise had left in the lives of him and the rest of the family. It was hard to believe that Cecile would no longer be popping into the boulangerie to indulge in her favourite treats. Nor would she be there guiding Telo, a calming influence that Maurice had been glad of since the loss of his own dear wife. As he sat back down, Simone Dupuis leaned forward and placed a hand on her friend's shoulder, proud that he hadn't cracked, relieved that the service was nearly over.

As the procession was led outside to the Vidal's very grand family tomb, Jack Hobbs stepped lightly to one side in order to meet up with the Inspector.

'Alright, sir?' he asked, noting the unusual pallor of his boss's face.

'Do you remember what you said to me about killers having a strange need to turn up at their victims' funerals?'

Hobbs nodded. 'I do. Why?'

'Isobel Green was just here, Jacques.'

The younger man's eyes widened. 'You're kidding!'

Max lowered his voice, 'No, she was right here, acting as though it were normal to come and pay her respects.'

'I don't think the rest of the mourners would have been impressed if they'd seen her. Where's she gone now?'

Mallery jerked a thumb towards the village. 'Back to the boulangerie, I presume. The foolish woman just can't keep out of trouble.'

'Guilty conscience?' Jack pondered.

'My thoughts, exactly.'

Gabriella Dupont got out of the car and stretched just as Isobel Green appeared around the corner. The women exchanged glances, a glimmer of recollection dawning on Izzy's face. She'd seen the woman somewhere before, minus the straw hat and dark sunglasses, but where exactly was a mystery. Noting the confused look on Izzy's face, the detective ducked out of sight, pretending to tie a lace on her running shoes.

'Shit,' she muttered into her two-way radio. 'Thierry, where are you? We need to move.'

The signal crackled into life as her partner's voice responded. 'Round the back of the boulangerie, checking if the Beetle's been driven lately.'

'Get out of there now, Green's on her way back.'

Thierry thrust both hands deep into the pockets of his jeans and sauntered around the corner of the bakery, narrowly avoiding bumping into the returning Englishwoman.

'Can I help you?' Izzy asked, her question automatic, in English and abrupt.

'*Pardonnez-moi*,' Thierry quipped, proud of his natural ability to think quickly, 'I wanted to buy a loaf of bread.'

'The boulangerie is closed,' Isobel replied curtly. 'It will be open tomorrow.'

She watched the strongly-built dark man walk towards the parked car and greet the familiar woman. The couple then drove away, but not before making a witless mistake. As they passed detectives Mallery and Hobbs leaving the church, the man in the car raised a hand in acknowledgement, which was returned with two waves, one from each policeman.

Izzy stood in awe. Now she knew for certain that they had been watching her.

'What the hell do you think you're doing, having me followed?' Isobel spat, her cheeks reddening in anger as she ran back towards the detectives.

Max Mallery, unfazed as ever, caught her elbow and steered the woman away from the church walls, mindful of the congregation gathering in the graveyard.

'Mademoiselle Green, please lower your voice. We are completely within our rights, as you are not yet eliminated from our enquiry.'

'And I have rights, too,' she continued, hesitating to look at Jack Hobbs who stood sheepishly at his boss's side.

The Inspector shrugged, a carefree gesture that he hoped would conclude the altercation before any of the grieving villagers noticed, and then he let go of her arm.

'As I said, we are just doing our job, Mademoiselle Green.'

'Did you even bother to follow-up on what I told you?' Izzy hissed. 'About the blood on Gaston's shirt and Telo using my car?'

Max sighed. 'Yes, we did, and both men had reasonable explanations. It appears your accusations were without foundation.'

'That's impossible! I know what I saw!'

Jack stepped closer to the ranting woman, trying desperately to neutralise the negative energy. 'Miss Green, today is not the day to start getting fired up about the situation. If you wish to talk to us tomorrow…'

Izzy caught on to the detective's meaning instantly and looked over to where Father Claude was speaking next to the Vidal family tomb.

'Until I have my passport back and this whole situation is over, I won't rest.'

Hobbs nodded. 'I wouldn't expect anything less.'

Max coughed. 'Perhaps now you will go back to your apartment, out of sight, if only to let these good people mourn their friend in peace.'

Isobel sat smoking a cigarette at the window and failed to notice the falling ash that dropped silently to the carpet. She was certain that nobody could see her, so close to the wall was her chair, yet her angle afforded a good view of the departing cars as they headed out of the village towards the Saint Margaux vineyard.

'Thank you all for coming,' Hubert Vidal announced, tapping the side of his glass with a silver spoon, 'it is much appreciated. Cecile would have been glad to see so many of you wishing her farewell. Thank you very much.'

The group raised their drinks in a toast to the winemaker's wife and quiet respectful chatter soon continued as Hubert made his way over to Maurice.

'Your eulogy was perfect,' he whispered, embracing the baker tightly. 'I don't know what the children and I would have done without you this week.'

'Hubert, there's something I've been meaning to talk to you about,' Monsieur Fabron confessed, pulling his brother-in-law to one side. 'Can we go into your study, away from the guests?'

'Of course. After you.'

Simone Dupuis watched intently as the two men exited the sitting room, wondering what the topic of conversation could be that warranted them leaving the group of mourners. She tapped Gaston on the arm and pointed.

'Where are those two going?'

The artist feigned disinterest. 'I have absolutely no idea. Maybe they just want to talk about the funeral in private.'

Simone was unconvinced, her curious nature pushing to the fore. 'Surely not?'

Hubert's desk was littered with scraps of paperwork and unopened letters, suggesting to Maurice that the widower hadn't been focussed on his business of late and wondered if he might be able to offer some assistance. However, it wasn't help that was bothering him at that moment and Maurice set down his glass on the ornate mantelpiece.

'What is it?' Hubert asked. 'Is this about Cecile? You look worried.'

'Well, I'm not sure,' the other man began, 'But there's a matter that's been bothering me constantly since the day of her death. I'm puzzled about the robbery… well actually, the crime that didn't happen, when your safe was found open. Don't you think it a strange coincidence that Cecile was murdered just three days after someone broke in?'

'Ah, Maurice, I've thought of nothing else. Both you and I are aware of the contents of those documents, yet I can see no reason at all for someone else to be interested in them. Besides, nothing was taken, so how on earth could a person benefit from reading such a thing?'

The baker ran a hand through his hair and shook his head. 'I really have no idea, Hubert, yet I'm worried that it might be connected.'

Hubert sipped at his wine, thoughtful and tired. 'Presuming that there is some kind of connection, who would be curious to know what we had agreed? Only my children or Telo, correct? Anyone outside of the family has nothing to gain from knowing that you now own Cecile and Valerie's family home outright.'

'You're absolutely right,' Maurice concluded, 'but I still have a strange feeling about it. Don't you?'

'Yes, but I'm not going to let it bother me any longer, and neither should you. The most important thing now is for the police to catch Cecile's killer. Come, Maurice, let's return to the lounge. There are many people wishing to offer us their condolences.'

Back at the police station in Bordeaux, Max Mallery was on the warpath.

'You two have to be the worst undercover detectives I've ever met in my life!' he thundered, pointing a finger at Gabriella and then slowly turning it on Thierry.

'Sorry, sir,' the young police officers said in unison, embarrassed to be brought to task in front of Jack and Luc.

'I mean, what on earth were you thinking, sneaking around the back of the boulangerie in broad daylight? No, don't answer that,' he snapped, as Thierry made to open his mouth in protest. 'Foolish, that's what it was!'

Ever the peacemaker, Jack Hobbs attempted to calm his boss down. 'There's no harm done, sir. At least Isobel Green is unlikely to make a run for it.'

Mallery swung round, his anger not dissipating one ounce. 'Make a run for it? Well, Jacques, how would she do that anyway, without her passport? Do you suppose Miss Green to be a master of disguise?'

Hobbs decided to let the ignited flame of Max's fury burn out, which he knew it would eventually, and sat tight-lipped at his desk.

'I need some coffee,' the Inspector muttered, striding out of the room. 'When I get back, I expect somebody to have come up with a plan of action. We're no further along with this case than we were almost a week ago. At present, we are an embarrassment to the force.'

The team signalled their agreement by unified silence and watched Mallery leave, his paces long and heavy-footed.

'He's right, you know,' Gabriella told the rest of the group. 'We haven't got anything to go on. Without evidence, we have no suspects or conviction. Mind you, I guess we're out of practice. There hasn't been a murder in Bordeaux for almost three years.'

Thierry handed around a bag of sweets, contemplating his colleague's assessment of the situation. 'We're a good team. Besides, I still think it's Isobel Green. It has to be her. She's not exactly a stranger to murder.'

Hobbs dipped his fingers into the paper bag and popped a hard-boiled sweet into his mouth. 'I'm not so sure. Ninety-nine per cent of killers have a reason behind their crimes, yet we have no connection at all between Green and Vidal. I think we'd better get our thinking caps on before Mallery gets back.'

Jack tapped the side of his head with two fingers so that the French team members could grasp his meaning.

The constant tapping on a keyboard, that had been present since the team had gathered twenty minutes earlier, suddenly stopped and Luc stood up. He turned the screen to face the centre of the room and beckoned the others to come over and look.

'I have it. Here is Isobel Green's Beetle parked in a side street near the town centre last Wednesday morning. The CCTV camera shows the time as eight thirty-two.'

The three detectives came closer to get a good look at the pale blue VW.

'So,' Luc explained, 'it's impossible that Isobel Green was on the train from Saint Margaux. She simply wouldn't have had time to return, fetch her car and get back to Bordeaux for that time.'

'Could she have got off the train at the stop after Saint Margaux and doubled-back?' Jack queried. 'Perhaps having already murdered Cecile Vidal?'

Luc shook his head. 'No way. I've already checked the train timetable. If she'd got off at the next village, which is Salbec, and then waited for a train back to Saint Margaux, it would already be eight twenty-five. That's not enough time for her to collect the car and drive to Bordeaux.'

'And she definitely couldn't have dropped off the car the previous night,' Thierry added, pulling out a file, 'as we have a statement from Hubert Vidal that he saw Green at the station on Wednesday morning when he dropped off his wife.'

'We'd better tell Mallery,' Luc sighed, reaching for another sweet. 'Who wants the task?'

Every eye in the room turned to look at Jack Hobbs.

'What? Why me? That's not fair!'

'You seem to have a good relationship with the boss,' Gabriella reasoned, 'and after his certainty that Isobel Green was guilty, I think you'd be best to break the news gently. Off you go.'

Jack's freckled complexion took on a pink hue as he started to blush. 'Well, thanks. Thanks a bunch.'

Inspector Mallery scrolled fruitlessly through his phone messages while enjoying a macchiato, the sugar hit much needed after missing breakfast that morning. There was still nothing from Vanessa and he was beginning to wonder if she would ever return his calls. Perhaps it was time to set his sights elsewhere. There were few women in the force that held his attention, yet Max yearned for some female company, especially to have conversation with over dinner.

A knock at the office door roused Max from his thoughts.

'We have an update, sir,' Jack explained. 'It's about Isobel Green.'

Max sat completely still, his hot drink abandoned and growing colder with each passing minute, as Hobbs gave him the details of Luc's CCTV findings.

'I can't believe it,' he eventually said, in an exasperated tone. 'It's taken nearly a week to find a sighting of her car, and now that we have it, well…'

'It definitely puts her out of the frame,' Jack commented, 'unless she drove at over a hundred kilometres an hour to get to Bordeaux.'

'Which is highly unlikely, given the usual morning traffic on the highway and the age of her car. That leaves us with no suspect at all. Do you realise that?' Max growled. 'We cannot release this information, not yet, or the people of Saint Margaux will probably crucify us. This is the worst possible news.'

'Right!' Inspector Mallery announced, striding into the Incident Room with renewed vigour. 'Back to the beginning. I want every single detail gone over twice – no, three times, or at least until we find something to go on.'

Thierry groaned, already feeling lethargic from the late nights and early mornings he'd spent keeping an eye on their English suspect.

'Does that mean surveillance on Green is off now?' he asked tentatively.

Max bit the skin around his thumb. 'Yes… no, let's keep an eye on her. Perhaps there is some connection to her chance meeting with the drug dealer. Or maybe someone else drove the Beetle to Bordeaux. I still have a bad feeling about her.'

'Who else could have driven the car?' Jack piped up.

'Well, Telo Fabron has already admitted that he used Green's car to collect Gaston Lauder from the airport…'

Hobbs didn't buy it. 'There's too much animosity between him and Green for them to be in cahoots together.'

'What is that famous saying by Sherlock Holmes, Jacques?' Mallery enquired.

'When you have excluded the impossible, whatever remains, however improbable, must be the truth.'

'Exactly!' Max exclaimed, looking triumphant. 'First, we exclude the impossible.'

A room full of puzzled faces looked back as the Inspector clapped his hands together in a dramatic manner. 'Somehow, somebody drove that car to Bordeaux. Perhaps it was Mademoiselle Green, or perhaps it was someone else, but it is our job to find out the truth.'

Thierry rustled the small paper bag as he extracted another boiled sweet, trying to carefully devour it without crunching and breaking the silence in the room.

It was too late. Mallery had already noticed and raised an inquisitive brow. He looked down at the last remaining sweet with interest.

'Where did you get that?!'

Thierry jumped, startled at the raised tone. 'At the gift shop, sir, the one in Saint Margaux. We went in to chat to the shopkeeper.'

Using two fingers to carefully lift the striped pink and white candy, Mallery held the item aloft for all to see.

'What do we have here?' he said, with a broad grin.

Jack Hobbs was the first to gasp out loud. 'Blimey, it's exactly the same as the sweet that was lodged in Cecile Vidal's throat!'

'At last, a clue!' Max exclaimed triumphantly.

CHAPTER FIFTEEN – ACCUSATIONS FLY

By Wednesday morning, the news that the Saint Margaux residents had an ex-convict in their midst circled like wildfire, spreading from house to house, shop to shop and back again. Speculation regarding Isobel's arrest and subsequent involvement in Cecile Vidal's murder grew to new heights, every face inquisitive and accusing. Subsequently, the boulangerie was busier than ever, with customers eager to get a glimpse of the English killer, unwilling to give her the benefit of the doubt, their emotions running high on hearing of her release from the police station.

Simone Dupuis had spilled the beans. In a moment of drunken chatter, she had confessed Isobel's past to her friend Dominique Fabre, who in turn passed the news on with relish, adding a few sordid details of her own. As morning broke, the Saint Margaux grapevine was alive with the news that Isobel Gilyard had a different identity and had once been convicted of a heinous crime.

Maurice Fabron was struggling with all the unwanted attention that day, despite his bakery sales rocketing, as each face at the counter lingered far too long, undoubtedly there to dig for more information. As advised, Izzy had stayed in the back kitchen, trying to focus on new bakes and exquisite decoration, but she could hear the constant flow of business and knew exactly why Maurice's bread was suddenly in such great demand. The cakes, however, were not selling as well as they should, for the villagers feared that the murderer could strike again at any given time, perhaps even poisoning the chocolate éclairs, so warped was their way of thinking.

Simone Dupuis had already called in three times before ten o'clock, once for an early espresso, again to ask Monsieur Fabron for change and then once more with the excuse that she had previously forgotten to purchase a fresh baguette.

Maurice knew exactly the purpose behind his friend's pretence, for he had heard the idle gossip and regretted the very moment he'd told Simone about Isobel's past. In a way, he felt guilt, too, for a trust had been betrayed between employer and employee. Izzy had been honest with him and in return, the baker had taken those secrets and gone running to tell all to his friend. Maurice was angry with Madam Dupuis, but chose to hold his emotions in check until a suitable time when he could politely express his disappointment at such a heartless faux pas.

'Izzy,' Maurice coaxed, 'would you like a coffee? A cappuccino, perhaps?'

Isobel looked up from the apricot buns that she was carefully icing, trying to decide whether dark chocolate might compliment the bakes, too, and hesitated slightly before saying, 'That would be lovely, thank you.'

The baker stood in the kitchen doorway and told her, 'Eventually, things will get back to how they were when you first arrived. People forget, they move on. As soon as the police arrest someone for Cecile's murder, you will be…'

His words trailed off, failing to find the right English expression.

'Vindicated?' Isobel offered. 'I don't think so, Maurice. I've heard people asking, whispering. I know that my secret's out.'

Monsieur Fabron blushed deeply and looked down at his feet in embarrassment. 'I'm so sorry. I confided in one very dear friend, somebody who I thought could be trusted. It was so hard to hold in what you had told me about your past. I suppose I just needed to talk about it.'

'It doesn't matter,' Izzy countered, her face blank, 'they would have found out sooner or later anyway, but it would have been much easier if they'd found out after I'd gone.'

'Gone?' Maurice repeated, looking startled. 'Surely you're not thinking of leaving?'

Isobel sighed. 'What choice do I have? There can't be a future for me here. As soon as I've saved a bit of money and the police have returned my passport, I'm going to start looking for another job.'

The baker's shoulders lifted slightly, almost as if a huge weight had been lifted from them.

'Where will you go?'

'I have no idea yet, Maurice. But I'll be sure to give you notice when I know.'

Monsieur Fabron nodded. The relief he felt was welcome, yet he couldn't help feeling guilty about his role in Izzy's decision. 'I'll fetch your coffee.'

Isobel turned back to her work, biting at her bottom lip to keep the tears from falling. It had been so painful listening to the morning's gossip, straining her ears and then struggling to translate the words from French.

'*Le rapport de police. La déposition. Ça s'est passe quand?*' she'd heard.

The police report. The statement. When did it happen?

It hadn't escaped her notice that Telo had been using the front door of the boulangerie for the collection of goods ready for delivery, either. Obviously, the young man still doubted Isobel's innocence and probably hated her for making him confess about using the Beetle, she thought. Life was getting too damn complicated for Isobel Green and she couldn't wait to leave, although making yet another fresh start might be a task in itself.

'Dinner later?' Simone Dupuis asked tentatively on her fourth visit to the boulangerie before noon, as the baker stood wrapping bread rolls.

Maurice shook his head. 'No, Simone. I plan a quiet night with Telo.'

The florist flushed slightly, embarrassed at receiving such an obvious snub in front of a customer, and pretended to look at her perfectly manicured fingernails.

'If you want to see how Isobel is doing, go through to the back,' Maurice whispered, certain that Simone should apologise to the other woman about her erroneous gossiping. After all, he considered Simone as much to blame as himself in some ways.

'Okay,' Madam Dupuis muttered, excusing herself and disappearing behind the counter, her soft leather loafers squeaking on the polished floor tiles as she went.

Inquisitive eyes followed as the female customer stood with her mouth agape, straining to hear any fragments of conversation between the florist and the Englishwoman. Maurice coughed to attract the lady's attention. '*Six Euro, s'il vous plaît, Madame.*'

'Isobel,' Simone called out softly, 'may I speak with you for a moment?'

Izzy turned sharply, startled at hearing a woman's voice. 'Yes, of course, what is it?'

'I think I owe you an apology,' Madam Dupuis began, clasping her hands together. 'Maurice told me about your past in confidence and, in a moment of stupidity, I repeated the details to someone else. It now seems that everyone in the village knows. I am truly sorry, I had no idea that this would happen.'

Isobel remained silent. A part of her wanted to slap Simone across the face, but a voice in her head suggested it was better to stay calm, allow the vulture to say sorry and then make her feel even more guilty by being friendly and forgiving.

'It doesn't matter, Simone. After all, I'm an outsider here.'

'Please, let's try to be friends,' the florist insisted, stepping closer. 'Can we?'

Izzy picked up the sharp knife that she was using to chop chocolate shards with and considered it for a moment, turning the handle slowly in her hands. 'Yes, Simone. I'd like that.'

The motion wasn't lost on Simone and she fought to regain her composure, leaving just enough time for Izzy to deliver her own piece of news.

'I know about you, Simone,' she smiled sweetly, holding the florist's gaze.

'Sorry? What do you know?'

'That you were in Bordeaux on the day of Cecile's murder.'

'I think you must be mistaken,' Madame Dupuis insisted, looking down at the knife still twisting around in Isobel's right-handed grip. 'I was not there.'

Isobel Green slipped her left hand into the deep front pocket of her apron and pulled out a slip of folded white paper. 'That's very strange. You see, I found a receipt for the dress you lent me. It was in the bottom of the bag, and guess what? It's dated last Wednesday.'

Simone stretched out a hand, intending to lift the receipt from Izzy's fingers. 'May I see?'

The Englishwoman shook her head. 'No, you may not. The police might be interested in seeing this. It could be used as evidence.'

'The police!' Simone gasped. 'Evidence? Whatever are you talking about?'

'Well, perhaps you were on the train to Bordeaux, Madame Dupuis. Maybe you were the one that killed Cecile and then calmly went shopping afterwards.'

Simone lifted a hand to her mouth. It trembled slightly as she gathered her thoughts. 'What a ridiculous accusation! Isobel, please look at the time on that receipt.'

Izzy glanced down, noting the numbers. 'Eleven,' she uttered, looking questioningly at Simone. 'So?'

'You see, Cecile was already dead by that time. I drove into Bordeaux at ten for shopping last week and returned straight after visiting the boutique. I cannot believe you would say such a terrible thing. Cecile Vidal was my best friend.'

Izzy watched as Simone Dupuis stormed out of the kitchen, flustered and upset.

Looking back down at the *ETIENNE* receipt, she realised that if Simone was telling her the truth about driving into Bordeaux, then she was also correct about Cecile being dead some hours before. Even if Simone had caught the earlier train, Isobel reasoned, she would have arrived in the town covered in blood. It just didn't stand to reason that someone could have exited the train with blood on their hands and calmly walked away without being stopped.

'Oh, shit,' Isobel muttered to herself, putting the knife back down onto the workbench in front of her. 'What have I done now?'

'Is this true?' Maurice demanded, putting both hands on his hips in anger, 'Have you really just accused Madame Dupuis of murdering Cecile? After all that woman has done to try to help you? I have no words to describe my feelings.'

Izzy rubbed her palms over her face. 'Yes, I'm sorry, Maurice, I wasn't thinking. I'm just desperate to clear my name, you must understand that. And Simone did go to Bordeaux last Wednesday. I can prove it.'

'A slip of paper for an innocent shopping trip proves nothing! And you think that, by throwing around false accusations, this will help your case?' he growled, stamping a foot on the floor like a petulant child.

'No, it's just, when I found the receipt for the dress, I thought...'

'No, that's it exactly!' Maurice cut her off. 'You didn't think at all. Perhaps it would be best that we terminate your contract right now. I will pay you to the end of the month and you can stay in the apartment until the police return your passport, but after that, Mademoiselle Green, or whatever your name is, please do not bother me or the other Saint Margaux residents again.'

Isobel was speechless. All morning, she'd been turning over the possibility of Simone Dupuis being Cecile's killer – after all, she had been in Bordeaux the same day – but it had turned out the woman had a perfectly rational explanation. Once again, her smart mouth and impulsive behaviour had caused trouble.

Maurice dipped his head toward the apricot buns, perfect in their decoration, the chocolate shards giving an edgy contrast to the pale fluffy sponge and white icing. He couldn't deny the Englishwoman's eye for detail in her baking skills.

'Are these finished?'

Izzy nodded, 'Yes, all done.'

'Then so are we,' the baker sighed, picking up the tray of cakes. 'Good day.'

Upstairs in the apartment, Isobel changed out of her cotton summer dress and pulled on a pair of yellow shorts and a simple t-shirt. She had no idea what to do in this sudden turn of events, but she was desperate to get away from the boulangerie for the rest of the day for fear of upsetting yet more of the villagers. She had no friends, little money and was reluctant to turn to her family even if she was in dire straits, so the rational option for now was a long walk in the fresh air to conjure up a plan of action.

There was a narrow path that ran along the rear of the boulangerie building, easy enough to walk along, yet in parts overgrown with wildflowers and long grass. It was seldom used by the Saint Margaux residents, most of whom preferred to walk their dogs past the church and along the river banks, therefore Isobel's fear of running into any other villagers was a minimal risk along that route.

Wearing dark sunglasses and a baseball cap to cover her signature bleached hair, the Izzy strode carefully along, avoiding dips and being mindful of wildlife that might be nesting in the hedgerow. It was a cloud-free and hot morning, the sun not yet having peaked at noon, and Isobel felt uncomfortably warm after just a few hundred metres. As the path veered off into a fork, she took the right turn, away from the village and continued on until she heard the rush of a waterfall a bit further along. Sticky with the exertion of her walk, Izzy looked around for some shade in which to sit and watch the steady trickle of the flowing river as it tumbled onto rocks below. However, her peace was shattered when a voice called from around the slight bend in the riverbank.

'Mademoiselle Gilyard!' Gaston called cheerily. 'Are you not working today?'

'Green.' Izzy turned to face the artist and snapped, 'I'm sure you're aware, as everyone else seems to be, that my name is actually Isobel Green.'

Gaston nodded from behind a tall easel, his dark eyebrows shooting upwards. '*Oui*, I knew that. I just wondered if you knew that I knew.'

Izzy shot him a puzzled look and stood deliberating whether to find a spot somewhere else in which to sit.

'Look, why don't you sit down, have a rest? I've got some cold bottles of water here and you look in need of a drink,' the man offered.

Isobel watched as Gaston put down his paintbrush and picked two plastic bottles out of an insulated bag. The sight of them caused saliva to build in her mouth.

'Here, take one of these,' he offered, coming alongside Isobel, 'have a drink.'

She took a bottle and twisted off the top. 'Thanks, I guess I am quite thirsty.'

Gaston eased himself down onto the grass, dangling his long arms over bare knees, and patted the warm spot beside him. 'Sit down, I don't bite.'

Izzy snorted. 'You must be the only person around here that doesn't, then.'

'Why, what has happened?' The question seemed genuine.

Isobel noted that the artist's French accent was much heavier than that of the locals and she wondered if he'd always lived in Paris. However, given Gaston's close relationship with Simone Dupuis, she had no intention of spilling the beans just yet. He'd find out soon enough.

'Nothing. I'm just fed up, that's all. I need some time to think.'

'Fair enough.' The man shrugged, swigging the water and trickling a little down his open shirt and onto his chest to help cool off. 'But can I ask you something before I leave you with your thoughts?'

Izzy looked up, blinking as the sunlight blocked Gaston's face from her line of vision. 'Sure, why not?'

'Why did you accuse me of having blood on my shirt?'

Isobel closed her eyes. It seemed that her trail of destruction was never-ending. 'Because, at the time, I honestly thought it was.'

Gaston pointed down at his navy shorts. 'Like this red mark here, which is paint, and this one over here, when I had been working on an oil of the poppy field. Do you see? Naturally, it would stand out even more on a white shirt. What can I say? I'm clumsy with my oils.'

His long thick fingers darted over the fabric, pointing out every speck of dried, blood-red pigment.

'I can see that now,' Isobel admitted, dropping her head. 'I was desperate.'

'I don't suppose it was easy being in that police cell,' the artist continued, shooting his companion a sideways glance. 'I can understand how you would want to blame someone else for the crimes. But I assure you, I am not a killer.'

'And I am? Is that what you mean? Because of my past. You seem to forget that I am actually innocent,' Izzy retorted sharply, before taking another sip of water. 'No matter what everyone thinks, I did not murder Cecile Vidal.'

'So you say, but I also witnessed the murder weapon being pulled from your car. That's pretty damning, isn't it?'

Isobel breathed deeply, trying to maintain her composure. 'Gaston, somebody must have put it there, because I certainly didn't.'

A deep silence fell between the pair as they contemplated how to continue.

'It is unbelievable,' Simone Dupuis was telling Dominque Fabre during one of the gift shop owner's many coffee breaks. 'Now that woman is accusing me of murdering Cecile. I think she has gone completely crazy! She should be locked up. Who knows who she'll point the blame at next?'

Dominique watched as her friend fussed with a bouquet of yellow roses and freesias, in awe of Simone's attention to detail.

'Now Simone, don't let it stress you. The police will have Isobel Green under arrest again soon, you wait and see. We all know she's capable of murder, now, don't we? She's already served one prison sentence. It's a nasty business, it really is, but I'm sure that those two lovely detectives will find enough evidence to put her away for a long time.'

Madam Dupuis cut a length of pink ribbon and considered Dominque's words before replying, 'You're so right. And to think I tried to help her, too!'

'What does Maurice think of all this?'

Simone breathed out gently. 'He's finally seen sense and told Isobel she has to go as soon as she's got her passport back. He's still mad at me for telling you about Mademoiselle Green's past though, Dominique, and I'm not very happy with you for gossiping to others. I told you in the strictest confidence.'

The larger woman coughed, took a sip of coffee and replied, 'Simone, we have a duty to our fellow neighbours to divulge something so serious as having a murderer living amongst us. Mmm, don't you think?'

The florist agreed, gripping Dominique's hand in hers, 'Do you know, you're absolutely right. Isobel Green murdered her boyfriend and she was seen at the station on the day of Cecile's murder. The discovery of that knife in her car only secures her guilt further. The police were errant in releasing her. She has to be brought to justice, the sooner, the better.'

'But what can we do, Simone?'

'A petition,' the florist said, smiling broadly. 'We start a petition for the re-arrest of Isobel Green. If we get enough signatures, Inspector Mallery cannot ignore it.'

As noon arrived, Isobel and Gaston lay back on the riverbank enjoying the heat on their faces, sunspots dancing behind closed lids as they soaked up the warmth while allowing the silence to become less strained between them.

'Where will you go?' Gaston ventured, turning to lie on his side, facing Izzy.

'How do you know I intend to leave?' she murmured, keeping her eyes shut but aware of the artist's fresh breath close to her face.

'Because I would,' the man admitted, plucking a daisy from the grass. 'With all the bad blood, I couldn't stay where I wasn't wanted.'

Izzy allowed the words to float in the air for a while, rearranging them in her mind before choosing the best way to respond.

'I don't know. Maybe Spain, or Holland. I haven't decided yet.'

'Not back to England?'

There was a slight tensing of the woman's shoulders and she opened her eyes, blinking against the bright blue sky. 'No, there's nothing there for me.'

'No family? Parents, brothers or sisters?'

'Nobody. I don't think I'll ever go back.'

Maurice Fabron was allowing himself a much-needed sit down after the busy morning trade. It hadn't escaped his notice that, without Isobel working in the back kitchen, the customers had reduced to a trickle as there was nobody in the boulangerie to speculate about any longer. A steaming mug of black coffee and an untouched ham baguette sat on the table in front of him.

There was the familiar rev of an engine as the Citroën delivery van came into view, causing Maurice's heart to fill with joy for the first time that day.

'*Bonjour, Papa*,' Telo called as he stepped in through the open front door. '*Où est Mademoiselle Gilyard?*'

The boulangerie owner hadn't yet explained to his son about Isobel's name being Green and that she hid a dark past. It wasn't going to be an easy conversation, yet he would have to broach the subject soon, before Telo caught wind of the villager's gossip. Perhaps tonight would be a good time, he mused; just the two of them, with plenty of opportunity for questions and explanations.

Maurice explained that Isobel was no longer employed there, but might need to stay for a few more weeks until she had her passport returned. Telo's expression changed noticeably from a deep frown to a faint smile as his father spoke. It seemed that although he didn't relish the idea of Izzy staying in Saint Margaux, he definitely saw light at the end of the tunnel with an imminent departure.

'*Très bien,*' he replied simply, as the baker got up to give his son a hug.

Maurice motioned to the chilled chocolate milkshake sitting on the counter, a thick whirl of fresh cream and squishy marshmallows sitting on top,

As Telo Fabron sipped at the delicious drink, he listened carefully as his father explained how there were going to be changes at the boulangerie. He intended to hire a new delivery person and would train Telo in basic bread-making skills in order to keep the Fabron family tradition alive. It was something he should have done a long time ago, in Maurice's honest opinion. The young man smiled eagerly, happy to go along with his father's new plans, anything, so long as they didn't include Isobel.

Just as Dominique Fabre took the last sip of her coffee, a familiar red BMW pulled up alongside her gift shop.

'Well, well, look who's here?' Simone declared, motioning towards the vehicle. 'I wonder what Inspector Mallery wants this time.'

'I'd better go and see,' Dominique replied cheerily, her ample behind swaying as she sashayed out of the flower shop. '*Au revoir, Simone.*'

Madame Dupuis watched as the detective looked at the *Closed* sign on the shop door and then saw the tall man gaze around the square inquisitively. Seconds later, Jack Hobbs appeared from the passenger's side of the car, a phone held to his ear. He was talking animatedly and running a hand through his thick ginger hair. Simone looked at the two as they hovered around, waiting for Dominique to make her way across to them and wondered which of the men, if either, were single.

She frowned as Dominique slipped a key into the door of her premises, smiling up at the Inspector with pearly white teeth and a red-lipsticked smile.

Simone loved her friend dearly but perhaps it was time to have a few words about the art of flirtation, or, at the very least, a little education in how to act coy, she pondered. It wouldn't do at all to have the shapely brunette throwing herself at Max Mallery in such an obvious display of lust. He was an incredibly handsome man, she had to concede, and poor Dominique Fabre was sure to get her fragile heart broken, as she had done over and over at school when the boys had preferred Simone's slender silhouette. Or, even worse, the florist told herself, the dashing Inspector might fall for Dominique's charms and that would never do!

CHAPTER SIXTEEN – MORE CLUES

Inspector Max Mallery stepped inside the fragrant gift shop, his eyes automatically wandering down towards Dominique Fabre's ample behind which gently moved up and down as she walked. He noted that the interior of the building was predominantly furnished with pastel-coloured accessories, with the goods neatly presented on antique dressers and shelving.

Max cast his obsessive-compulsive eye over the room for dust but there was none. The aroma of scented candles permeated every inch of the floor-space and it overwhelmed his senses somewhat, filling his nostrils with the heady perfumes of vanilla, lavender and citrus. He wondered if there was such a thing as a coffee-fragranced candle to curb his constant caffeine craving.

Madam Fabre slipped behind the counter and coughed politely to draw the man's attention, assuming an air of importance in her role as shopkeeper. Intent on the task at hand, Max leaned forward to where rows of boiled sweets were lined up in their containers like multi-coloured soldiers standing to attention. Dozens of pink-striped sweets filled a huge glass jar. This was what he needed to question the delightfully scary Madam Fabre about.

Outside, Jack Hobbs was attempting to extricate himself from an emotional phone call with his wife. Angélique was a highly-strung woman at the best of times, but today she was more so than usual as it was her mother's birthday. She had called to remind Jack to finish work early in order to look after their son, while she created a special dinner for them all that evening.

'I promise, I'll be home by five,' Jack was saying in a low voice, as he paced up and down beside his boss's car. 'I don't think I can make it any earlier.'

'That's no good!' Angélique returned, her voice becoming high-pitched and irate. 'My parents will expect to eat at seven and I have so much to prepare. Honestly, Jack, I am asking you to do just one thing.'

'Why not ask them to come over earlier, then your mum can look after Tom while you cook?' her husband reasoned, desperate to find a solution, yet determined not to let his domestic problems compromise the murder investigation. It was bad enough having this altercation while standing in the middle of the village in Saint Margaux. There was a loud sigh and then the line went dead, leaving a buzz in Jack's ear.

Hobbs stared at the mobile in his hand, debating whether to call back, but concluded that letting Angélique calm down for a while was the best bet. There would be more tears and tantrums later, Jack could virtually guarantee it, but he'd face the music when he got home, not now. Slipping the device into his trouser pocket, the young police officer followed Mallery into the shop.

'Madam Fabre, this is my colleague, Detective Hobbs. As I explained, his French is not quite perfect yet, so if you wouldn't mind, can we speak in English?'

Jack blushed as the Inspector made courteous introductions, the red hue of his freckled face causing his ginger hair to become a more prominent feature.

The busty woman fluttered her long dark lashes and smiled widely. '*Bonjour*, hello, I'm happy to practice my English. How can I help?'

Jack took the outstretched hand, noting that the woman's soft, pudgy fingers were warm and clammy, offering a polite greeting as he did so.

'Now, the reason we are here, Madame Fabre,' Max explained, 'is due to these pink candies here. The strawberry ones.'

He lifted the jar and set it on the wooden counter in front of the shopkeeper.

Dominique looked puzzled. 'I don't understand, Inspector.'

'Would it be possible for you to make a list of everyone who has purchased these in the last, say, two weeks?'

The woman puffed out her cheeks and pondered the question for a few seconds. 'Well, maybe, but these are my most popular brand, Inspector. I sell at least six or seven bags a day. Why do you need...'

'It's very important, Madame. Do you think you could try?'

Dominique nodded and pulled a notepad towards her, licking the tip of a pencil before beginning to write slowly and carefully.

While the task was in process, Mallery excused himself and stepped outside to smoke, leaving Jack to peruse the array of trinkets and gifts adorning the shelves. The pungent mix of aromas was beginning to give the Inspector a headache and he desperately needed to clear his head before going back inside. Besides, it would give him chance to check his mobile for text messages from Paris. Sadly, there were none.

A good five or six minutes later, Madam Fabre's list was complete, and she proudly handed it over to Detective Hobbs.

'This is it as far as I can remember,' she explained, pointing to the names. 'But there were also a lot of tourists who may have purchased them, including a young couple the other day, a blonde woman with a straw hat and a dark man.'

Jack nodded. He recognised the description of his colleagues, Gabriella and Thierry and marvelled at how they'd both failed to notice the significance of the pink sweets when the purchase had been made. However, he had to concede that if the detectives hadn't bought the bag of confectionery, he probably wouldn't be standing in the shop with Madam Fabre at that very moment.

A tinkling of the little bell over the door and Mallery appeared, a faint whiff of tobacco emanating from him as he peered over Jack's shoulder.

'A lot of names,' he commented gruffly. 'Some very familiar ones, too.'

Hobbs agreed. Most of the Saint Margaux residents that he'd met so far had purchased a quantity of the striped candy, including Cecile Vidal and Isobel. He noticed that Madam Fabre had written the Englishwoman's surname as 'Green' which suggested that she was already privy to the sordid details of the newcomer's past.

'Madam Fabre, you were a good friend of Cecile Vidal, were you not?' Max asked, almost as an afterthought.

'Why, yes, we were very close,' Dominque acknowledged, pulling out a cotton handkerchief in anticipation of the few tears that might fall.

'And when was the last time you saw her?'

The woman bobbed her head, sniffling. 'We had coffee the day before she died. Cecile was so excited, chatting about collecting a gift for Hubert's birthday. If only she hadn't gone to Bordeaux…'

A fat, round tear rolled down Dominique's cheek.

'*Merci,* Madame,' the Inspector acknowledged, turning to leave, 'I am so sorry to have upset you. Jacques, do you wish to make a purchase before we go?'

'Erm, no, I don't think…' Hobbs stammered, looking around bemused.

'I think your wife might appreciate…'

'Oh, yes, she would!' Jack agreed, picking up an ornate jewellery box and examining the price tag. 'Thanks.'

Max lifted Dominique's neatly written list from the younger man's fingers and made to leave, aware now that Hobbs was slightly embarrassed that his new boss had picked up on the heated conversation on his phone as they'd exited the car. It occurred to the young detective that Mallery knew the mystical mind of a woman better than he did.

Madam Fabre's eyes followed the Inspector intently as he opened the door.

'Is he single?' she whispered, wrapping an auburn curl around an index finger, the damp handkerchief still clutched in her other hand.

'What? Oh no, he's very happily married with six children,' Jack blurted, catching on to the not so subtle hint.

Dominique's round shoulders visibly sagged as she took in the response. 'Oh, what a pity. He is such a handsome man.'

As Hobbs stepped outside with his expertly wrapped purchase, Max was poised with his cigarette lighter in hand.

'Okay, Jacques?' He smiled, looking at the gift bag. 'I may have saved you from some trouble tonight, *oui*?'

'Hah, we're quits now!' Hobbs laughed, jerking his head towards the shop. 'I just saved you, too!'

'Eh? From what?'

Jack shook his head, aware of Madam Fabre peeping at them through the layers of bunting in the window display. 'Never mind, sir, I'll tell you later.'

'Well, okay. Put that in the car, I think we might as well visit Monsieur Fabron while we're in the village. I've just thought of something.'

'*Bonjour*, Inspector Mallery, Detective Hobbs,' Maurice greeted the men as they stepped into the boulangerie and inhaled the incredible aroma of warm bread.

'Is it convenient to ask you a couple of questions?' Max asked, already pulling out a chair and eagerly eyeing the coffee machine.

'Of course. Coffee?' the baker offered, automatically picking up three cups.

The detectives dipped their heads in unison, both rapidly building up a thirst for the excellent cappuccinos that they knew would be forthcoming.

Seated at the table, after first checking that Telo was on hand to help out should any customers need service, Monsieur Fabron splayed his fingers. A dusting of fresh white flour was caught in the cuticles, evidence of the baker's passion for his work. 'What brings you to Saint Margaux again, so soon?'

Jack Hobbs looked expectantly at Max, wondering what it was that had urged his boss to come over to the boulangerie. He didn't have to wait long to find out.

'As you know, Monsieur Fabron, the murder weapon used to kill Cecile Vidal was from your kitchen. So, I want you to be absolutely certain about the last time you saw it.'

Maurice rubbed his chin, deep in thought. 'Well, Inspector, let me think. As I told you previously, it must have been on the Sunday of last week. It's difficult to remember exactly.'

'Right. So that means it was before Madam Vidal was murdered. Correct? Please think very carefully, Monsieur. Is it possible that the knife went missing some days before?'

The baker looked down into his cup, as though searching for clues, and then suddenly perked up as the answer came to him.

'No, definitely not! You see, as I told you before, I remember having to ask Gaston to come over here on Wednesday night to get a knife from the back kitchen as mine was missing. Isobel got one for him. We were having a simple supper of bread and cheese.'

Max clasped his hands on the table. 'Now, please be sure. Could it have gone missing on the Saturday and not the Sunday?'

Maurice pondered for a while, allowing the detectives to enjoy their coffees. 'No, it must have been the Sunday. Yes, definitely, it was. Isobel arrived on the Saturday and I invited her to dinner on Sunday evening. I used it to cut the loaf that we ate with our meal. I have no doubt in my mind that Sunday evening was the last time I saw it.'

Mallery and Hobbs looked at each other as the boulangerie owner spoke, each feeling frustrated.

'Monsieur, was Telo also at home on Sunday night?' Jack clarified.

'Yes, yes he was. Telo wasn't happy about Isobel coming over, but we all ate together.'

'Just the three of you?' Max jumped in, beginning to join the dots in his head. 'Now please, this is most important. Do you remember seeing the knife after the meal that night?'

The boulangerie owner seemed clear in his mind now and said confidently, 'Do you know, Inspector, I don't remember seeing it at all after that!'

'Monsieur Fabron, is Isobel working today?' Jack asked, casting a glance at the doorway leading to the back kitchen.

Maurice let out an audible sigh. 'No. Sadly, she is no longer employed here.'

Max shifted in his seat. 'I see. Do you mind telling us why that is?'

The baker raised his coffee cup to drain the last dregs. 'Because I fear that you were right in arresting her, Inspector. Isobel Green is nothing but trouble.'

Having established that Isobel Green was no longer working at the boulangerie, but that Monsieur Fabron had agreed to let her stay in the apartment until she could find an alternative arrangement, Mallery and Hobbs stood at the rear door of the bakery. There was no response to their urgent knocking and Max's patience was beginning to wear thin.

'Do you think Monsieur Fabron could be mistaken at all?' Jack ventured.

Mallery puckered up his lips. 'No, he seems pretty certain. Although unless Isobel Green tells us the same, it could put both Telo and Maurice in the frame for murder.'

'You're joking! No way would either of them have murdered Madam Vidal.'

Max turned a beady eye on his colleague. 'And why is that, Jacques?'

'Maurice just seems really straight, and Telo is the sort of chap that couldn't tell a lie without giving himself away. Cecile Vidal was his aunt, after all.'

'Maybe,' Max agreed, 'I can't see him attacking anyone, either, but nobody in Saint Margaux is innocent until we have the murderer behind bars, right?'

Hobbs was of the same mind. 'Yep, you have a point. I wonder if Isobel Green will be able to shed any light on what Maurice Fabron told us just now? We have to find her.'

'The car is still here,' Mallery pointed out, gesturing to the battered VW Beetle, 'So she can't be far away, unless she caught a train, of course.'

'Perhaps she's just gone for a walk,' Jack replied. 'Why don't you drive down towards the river and I'll ask around here. Maybe someone's seen her.'

'Okay, why don't I meet you back here in half an hour, Jacques?'

Detective Hobbs exited the small courtyard behind the boulangerie and stood with his back to the wall of the building, watching his boss return to his expensive car, and contemplated where to go first. He didn't fancy another grilling about Mallery's love-life by the voluptuous Dominique Fabre, so he decided to work his way clockwise around the square, the opposite direction to the gift shop.

His first port of call was to the flower shop next-door, where he at least felt confident in being able to communicate easily in English with Simone Dupuis.

The lady in question was tying together an extravagant bouquet of white lilies and pink roses, fussing with a length of ribbon until it reached perfection. Jack watched from the open doorway until the florist gave a satisfied grunt and placed the display in an oversized green bucket.

'Madame Dupuis?' he called. 'I'm sorry to interrupt.'

'Oh, how long have you been there?' Simone gasped, placing a slender hand at her throat. 'You frightened me, detective.'

'I'm very sorry, it's just that I could see you were busy.'

The woman flipped a hand at Jack and beckoned him inside. 'I'm sorry, I'm just tired. Please come in. Is it a bunch of flowers that you need?'

Hobbs began to shake his head but stopped mid-way, instead darting his eyes to the pretty floral bouquet that had just been completed.

'Well, no, I came to ask a question actually, but perhaps you have a point, my wife might like some flowers.'

The florist followed Jack's eyes to the lilies and gave a delighted chuckle. 'Yes, I think she would love those. You have a very lucky wife, Detective Hobbs.'

Reaching into his wallet for a debit card, Hobbs felt the familiar embarrassment as he struggled to ask for the price, a seemingly delicate matter when making purchases for his beloved. Simone righted the matter there and then.

'Forty Euros,' she said with a smile, taking the card deftly and inserting it into a machine.

Jack gulped. This was turning into a very expensive day.

As the transaction was concluded, the detective donned his proverbial professional cap and got to the point of his visit. 'Madame Dupuis, did you happen to see Isobel Green at all today?'

It was as though the gates of hell opened up then, with the florist embarking on an incensed rant about her altercation with Izzy that morning. Jack stood riveted. The news of Isobel's accusation was startling, and he began to wonder whether the Englishwoman had completely lost the plot.

'Do you recall what started the argument?' he pressed. 'Why she accused you of the crime? Did something trigger it?'

Simone looked sternly at him, her eyes shining with intense anger. 'Detective Hobbs, that woman is completely mad. Not only has she accused me, but also Gaston and Telo. I tell you, she needs locking up! None of us are safe until she is in a high-security prison.'

Armed with the fabulous, but what he considered to be a staggeringly expensive, bouquet in one hand and his police identity card in the other, Jack Hobbs strode around the square, calling in at several more of the street's premises, yet each time being met with a negative response. None of the Saint Margaux residents had seen the Englishwoman for several hours and, judging by the air of hostility, they were all glad that she wasn't hanging around the village. At the bistro, Hobbs was offered a discount card and promised to bring his wife for lunch when time allowed. Yet all the time, Isobel Green remained elusive.

While the detectives searched for their main suspect, Isobel Green lay alongside Gaston Lauder on the riverbank, unaware of her name being bandied about the village like a common criminal. For an hour, she had been able to push recent events to the back of her mind and, instead of worrying about the future, Isobel was making general conversation with the Parisian artist.

'Why do you come to Saint Margaux every year?' she murmured, enjoying the sensation of the warm grass against her bare legs.

'Why not?' Gaston replied, plucking a poppy and tucking it in the woman's hair. 'This area is so beautiful. It gives me a lot of inspiration to paint.'

'Do you only work on landscapes? Or do you sometimes paint people?'

The artist studied Isobel's face carefully, unsure as to whether their minds were on the same track. She hadn't flinched, her eyes were still closed, her lips puckered.

'Would you like me to paint you?' he ventured.

The Englishwoman opened one eye and considered her response. 'Maybe.'

There was something dangerous, yet seductive in the way that Isobel looked at the man. It caused blood to rush to his private parts and he turned away quickly. It hadn't escaped Gaston's notice that Mademoiselle Green was incredibly attractive in a boyish way, her cropped hair perfectly suited to the elfish facial features. Yet, he told himself, the woman had served ten years for murder. Not only did that one fact place doubt in his mind about her willingness to be kissed, but it also cast a shadow on any intention he might have to become intimate with her. After all, did anyone know the whole truth about Isobel Green?

Cruising over the humpbacked bridge at a much slower speed than the sporty BMW was comfortable with, Max Mallery rested an elbow on the ledge of the open window and gazed out across the poppy-strewn riverbank. There, almost out of sight where the water disappeared around a natural curve, he caught a flash of yellow and then something white. He wasn't entirely sure what he'd seen, but it was enough to spark the detective's interest and he pulled the car into a farm gateway a little further along, before striding across the lush long grass.

'Inspector Mallery?' Gaston called out, squinting in the sunlight.

Isobel followed the artist's gaze and groaned at the sight of the tall policeman. 'Oh, shit. Not him again! What now?'

'*Bonjour.*' Max raised a hand and walked closer to the reclining couple, eager to know what had brought them together at this location. He noted the way in which the man's body was angled towards the female at his side. There was a heavy bulge in the artist's shorts which he quickly covered with one hand on noticing the Inspector's wandering eye. The woman, however, seemed oblivious.

'*Bonjour,*' Gaston replied, now pulling his knees up to his chest.

'What do you want?' Izzy sighed, shuffling up onto her elbows.

Gaston tapped her leg with his paint-smudged fingertips, frowning. 'Be polite, Izzy. Maybe the Inspector is here with good news.'

Isobel ignored the comment and pushed herself into a sitting position, 'Well?'

'Just a few questions,' Mallery said steadily, crouching down to get the irate woman in his line of vision, 'if you don't mind.'

'And if I do? Are you going to ask anyway?'

Max ignored the retort and continued, 'Did you happen to purchase some pink striped strawberry candies from Madame Fabre last week, Isobel?'

'I don't know. Maybe,' Izzy snapped, rubbing a hand through her short hair 'Is it a crime to buy a few sweets these days? Oh, don't tell me. Not only am I a murderer, I'm being accused of stealing now!'

'Not at all,' Mallery replied, his gaze unwavering. 'Please just think, did you?'

Gaston tilted his head, waiting for Izzy to respond.

'Alright, yes, I did. I didn't eat them though, they were disgustingly sugary.'

The Inspector gave a satisfied nod. 'I see. And just one more thing, Mademoiselle Green. Do you recall seeing a bread knife in Monsieur Fabron's kitchen when you went there for dinner on Sunday of last week?'

Isobel scrambled to her feet, sweat beading across her forehead. 'What?'

'Mademoiselle, answer the question, please.'

Izzy bit her lip, as she always did when feeling under pressure, a thousand thoughts racing through her mind. She closed her eyes for a second, trying to work out the best response. If she said yes, would she be arrested again? But if she said no, would Maurice testify that she had seen the knife?

'Isobel?' Gaston urged, squeezing her arm gently.

'Yes, I think so,' she answered quietly, afraid that lying would cause a tangle of knots in the already complex case against her.

'Where did you see it?' the policeman pressed. 'Think carefully, Mademoiselle.'

Izzy closed her eyes, feeling sick in the pit of her stomach. She replayed the moment when she'd entered Monsieur Fabron's elegant kitchen and tried her best to recall the item. She had seen it, she was sure. It was one of those old-fashioned serrated knives with a carved wooden handle.

'It was on the side, on top of the wooden board. I remember now. Maurice asked me to take the loaf into the dining room and I remember it being there then. I didn't touch it, if that's what you're thinking.'

Max stood, eager to see the expression on Isobel's face clearly. He was sure that he could identify if she was lying, after all their hours of questioning the weekend before. However, he was certain that right now, she was telling the truth.

'You're absolutely sure it was there, in the kitchen, on that Sunday?'

Izzy seemed resolute. 'Yes, Inspector. I'm sure. If you don't believe me, ask Simone Dupuis. She must have seen it as well.'

Mallery squeezed his eyes shut, then opened them rapidly. 'Madame Dupuis was there for dinner, too?' He cursed silently. Why hadn't Maurice Fabron mentioned the florist?

The Englishwoman folded her arms, now suddenly forthcoming with information. 'No, she didn't stay for dinner, but she was at Maurice's house when I arrived. It looked like she'd been there for a while. They were drinking wine in the kitchen, but she left, saying she had to prepare things because Gaston would be arriving.'

Max let the words sink in slowly, turning them over in his mind.

'Thank you, Mademoiselle Green. It's possible that I may need to speak with you again, so please don't leave the village. Sorry to have disturbed you.'

Isobel spat out her final words as Mallery turned to leave, the colour rising in her already flushed cheeks. 'Well, I can't, can I? Somebody has my bloody passport!'

Max didn't respond. Instead, he walked purposefully back to the gleaming red sports car, the dots that he'd previously joined in his mind beginning to unravel themselves in quick succession. Simone Dupuis had also been at Fabron's house. What on earth was going on?

CHAPTER SEVENTEEN – BAD VIBES AND ALCOHOL

On Thursday morning, just over a week after the murder of vineyard owner and Saint Margaux resident Cecile Vidal, the mood in the village was sombre and tense. People were afraid to go out after dark for fear of meeting the fiend in a dark alleyway, or, worse still, bumping into Isobel Green whom they still regarded as the main suspect.

Maurice Fabron was tired. He was once again coming to terms with completing the boulangerie bakes by himself, no mean feat for a man who was used to having a woman's touch around the place. He'd been impressed with the creations that Izzy had served up, patisserie with creative flair and afternoon fondant fancies with delicate fillings, and although he wouldn't admit it out loud, the baker wished that he'd been a bit more astute in keeping her on. The knowledge that Isobel had gained her skills on a course whilst in prison was a bitter pill to swallow, yet she'd brought a ray of sunshine into the shop and a much-needed increase in trade.

Monsieur Fabron had spent the previous night tossing and turning, wondering whether he should offer Isobel her position back, at least until she moved on, or if it was time to create a new advertisement, this time for someone local to help out with the business. The middle-aged man knew that he wouldn't have found himself in this position if his beloved Valerie were still alive. She would have been there, chatting with customers, carefully preparing luxurious coffees and wrapping up their purchases in neat boxes with delicate ribbon. It wasn't just the loneliness of his wife's death that had affected Maurice, either. He missed sharing a meal with someone, clinking glasses over dinner and even biting his tongue when he knew he'd stepped over the line during an argument.

The boulangerie owner had seen all of Valerie's traits in her beautiful sister, too, although Cecile was more hot-headed and impulsive, whereas Valerie liked to think matters through to ensure the right decision. Maurice missed his chats with Cecile. She'd been the only one who'd really understood how the loss of his wife had affected him, comforting him with kind words and urging him to keep going on the days when he'd rather just have stayed in bed and shut out the world.

Cecile had also stepped in to help deal with Telo, a young man lost in his own world, who had buried himself even further after the loss of his mother. Maurice found his son's constant mood swings difficult to handle on top of everything else, especially over the past week, when they'd had to come to terms with Isobel's involvement in the most terrible of crimes.

On that particular morning, Monsieur Fabron had been far too busy to dwell on matters that were out of his control, yet at half-past eleven, when the traffic of footsteps into his shop came to a halt, he poured a cup of coffee and sat down exhausted. It was at that moment that a torrent of grief washed over Maurice and he made a decision; not a big one, but a step to get his life back on track. Finishing his hot drink, the baker turned the door sign to *FERMÉ* and slipped out.

Simone Dupuis was taking a ten Euro note from a customer when Maurice appeared at the door of her florist shop and failed to look up until the transaction was over. When she did spot him, Simone called out his name and rushed over immediately.

'Maurice, whatever is the matter?' she fussed. 'Please, sit down.'

'I can't stay,' Monsieur Fabron told her, extricating himself from the woman's grasp, 'but I have come to apologise for my rude behaviour yesterday…'

It seemed that the florist had already forgotten the previous day's slight and gave a simple shrug. 'You were busy. It's fine.'

Maurice cleared his throat and began again. 'Simone, I was very blunt when you invited me to dinner. I wonder if you would accompany me to the Bistro this evening? Some good food and a bottle of wine is just what I need.'

The florist stood back. She had to admit that, even in his white apron and faded jeans, Maurice Fabron was quite a catch. Besides, he was also one of her closest friends and the response fell instantly from her pink-stained lips.

'I would love to, thank you, Maurice. But what about Telo?'

The boulangerie owner shrugged. 'I will ask Gaston if he can keep Telo company tonight and will leave something for their dinner. See you at eight?'

Simone smiled, her eyelids closing for a few seconds.

'That's fine. See you later.'

Above the boulangerie, Isobel Green was feeling a few degrees more positive than she had been the previous morning. Even though Inspector Mallery's incessant questions were driving her crazy, at least the detective had gone away with a few new leads. She wondered why Maurice had failed to mention that Madam Dupuis had been at his house on that first Sunday night. After all, it seemed that he'd been quick to give Izzy's name. There was something not quite right about the way in which the residents of Saint Margaux protected each other, she mused, and their readiness to blame the newcomer hadn't escaped her notice, either.

On a positive note, Isobel was feeling more comfortable about her conversation with the artist the day before. Gaston now seemed to believe her story, although Izzy guessed that could change at any given time, just like the way that Monsieur Fabron had cast her out from the role as bakery assistant. She missed working, doing something with her hands and occupying her otherwise distracted mind in the long summer days.

She wished that Maurice would give her another trial run. Regardless of the negativity surrounding the period when she was locked up, Izzy knew that she was more than capable of contributing to the boulangerie and just needed a second chance to prove herself. After all, no matter what had gone on, Mallery and Hobbs would eventually catch the murderer and Maurice Fabron would be sorry for his actions, of that she was sure.

Before leaving in opposite directions after their chat at the riverbank, Gaston had invited Isobel to join him for dinner. She had said yes, and tonight would be her first venture into the public eye since returning from the police station. Izzy was nervous about how the other diners would react, but the artist had convinced her that the only way to let them believe in her innocence was for Isobel to carry on living normally, and that included going out for a meal.

She doubted whether Gaston saw the upcoming encounter as an actual date. After all, it had only been a couple of days since she'd reported to the police that she'd suspected him of having Cecile Vidal's blood on his shirt, but the artist held no bad feelings and the air had been cleared.

Isobel Green didn't really care what the French villagers thought of her. The most important person in her new life abroad had been Maurice Fabron and in that particular area it seemed that all was lost. The boulangerie owner had hardly been able to look Izzy in the eye after her altercation with Madame Dupuis, proving once and for all where his loyalties lay. If only things had been different, Isobel thought. There was, however, one positive side to her recent ordeal, and that was the fact that her parents and sister were still oblivious to her plight, meaning that they were unable to play judge and jury with her life this time.

Gaston Lauder had packed away his paints early that day, eager to get cleaned up and ready for his rendezvous with the Englishwoman. He had ironed a fresh shirt and shaved, leaving a couple of hours free to contact his agent in Paris and fulfil one last task before collecting Isobel from her apartment. The artist took a deep breath and headed out of Simone's cottage with a heavy heart. There was something he needed to confess to Maurice.

Monsieur Fabron was busy sweeping up crumbs from the boulangerie floor when Gaston arrived, a look of determination on his face as he battled with the prospect of dinner with Simone. It felt like a huge indiscretion, a slight to his late wife's memory, yet life had to move forward and it had to begin today.

'Hello, Gaston,' he greeted the young man. 'Do you want a baguette?'

The artist shook his head, unsure where to begin, but when he did, the torrent of words explaining that he was taking Isobel Green to dinner fell easily from his lips. They were not met with pleasure or with distaste; instead, Maurice Fabron looked bemused and surprised by the divulgence.

'Where are you taking her?' he asked simply.

'The Bistro.'

Maurice greeted the response with a frown, unable to comprehend that Gaston intended to take Izzy to dinner at the very same place he had promised to take Simone. He asked if there was a chance that the couple could change their reservation to a different night, but Gaston said no, Isobel needed to be seen before more accusations about her started circulating in the village.

'Never mind, it's not a problem,' the baker told Gaston.

At ten minutes to eight that evening, Maurice Fabron knocked lightly on Madame Dupuis' front door. He stood patiently watching for her shadow to appear in the hallway, hands balled up in frustration, brow furrowed in anticipation of an emotional outburst when he broke the news. Presently Simone's svelte silhouette made its way down the passage, slender and neat, perfectly dressed in a tightly-fitted red shift dress. The woman paused before turning the handle, presumably to check herself in the full-length mirror, and then swung the door wide to greet her friend.

'May we go inside for a moment?' Maurice asked softly, as Simone reached for her clutch bag. 'It won't take long.'

Madam Dupuis was an instinctive woman and knew immediately that all was not well 'Tell me, Maurice, what is it?'

She cast an eye over the man's tailored navy trousers and expensive pale blue shirt, noting that she hadn't seen the baker this well turned out since the death of his wife.

Monsieur Fabron wasted no time in explaining that Gaston and Isobel would be dining together at the bistro that night. He offered to cancel, fully understanding if Simone couldn't face the pair.

Instead, she sniffed, stepped outside and offered her arm to Maurice.

'How interesting!'

The bistro was half-full when Maurice arrived with Simone. The room was illuminated with soft downlights and, in typical French style, every table was adorned with a red gingham cloth and pillar candle. The owner fussed over his guests, ensuring that nothing was too much trouble, yet you couldn't help noticing that his eye kept wandering to a couple seated in the far corner.

Gaston turned awkwardly in his chair as the door opened. He had been anticipating Maurice's arrival for the past hour, secretly hoping that his friend might have persuaded Simone to stay home that night. He'd pre-warned Isobel of the expected appearance of the two villagers, and her inward groan had spoken volumes about the incensed feelings it conjured up, yet they were here and so, too, were Maurice and Simone.

'Do you want to try some of this?' Gaston offered, attempting to distract his companion's eyes away from the newly arrived guests.

'What is it? Chicken?' she asked, slowly moving her focus to the plate in front of her dining companion.

'*Cuisses de grenouille*,' he informed her, lifting up the fork. 'Frog's legs.'

Izzy crinkled her nose. 'No, thanks. I'll stick with the avocado.'

'You're not getting very far,' Gaston commented, after polishing off his own starter. 'Not hungry?'

His companion winced. 'Stupid question, don't you think?' Isobel kept her eyes on the plate in front of her. 'I'd love to be a fly on the wall over there.'

'A fly? Why?'

'To hear what they're saying,' she muttered, flicking a glance at the artist. 'It's a daft English expression.'

Gaston turned his head just enough to see Maurice and Simone perusing their menus. 'They're just here for dinner, the same as us. Ignore them.'

Maurice ordered a medium-priced bottle of red wine, unsure whether a cheap one might offend Simone, or an expensive one give her the wrong idea about their night out. He was loath to think of this meal as a date, preferring to look at it as a gesture of goodwill rather than anything more intimate. This was his apology, a way to make amends after being so unsociable, and the first step in moving forward with his life. He would never contemplate courting Simone, not after Valerie's warning about her friend, yet Maurice considered her a good listener and delightful dinner guest.

'She's a gold-digger.' Monsieur Fabron's wife had warned one evening. 'A good friend, but nevertheless not one to be trusted with other women's husbands.'

At the time, Maurice had dismissed Valerie's remark as unwarranted but, turning the words over in his mind some time later, he'd wondered whether there was any truth in his wife's vindictive comment. Still, it was too late to find out now, he mused, as whatever had caused the outburst was well and truly buried.

Casting an eye at the woman across the table, the boulangerie owner noticed a pink flush in Simone's cheeks as she drank back the first glassful of wine, almost as though she were in a hurry to get drunk. Maurice dismissed the thought and put her eagerness down to the couple sitting at the back of the room and the brittle air they'd caused amongst the other village diners.

'Maurice,' Simone said softly, looking cautiously around the room, 'Dominique and I thought we might start a petition. I know we can rely on your support, of course…'

The baker leaned back, allowing the waiter to put a dish of mussels in front of them both and then waited until the man had retreated. 'A petition for what?'

Madame Dupuis looked down at the shellfish and then lifted her gaze upwards. 'Why, to force Isobel Green to leave Saint Margaux, of course.'

'You must be joking!' he blurted. 'She has nowhere to go and the police still have her passport. It's a ridiculous idea.'

Simone curled her lips, fighting back the urge to get up and leave. 'That woman has caused nothing but trouble, Maurice. After she accused Telo of being involved in Cecile's death, I would have thought you, for one, would be glad to get rid of her.'

The florist had undoubtedly underestimated her friend and became even more indignant when he replied, 'I will have nothing to do with your petition. Although Isobel wasn't honest with me about her past, I feel that's all it is – her past. Being involved in someone's death over a decade ago does not mean she is guilty this time. Anyway, as soon as she can, Isobel will be leaving.'

'Pah! How on earth can you be sure of that?'

Maurice looked steadily across the table and lifted a fork to eat his entrée. 'Because she told me so, and I happen to believe her.'

Down the street in Monsieur Fabron's 'Maison de Maitre', Telo had finished the *croque-monsieur* that his father had left for supper and was upstairs in his bedroom. A French copy of *Dracula* lay on the top of the bedcover, but the young man was distracted by something that sat in his bedside drawer.

Slowly sliding out the piece of blue tissue paper, Telo unfolded the edges and peered at the gleaming gold brooch inside. It was formed in the shape of a leaf and was studded with purple amethysts, a pretty antique piece of jewellery that was worth a few hundred Euros at least. He rubbed a thumb over the smooth surface, marvelling at how the gemstones sparkled under the light from his bedside lamp. Telo wasn't stupid and knew that he shouldn't tell anyone that he had this brooch, yet the burning desire to confess to his father was eating him up. Maybe when Papa comes home, he thought. Maybe later.

'Are you done?' Gaston asked, gesturing with his knife towards Isobel's unfinished sea bass and vegetables. 'May I?'

Izzy pushed the plate forward, amazed that the artist could manage to eat the rest of her meal after polishing off a plate of frog's legs followed by a sirloin steak and fries. 'Sure, go ahead.'

Gaston pushed his own empty plate to one side and tucked into the fish. 'This sauce is superb. What was it, lobster?'

Isobel nodded, her eyes straying over to the front of the restaurant where her former employer seemed to be having an altercation with Madame Dupuis.

'Erm, yes, it was. It's delicious but I'm just too full.'

The artist pushed another forkful of fish into his mouth and swallowed. 'Nothing to do with a certain couple over there, then?'

Izzy shrugged. 'Well, it doesn't help. Of all the nights to choose to come out…'

Gaston set down his cutlery and touched her hand 'It doesn't matter, you're going to have to face everyone sooner or later. I think Maurice is worried about you. He feels bad for what has happened.'

'Well,' Isobel murmured, 'he doesn't need to.'

'Look, as soon as the police arrest Cecile's murderer, the easier things will get for you. Trust me, I promise.'

Gaston's face looked sincere and bright, definitely not the visage of someone hiding a deadly secret, yet, after all that had occurred in the past week, Isobel was unsure whether she could trust anyone completely.

'Do you know who murdered Cecile?' she asked, unsure of what to expect from the handsome gent across the table.

'No, Isobel, I don't,' he said openly, 'and I'm very disappointed that you asked.'

An hour or so later, Maurice Fabron left the bistro with Simone on his arm. She had drunk far too much wine and was as talkative as ever, although not everything coming out of her mouth made sense to the baker.

'Won't you come in, please?' she begged, tugging Maurice towards the white cottage. 'Let's have another drink. What about a cognac?'

Monsieur Fabron lifted the woman's fingers from his shirt and stood waiting while she hunted for the front door key. 'No, Simone. I'm going home.'

Madam Dupuis blew out her cheeks and made a huffing sound. 'Please yourself. Goodnight, Maurice.'

She lurched forward, open-mouthed and ready for a full-on kiss but Maurice deftly stepped to one side avoiding the collision.

'No, Simone.'

The man waited until he was sure the florist was safely inside and then strode across the village square towards his own residence. He could clearly see a light on in Telo's bedroom and smiled. He would be able to spend a few minutes with Telo before bed, which would no doubt include the usual milk ritual.

'Goodnight, Gaston,' Izzy was saying as she leaned against the doorframe that led up to her cosy apartment. 'I'll see you tomorrow.'

'Aren't you going to invite me in?' he grinned, tilting his head to one side in mock dejection.

'Not tonight,' she said automatically. 'I just don't think it would be a good idea, do you?'

The artist shrugged, taut muscles tightening under the cotton seams of his shirt, 'What difference would it make? After all, I know you're attracted to me...'

Isobel pushed her key into the lock and turned back to look over her shoulder. 'Is that so? Goodnight, Gaston.'

She swiftly slid inside and closed the door before her companion could utter another word. It had been a strange evening and an extremely stressful day, yet Isobel feared that Gaston could be right. She might actually be very attracted to him indeed.

As Monsieur Fabron reached the top of the stairs, he paused to watch his son through the crack in the doorjamb. Telo was rolling something over in the palm of his hand and it sparkled against his pale fingers.

'Telo, do you want some milk?'

The young man jumped at the sound of his father's voice, yet was too slow to hide the golden brooch from Maurice's eyes as he entered the room.

'What is that?'

Telo dutifully opened out his fingers to reveal the treasure.

'Ah, your mother's,' his father sighed, recognising the brooch as the boy's mother's favourite piece of jewellery. He recalled that Valerie and Cecile had been given identical brooches by their father one Christmas. The women had proudly worn the items on their coats, jackets and cardigans every day, signalling the bond between them as sisters.

Telo shook his head, loosening his grip on the brooch. 'No.'

Maurice looked puzzled. He was sure that he'd shown Telo all of the pieces in Valerie's trinket box. Nevertheless, he was too tired to disagree and instead reached for the empty glass that sat rimmed with milk on his son's bedside cabinet. It irritated the baker that he'd arrived home too late to make Telo a bedtime drink. He leaned forward and kissed the young man's head.

'Goodnight, my dear son.'

Undressed and standing in the bathroom, Maurice looked at his reflection in the wide vanity mirror. He considered himself to be fairly fit for a man in his mid-fifties, yet there were tell-tale signs that he didn't hold with a regular exercise regime in the form of a slight thickening of his waist, loose skin on his upper arms and the beginnings of a double chin. He wasn't half as handsome as he had been on the day that he'd married his beloved Valerie. Still, nowadays there was no-one to impress, no queue of women ready to fill his lonely hours, nobody special to wine and dine.

Monsieur Fabron wondered whether taking Simone out to dinner had been a mistake. Her intention to raise a petition against Isobel was cruel and unnecessary, showing the florist's true colours and he hadn't liked what he'd seen. Maybe Valerie had been right about her friend. Simone had certainly shown her vindictive side tonight and, with too much wine inside her, she had appeared more than willing to lure Maurice into her den. It wasn't what he wanted, not in any small degree. Despite Simone Dupuis being a good friend after his wife's death, the baker was neither ready nor willing to take it a step further. He would step back, starting tomorrow.

Before climbing into bed, Maurice paused to lay a hand on his wife's jewellery box. It hadn't been moved and he was curious as to why Telo would choose tonight to remove the leaf-shaped brooch. Gently lifting the lid, causing the tiny ballerina figure inside to start twirling to a tinkling melody, Maurice peered inside. There, on its tiny velvet pillow where it had always been, sat Valerie's golden brooch.

Monsieur Fabron gasped out loud, a look of fear and alarm crossing his face. If Valerie's brooch was still here, then the one that Telo had in his room could only have belonged to Cecile. So, how would his son have got hold of it?

Clammy with perspiration as his blood pressure rose, Maurice padded across the landing to his son's bedroom. The young man lay on his side, head pressed into the pillow, his fingers curled as he slept. Silently, Maurice prised the hand open and looked down at the purple gemstones. There was absolutely no doubt in his mind now that Telo was holding Cecile's brooch, the brooch that she had worn every day for the past twenty or more years. It could only mean one thing; either Telo knew who had murdered his sister-in-law, or the boy had been involved!

CHAPTER EIGHTEEN – NEW LIGHT ON THE MATTER

Jean Manon entered the Bordeaux Police Headquarters and stepped briskly up to the reception desk. He had returned from a vacation in Switzerland the previous evening and had been alarmed to find dozens of messages on his telephone answering-machine, some from his boss at the Railways office and others from the local force.

'*Bonjour, j'ai rendez-vous avec Inspector Mallery,*' he told the woman behind the desk, pulling off a pair of brand new sunglasses as he spoke.

'*Oui, asseyez-vous,*' the woman told him, gesturing towards a row of plastic chairs lined up against the wall.

Monsieur Manon took a seat and looked around the white-washed foyer. He'd been alarmed to hear the news of Cecile Vidal's death, partly because it had happened on a train line that he supervised, but mainly due to the fact that everyone knew the vineyard owner and thought very highly of her. His wife, Louisa, had been distraught to think there was a murderer in their midst and told Jean that she flatly refused to leave the house until he was caught.

It was typical, the stationmaster thought; the only time they had taken a vacation away from modern technology and this had happened! The trip had been a well-deserved anniversary treat and they'd relaxed more in those few days than ever he could recall in earlier years.

He watched the receptionist speak quietly into the phone and waited.

'Jacques,' Mallery called, sticking his head around the Incident Room door where four sets of shoulders were hunched over their computers, 'the stationmaster is here. Interview Room Three.'

Jack Hobbs closed his browser and took a sip of water from a plastic bottle.

'Yes, sir,' he replied, wiping his lips. 'Coming.'

Max strode out and took the stairs two at a time, eager to meet Jean Manon in person. With the stationmaster having been on holiday for over a week with no mobile phone coverage in his remote Swiss cabin, the Inspector had lots of questions to ask and didn't intend to waste time on small talk.

'*Bonjour, Monsieur Manon*,' Max greeted the portly gent, immediately noting the highly polished buttons on the man's uniform and perfect knot in his 'Railway' commissioned tie. There was also a strained look about the stationmaster. No doubt he had been shocked on hearing that the police needed to interview him urgently and Mallery decided to tread carefully.

Jack Hobbs appeared seconds afterwards and led the way to the interview room.

The Inspector made the usual introductions, asking Monsieur Manon if he was comfortable speaking in English so that Jack, the team's temporary recruit, could follow the line of questioning.

'No problem,' Jean smiled, taking in the fiery red-haired detective. 'My English is not great, but I will try my best to give all the information you need.'

'Now,' Max began, 'please could you think about the day before your holiday, the Wednesday. I believe you were in the ticket office that morning?'

Jean paused, then his eyes lit up. 'Yes, that's right. The usual attendant was late on that day, so I worked in the office until about nine-thirty.'

'Now, please think carefully. Do you know the Englishwoman who works for Monsieur Fabron in the Saint Margaux boulangerie? Her name is Isobel.'

The stationmaster looked perplexed and scratched his head. 'Isobel? Well, I don't know her, exactly, but I met her a couple of times.'

'Where?' Jack asked, looking up from his notepad.

'Now, let me see. Well, the first time was in Maurice's shop when I went in after work to buy some croissants. Then the second time was on that Wednesday morning, at the railway station.'

The two detectives looked at one another momentarily, relieved to see an immediate connection between Isobel Green and the day of the murder.

Max leaned forward, pressing his palms on the table. 'Now, Monsieur, this is vital. Do you remember if she bought a ticket and if she got on the early morning train to Bordeaux on that day?'

Jean Manon sat upright in the chair, proud that he had such a good recollection of events. It was one of his best traits.

'I certainly do, Inspector. She wanted to purchase a ticket but didn't have enough cash and our card machine wasn't working, so she walked back in the direction of the car park.'

'You're absolutely sure?' Hobbs pressed, biting the end of his pen.

'Yes, I have no doubt. The train arrived shortly afterwards, and the Englishwoman wasn't on it.'

'Now,' Max continued, 'do you remember seeing Madam Vidal that day?'

Monsieur Manon nodded. 'Yes, indeed. She bought two tickets and got on the train. We chatted for a few minutes. She was going shopping and having lunch with a friend. It is terrible what happened to her.'

Jean sniffed, trying to compose himself as tears welled up in his eyes.

'Two?' Jack said quickly. 'You said Madam Vidal bought two tickets?'

'Yes, that's right. Cecile's friend was running late, and she had to cut through the path at the back of the station. I saw her arrive just in time. She nearly missed the train completely!'

Inspector Mallery rose and laid a hand on the stationmaster's shoulder. 'Monsieur Manon, did you recognise this friend?'

Jean looked up, feeling the change in atmosphere as both detectives waited patiently for his response.

'*Bien sûr*. I know her very well. It was Simone Dupuis.'

'What the hell?' Mallery shouted, as soon as he returned to the Incident Room.

'What happened?' Gabriella asked, pushing her chair away from the cluttered workstation and looking expectantly at her boss.

'Madam Dupuis got on the train with Cecile that morning,' he explained, looking at the sea of faces in front of him 'But we only have Jean Manon's testimony. We have to go back through the CCTV footage.'

Luc began clicking his fingers over the computer keyboard, searching for the footage that he'd gone over dozens of times before.

'I guess it could be Simone Dupuis,' he said, squinting at the grainy image, 'Although whoever it is was dressed all in black, no front view of the face.'

Max paced the room thinking.

'Suppose she stabbed Cecile Vidal between Saint Margaux and Salbec. She could have got off the train there and then returned to Saint Margaux. Is that a possibility?'

'What about that boutique receipt that Isobel Green mentioned?' Jack asked, flipping papers around on his desk. 'If it was hers, then Simone Dupuis was in Bordeaux that morning.'

Mallery pointed a finger at Luc. 'There was no footage from the camera at Salbec, right?'

Luc pushed the long fringe out of his eyes. 'It wasn't working.'

'Right, come on, Jacques. We're driving out to Salbec to see if anyone remembers seeing Madam Dupuis at the station that morning. Grab that photo of her from the board and meet me downstairs.'

Salbec station was deserted. It was the kind of place that would have made the perfect television location for a period drama set at the turn of the century. The red brick ticket office was connected to a set of public conveniences and a tiny waiting room, all three blocks looking uninviting and neglected. Its windows had gathered so much dust that you could easily write your name in it and birds nested in the eaves of the ancient iron bridge that joined both sides of the railway track.

'It's like a ghost town,' Jack commented, as their heels clicked against the stone cobbled path leading to the platform. 'I'll check the ticket office.'

Peering in through the single square window, Hobbs cupped his hands to block out the sunlight. The shade revealed a huge bear of a man, fast asleep in a chair that looked ready to split in half from the weight of its heavy burden. Jack tapped gently with two fingers, but the man failed to wake.

'Monsieur!' Max shouted, banging loudly on the glass over Jack's shoulder and causing his companion to jump. 'Police!'

The huge figure stirred slowly, lifting his head to find the source of the disturbance. He focussed one eye on the men outside and struggled to his feet.

As soon as the station worker let himself out through the ticket office door, he was bombarded with questions by the irate Inspector. Have you seen this woman? When? Where did she go? Jack Hobbs struggled to keep up with his boss's interrogation but got the gist of the responses, thanks to the large railway employee's slow way of speaking as Simone's photo was thrust in his face.

Yes, he remembered seeing that woman. It's a quiet village and they don't get many pretty ladies catching trains from here. There was something odd, though, he recalled, scratching his head for a second. The woman had run quickly from the early morning train and had gone straight into the lavatory, as though she was desperate. Mallery asked why that should be odd, to which the man explained that she had spent over half an hour in there and she had been dressed in black going into the restroom but, on coming out, was wearing blue.

'Do you get that, Jacques?' Max asked, looking at the younger man. 'Simone Dupuis changed clothes here and then got back on the next train to Bordeaux.'

Hobbs sucked in his breath, feeling the thrill of the chase as they closed in on their newest suspect. 'Jeez!'

A few more words were exchanged in French before the station worker pointed towards the grim-looking ladies room.

'Come on,' Max urged. 'Apparently the bins in the public washrooms haven't been cleaned out yet. It's only done once every two weeks.'

The detectives raced forward, each keeping step with the other in anticipation of what they might find, before pushing open the door of the women's toilets. They were greeted with an acrid odour that suggested it had been far longer than a fortnight since the place had last been cleaned.

'You start from that end…' Max instructed, opening the door to the first cubicle, a hand over his mouth.

The call came after Mallery had been in the tiny compartment for a mere five seconds. 'Sir, I think I've found something.'

Stuffed into the bottom of the plastic waste bin was a long-sleeved black tunic and a pair of dark trousers, and both were heavily coated in dried blood.

After twenty minutes of additional questioning, Mallery and Hobbs were back in the BMW and heading down the highway towards Bordeaux with an evidence bag containing the bloodied clothing securely in the boot. They were now in possession of some vital information and needed the assistance of the team to pull out all stops in preparation for an arrest.

'*C'est bien*,' Max murmured as he pulled into the fast lane. 'This is good. But we made a fatal mistake, didn't we, Jacques?'

'Yes, sir,' Hobbs replied, mulling over the morning's findings. 'We should have checked the later CCTV footage at Bordeaux. Then we would have seen Simone Dupuis arriving on the later train.'

'Correct!' The Inspector smiled. 'But nevertheless, we got there eventually. How would you feel about becoming a permanent part of the team?'

Jack was slightly taken aback at the offer; he wasn't even sure if it was legally possible. 'Do you think you could swing it, sir?'

Max shrugged, keeping his eyes firmly fixed on the road. 'Why not? I've known stranger things than having a Yorkshire man on my team! You'd have to promise to improve your French, though!'

The younger detective felt proud that he might be able to find his feet in Bordeaux. It would also stop Angélique from worrying about their future together in France.

'In that case, yes,' he said, grinning. 'I'd be honoured.'

Back at the police headquarters, the team gathered for ten minutes before rushing off in different directions, each intent on fitting their own part of the case together.

Luc immediately connected with the national rail camera system and located footage of the nine o'clock train into Bordeaux, the one which they hoped to catch Simone Dupuis alighting from.

Gabriella raced to the forensics lab three blocks away, the plastic bag containing vital evidence on the back seat of her car.

Thierry was dispatched to the local café to fetch coffee and baguettes, Max insisting that the police canteen food just wouldn't suffice to fuel the hungry team.

In the meantime, the Inspector beckoned Jack over to the whiteboard that took up almost one full wall in the Incident Room.

'We still don't have a motive,' he pondered, circling Simone Dupuis' name with a thick black marker pen. 'Supposedly, the women were close friends.'

Hobbs rubbed his chin, thinking hard. 'I'm still puzzled over the break-in at the Vidals'. I'm sure it's connected.'

'But how? Simone Dupuis doesn't strike me as a burglar and what could possibly benefit her from looking in the Vidals' safe?'

Jack couldn't answer, although he felt the murder was definitely connected to the break-in. He could feel it in his bones.

In Saint Margaux, Maurice Fabron waited patiently for his son to return from the morning deliveries and stood at the door of the boulangerie, looking out for the arrival of their Citroën van. It wasn't long before the vehicle appeared along the main street, Telo holding on to the steering-wheel with both hands as he concentrated on navigating the parked cars and wandering pedestrians. Maurice felt guilty for having to ask the young man to look after the shop for an hour or so, but, after their conversation over breakfast that morning, there was a pressing matter to attend to.

'*Salut*,' the baker called as Telo entered through the back kitchen, holding up a jug of fresh orange juice. '*Tu veux le jus des fruits?*'

The youngster nodded eagerly and watched as his father picked up a glass.

'*Je vais partir maintenant,*' Maurice told him.

Telo nodded, stretching out his hand to pass over the van keys.

Maurice stepped forward and put both arms around his son, kissing him on the cheek. '*Pas de problème.*'

There was no reply, but Telo understood that his Papa must leave for a while to speak with Uncle Hubert. He knew that it was something to do with the brooch that he'd been given but couldn't comprehend exactly what.

Hubert Vidal was in the kitchen talking with Madam Paradis when his brother-in-law arrived. The grey-haired housekeeper stopped peeling vegetables and greeted Maurice warmly, asking eagerly about Telo and saying that she hadn't seen the lad for a while.

'*Telo est bon.*' The boulangerie owner smiled. '*Merci.*'

Hubert lifted a silver tray with a cafetière and cups on it, suggesting to his guest that they retire to the study.

Madam Paradis watched the men retreat before turning back to her task, thinking nothing of the two relatives getting together for a mid-morning coffee.

'You said on the phone that there was something urgent…' Hubert began, gently pushing down the filter on the coffee pot. 'What is it, Maurice?'

'It's quite a delicate matter,' the baker explained, taking a seat by the window yet still fixing his eyes on the winemaker. 'I need to ask you something.'

Hubert gave a short laugh. 'Come on, we're like brothers, you can ask me anything. What's wrong? Are you in financial difficulty?'

Maurice puckered his lips. 'No, of course not. It's rather a delicate matter, but very important nevertheless.'

Hubert splayed his hands. 'Go on, I'm listening.'

'On the day that Cecile… erm, passed away, was she wearing the leaf-shaped brooch that her father gave her?'

The vineyard owner frowned, surprised at the question and unsure of the answer. 'Well, I think so. She wore it practically every day.'

Hubert walked around to his desk and opened the bottom drawer. 'These are Cecile's belongings that the police brought here. As you can see, her wedding ring and watch are here, and the pearl earrings she loved, but no, no brooch.'

Maurice looked at the bag in his brother-in-law's hand, already knowing that the gold item wouldn't be there before he'd even looked. He dipped a hand into his own trouser pocket and pulled out something that had been carefully wrapped in blue tissue paper.

'Here. Here it is, Hubert.'

The tall man took the proffered parcel and opened it up, incredulous at what he was being given but still not fully understanding how the brooch could have ended up in Maurice's possession.

'Where did you get this, Maurice?' he asked, picking up the amethyst brooch.

'I'm afraid it was given to Telo a few days ago. I only found out last night.'

'Given to Telo?' Hubert repeated. 'But by whom?'

Maurice swallowed, feeling his throat dry up as he spoke. 'Simone Dupuis.'

'*Où est son Papa?*' Madam Dupuis was asking, as Telo prepared two espressos.

'*Je ne sais pas,*' the young man lied.

He could feel Simone's feline eyes boring into his back as he took due care and time over pouring the drinks, certain that the woman would be angry when she found out that his Papa had actually gone to Uncle Hubert's to show him Cecile's brooch.

Behind them, Dominique Fabre was becoming impatient and beckoned her friend to sit down and chat, asking Telo if they might have two slices of chocolate torte to go with their morning caffeine fix. She was excited about the petition against Isobel Green's residency but was astute enough not to say it out loud in front of the boulangerie owner's son.

Telo stood rigid with his back to the women, afraid that his Aunt Simone might get angry with him if she found out that Papa now had the brooch. He didn't know why Simone giving him the piece of jewellery was supposed to be kept a secret, but that's what she'd told him as she handed it over.

'*Telo,*' Simone repeated, '*où est son Papa?*'

The young man bit the skin on the inside of his mouth. He was a terrible liar, his father had always told him so.

'*Avec mon oncle Hubert.*'

Simone narrowed her eyes and put a hand on Telo's shoulder to forcibly turn him towards her. '*Pourquoi?*' she demanded.

Telo Fabron could feel the florist's sharp nails digging into his skin. The young man dropped his chin down onto his chest and instantly Madam Dupuis knew the reason. Telo had divulged their secret.

It was Dominique who spoke next, wondering why the espressos hadn't been forthcoming as rapidly as usual and she asked if everything was alright.

Her friend made a muffled sound and placed a hand to her mouth. '*Non, non.*'

As Maurice parked up the Citroën van and eased himself out into the midday sun, he was torn between finishing his day's work, immediately demanding an explanation from Simone Dupuis, or telephoning Inspector Mallery. As it happened, the choice was immediately taken from his hands as the florist darted around the corner to meet him.

'Maurice!' she cried, tears streaming down her face. 'Thank goodness you are back. There is the most distressing news. Telo has confessed!'

'What are you talking about, Simone? Please, calm down.'

The woman crumpled, laying a hand on her friend's arm for support. 'The boy, he told me what he has done. I am so sorry to break this to you, after all you are the most wonderful father, but Telo has told me everything.'

'Really?' The baker frowned. 'And pray tell me, what has he done?'

Simone searched her pocket for a handkerchief, avoiding Maurice's wary gaze. 'He told me that he stabbed Cecile. I'm so sorry that you have to find out like this.'

As the boulangerie owner stood incredulous in the rear courtyard, with Madam Dupuis hanging off his arm like a pet bird, Telo Fabron appeared in the kitchen doorway, his eyes pleading with Maurice to come inside.

'Papa,' he said simply, ignoring the crying woman. '*Salut.*'

'Don't be hard on him,' Simone begged, her whispering voice a hiss in the baker's ear. 'I don't think he understands. You know how Telo is prone to having temper tantrums. Perhaps that's what happened with Cecile.'

'Let me deal with this,' Maurice replied, leaving the weeping woman and bustling his son inside the kitchen. The bolt was drawn across without a single backward glance, leaving the florist's fate hanging in the balance.

With the boulangerie sign turned to *FERMÉ* to indicate that it was now closed, Maurice poured two cups of tea and told his son to take a seat. Telo remained silent, unsure of what Simone had told his father and determined to get his own mind straight about the events of that morning before saying anything. As soon as his aunt had burst into tears and declared his guilt in front of Dominique, Telo had panicked and run to the rear kitchen, leaving the women to express their shock and to console one another. He vaguely recalled Madam Fabre running out of the boulangerie in the direction of the gift shop, but he'd had no idea where Simone Dupuis had gone.

Maurice cajoled gently, asking again how Telo had come to possess his Aunt Cecile's precious brooch. Again, as he had done the night before, the young man repeated how Simone had given it to him for safe-keeping, telling him sternly that he wasn't to show the item to anyone else, nor to speak about it at all. It was to be their secret, she'd said, nobody else could know.

Satisfied that Telo was telling the truth, Monsieur Fabron rubbed a hand over his tired and weary face and then got up to use the phone.

'Inspector Mallery,' Max shouted above the din of the Incident Room, where both the clicking of keyboards and the intense chatter was at its highest level yet. '*Oui, Monsieur Fabron.*'

Mallery waved a frantic hand to calm the detectives around him, who were pulling out all the stops to wind together a tight case against the Saint Margaux florist. Everyone stopped what they were doing and stared at the Inspector. His face was tense and deep in thought, lines gathering at the bridge of his nose.

After a few minutes, Max pressed the 'close call' button and looked at his team.

'Telo Fabron has been found with a brooch belonging to the victim,' he explained, walking over to the whiteboard and picking up a marker pen. 'Apparently, she never took it off and, according to Monsieur Vidal, she would definitely have been wearing it on the day she was murdered. And we can all guess who gave it to him, can't we?'

'Simone Dupuis,' Gabrielle breathed. 'Do you think she was trying to set up Telo Fabron?'

'Sounds like it,' the boss replied, agitated that something so important had only just come to light. 'But, lucky for us, Maurice Fabron knows his son well enough and has managed to get the whole story out of him.'

A phone rang on Gabriella's desk and all heads turned in her direction as she made a short apology and answered it. '*Oui*?'

There was silence as she listened, scribbling a few notes on a pad as she did so.

'Sir,' Gabriella called, 'forensic tests are complete. The blood on the clothing found at Salbec station is a match for Cecile Vidal. There are also a few strands of dark hair and some skin cells which don't belong to the victim.'

The room fell silent as everyone contemplated the news. Their main suspect was now Simone Dupuis, who had thick, lustrous dark hair, but Isobel Green was also naturally dark, and Max was reluctant to rule out the possibility of her involvement in the murder.

Max ushered the rest of the group over to Jack's desk and put his hands on his hips. 'We need a DNA sample from Madame Dupuis. Any volunteers, Jacques?'

Hobbs groaned and picked up his car keys.

CHAPTER NINETEEN – THE SPIDER'S WEB

'Madam Dupuis, I am here to request a DNA sample from you,' Jack announced, pushing the door of the florist's shop closed behind him and turning the sign to *FERMÉ*. 'It's in connection with the murder of Cecile Vidal.'

'What? Don't be ridiculous!' Simone cried. 'Telo Fabron has already confessed to murdering my dear friend. It's him you should be asking for DNA.'

Hobbs was perplexed. 'I know nothing about that, Madame. As I said, I'm here to take a mouth swab and hair follicle from you.'

The slender, chic woman stood still, eyeing the detective as though he were a delicate morsel of prey. 'What if I refuse?'

'Are you refusing?'

Simone folded her arms and tilted her chin upwards. 'If you follow up my claim about Telo, then I am willing to comply.'

Hobbs nodded. 'Okay, I'll look into it.'

Walking down the street with Simone Dupuis' samples securely in his messenger bag, Jack Hobbs headed straight for the boulangerie.

Maurice Fabron was coming through from the back kitchen with a batch of custard tarts. He looked worn out, with dark circles beneath his eyes.

'Monsieur Fabron,' the detective began, tapping his fingers nervously on the glass counter. 'Do you have a minute to talk, please?'

Maurice slid the warm tarts onto a shelf and shrugged, the smell of nutmeg and vanilla wafting up towards Jack's nose. 'Of course. What is it?'

The detective delicately relayed Madame Dupuis' accusation, asserting his own belief that Telo hadn't been involved in the crime, but reiterating the fact that he was just following up on a serious allegation.

'There is only one way to solve this, isn't there?' Maurice replied, having stayed silent throughout Jack's explanation. 'Take a sample of Telo's DNA, too!'

'Monsieur Fabron, I'm sure there's no need for that...' Hobbs told the baker.

But it was too late. Maurice was already shouting for his son to come through to the café area, in animated French.

Sitting in his Ford Mondeo, having now accumulated two sets of DNA samples instead of just one, Jack Hobbs scratched his head in thought. There were still many dots to join in this case and, for him, one of the most aggravating was the strange break-in at the vineyard. It seemed to hold so many clues, yet didn't really connect with any of the evidence that they had so far.

On a whim, the young detective started up the motor and headed out of the village. But, instead of carrying on towards the main highway back towards Bordeaux, he turned off at the sign for the Saint Margaux vineyard.

Hubert Vidal was outside when Jack pulled up. He was helping a robust and jovial customer to heft cases of wine into the boot of an estate car. The winemaker looked unfazed by the exertion of lifting, but the same couldn't be said of his red-faced companion.

'*Bonjour*,' Jack called, hoping that he wouldn't be expected to continue the rest of the conversation in French.

'Ah, Detective Hobbs,' Hubert replied. 'What brings you here?'

Jack marvelled at the way in which the vineyard owner spoke English so effortlessly and made a note to himself to ask Angélique to practice French more often at home.

The men waited until the customer was well on his way down the long driveway before resuming their conversation.

'There were a few things I wanted to ask you,' Jack told Hubert. 'About the robbery, mainly.'

'The robbery? I thought the police would be more concerned with capturing my wife's killer!' Hubert didn't look irate but there was a slight sarcasm in his words as he spoke.

'It's just a hunch,' the detective confessed, 'but I think the two might be connected.'

'Come on into the house,' Hubert instructed, his interest piqued. 'I'll ask Madam Paradis to make a pot of English tea.'

'So, what's this all about?' Monsieur Vidal asked, as soon as they were settled in the study with tea and biscuits.

'Would you mind telling me what the combination to the safe was? I presume you've changed it now, but I mean on the day of the break-in,' Jack replied.

Monsieur Vidal was curious to see where the line of questioning was heading but complied without hesitation. 'It was Cecile's birthday, 02-06-63.'

'An easy number for someone to guess, I should imagine. And who else would have known that date?' the detective continued, taking out his trusty notebook and pen.

'Any of the family, I suppose. My children, Maurice, Telo, Madame Paradis. And most of our friends, too, as we always held a party for Cecile's special day.'

'Would that include Simone Dupuis?' Jack ventured.

Hubert didn't answer straight away, but paused to take a sip of his tea, eyes flitting to the side as though avoiding the question.

'Yes, Simone Dupuis was a friend.'

Hobbs immediately picked up on Hubert's use of the past tense and leaned forward in his seat. 'You said *was*, Monsieur Vidal. Does that imply that you no longer consider Madame Dupuis to be a friend of the family?'

'Did I? Slip of the tongue. She is still a friend.'

Jack felt that there was more to the matter than Hubert was telling and pressed harder. 'If there's something you need to tell me, now would be the time.'

There was a long silence, in which the detective waited patiently, experience in the Leeds crime squad having taught him that all good things come to those who wait.

'It was nothing,' Hubert began solemnly. 'Just one night.'

Jack nodded at the other man, gently urging him to go on.

'Oh, I suppose there's nothing to be lost by telling you now,' the winemaker sighed. 'Last summer, Cecile went away overnight to a spa with her friend Dominique. Usually, Simone would have gone with them, but she was busy creating a wedding bouquet that weekend. Well, anyway, on the Saturday night Simone turned up here, saying that she wanted to discuss a surprise for Cecile. She'd had a few drinks, I think and was very talkative. We drank wine, had a little supper and that's all I remember.'

'So, nothing happened? I mean you didn't… erm… have sex or anything?'

'Detective Hobbs, I loved my wife very much,' Hubert sighed, shaking his head. 'But Simone must have put something in my drink that night because I woke up in bed the next morning with her asleep at my side. I honestly don't remember if anything untoward took place, but I can assure you that I didn't intend it to.'

'Did you report this to the police? Drugging someone is a criminal offence?'

Monsieur Vidal rubbed his hands over his face. 'I couldn't. If I'd reported it, then Cecile would have found out. She never would have forgiven me.'

'So, what did you do?'

'I told Simone to leave immediately. She begged me to forgive her, said she was in love with me, crazy woman. I was so angry that morning, I told her never to cross my path again, but of course, as she was one of Cecile's closest friends, we had to tolerate each other's company now and again.'

'Did she ever mention what had happened to your wife?' Jack inquired.

'No, she said nothing. But every now and again there would be a look on Simone's face… It's hard to describe, but it was almost as though she was telling me that one day, she'd seek her revenge.'

'I know this might sound like a tough question to answer, Monsieur, but do you think Simone Dupuis was capable of murdering Cecile?'

Hubert Vidal looked startled. 'No, never. They were best friends!'

'Thank you. You've been very helpful. Now, if you could just explain to me again the details of the document that were removed from your safe on the night of the break-in…'

Maurice was alone in the boulangerie. He'd told Telo to go out and get some fresh air but to stay away from the florist's shop. The young man had no intention of going anywhere near his Aunt Simone's place after she'd told those lies about him to Papa and he headed home to sit in the garden with a book.

As soon as the boulangerie owner was certain that his son was safely back at the 'Maison de Maitre', he called upstairs to the apartment. Maurice had a lot to apologise for, he realised that now, and it was about time he spoke to Isobel.

'What's up, Maurice?' the Englishwoman asked as she closed the door to her personal stairway, her voice low and faint. Even in a few days, it was obvious to see that his former assistant had lost weight. The casual jeans and t-shirt she wore were hanging off Isobel's slender frame.

'Izzy,' the baker smiled, 'please come and sit with me… have something to eat.'

'Look, if this is about me going out for dinner with Gaston…'

'*Non*,' Maurice assured her, 'it has nothing to do with that. I just want to make sure that you are alright, and to apologise.'

Isobel took a seat in the café area and looked expectantly at her former employer, unsure of whether she could face another heart-to-heart, or whatever it was that he intended to get off his chest.

'I think the police are going to arrest Simone for Cecile's murder.' Maurice told her openly, bringing a fresh bagel filled with smoked salmon and cream cheese to the table. 'I am so sorry for everything, Izzy, I should have believed you. What you have had to endure has been terrible.'

'*Simone*?' Isobel repeated, hardly able to believe her ears. 'I knew it!'

'You did? How?'

'Well,' Izzy explained as Maurice fussed with coffee, 'on the night that the bread knife disappeared from your kitchen, Simone Dupuis was there. I'm sure she must have taken the lighter out of my bag while I was there as well. She was also in Bordeaux on the day of the murder. I found a receipt from that expensive boutique in the bottom of the bag she gave me to put my clothes in at the police station.'

Monsieur Fabron was quiet for a moment, mulling over what he'd just heard, and then came to sit down with two cups of fresh coffee in his hands.

'On that Wednesday,' he urged, eyes lighting up, 'you went to the train station, but you didn't buy a ticket, *oui*? Did you see Simone there?'

Izzy was sure that she hadn't. 'No, I only noticed Cecile. But I was only at the ticket office for about a minute. There weren't many people on the platform, but I didn't see Simone, I'm absolutely sure.'

'That's a pity,' Maurice sighed. 'You could have been an important witness.'

Isobel smiled for the first time in many days. 'I hope the police are on to her now. You had a lucky escape, Maurice. You were out on a date with Simone!'

The baker scowled, annoyed at such a supposition. 'I most certainly was not! Simone Dupuis and I were friends, nothing more. I took her out to dinner because I felt bad for being rude to her the previous day. At the time, I had absolutely no clue that she could have carried out poor Cecile's murder.'

Izzy took a sip of coffee and raised her eyes to the handsome man's face. 'Tell me, Maurice, why are you willing to believe that Simone is guilty now?'

'Because she dared to accuse my son of the crime, and in that moment, I knew that only someone with a twisted mind would say such a thing about Telo.'

Jack Hobbs handed the DNA samples to Gabriella, who immediately raced off to the lab with them. His mind was still full of unanswered questions but suddenly there was light at the end of the tunnel. There were still a few more links to work out, but when this was over, he was going to celebrate with Angélique.

Max Mallery was already seated in the Incident Room when Hobbs had arrived back in Bordeaux and eagerly listened as the young detective relayed all the new information that he'd gleaned from Hubert.

'So, why would Madam Dupuis want to break into the Vidals' safe?' the Inspector queried, pressing his fingers into a steeple as he pondered the information. 'What could she possibly gain from it?'

'Well, apparently, the house that Monsieur Fabron lives in was jointly owned by his wife, Valerie, and her sister, Cecile Vidal. They inherited it from their father, who was quite a prominent figure in the area. The documents refer to the complete signing over of the property to Maurice Fabron, officiated by a notary, so that he is now the sole owner. Madam Dupuis was desperate to see what was inside the papers, as her own financial situation was quite dire.'

'In what way?' Thierry jumped in, sliding his office chair across the room.

'According to Hubert Vidal, Simone is on the verge of bankruptcy due to her extravagant lifestyle. That's why she rents out rooms to Gaston Lauder every summer, to make extra cash.'

'I'm still confused,' Max admitted, a deep furrow appearing on his brow. 'How could that document benefit Madam Dupuis?'

'She's a gold-digger,' Jack said bluntly. 'Basically, with the knowledge that Maurice Fabron owned the large house outright and was also making a healthy living from the boulangerie, she'd set her sights on becoming his next wife.'

'So why murder Cecile?' the Inspector probed. 'It makes no sense.'

'It was revenge for being snubbed by Hubert Vidal, after she'd tried to seduce him,' Hobbs announced proudly. 'And she broke into the safe quite easily, as the code was Cecile's birthday, so it wouldn't have taken much guesswork.'

'It's all making sense now, Jacques. Simone Dupuis had the opportunity to steal the bread knife and she could easily have taken Madam Green's lighter and planted it on Cecile's body. We also know that she got off the train in Salbec and changed her clothes.'

'We have CCTV footage of her exiting Bordeaux station now,' Luc called across the room. 'An hour later than we first expected. Clear as anything. Even with all the police around, she just calmly walked off the platform and out into the street.'

Both men crossed the room to look at the video evidence looping on Luc's computer screen. It was still in black and white, but Madam Dupuis could clearly be seen wearing a lighter shade of clothes, exiting the station without a second glance at the uniformed officers milling around the taped area, where the earlier train had been cordoned off to preserve the crime scene.

'All we need now is a DNA match,' Max smiled, rubbing his hands together, 'and then we're ready to arrest Madame Dupuis.'

'It shouldn't be long,' Gabriella added, coming into the room. 'I've promised to go out for dinner with the lab guy if he gets the results within two hours!'

'Where is she now?' Isobel asked, peering out into the deserted village square.

'I'm not sure,' Maurice admitted. 'But with luck, the police will be here soon to arrest her. I told Inspector Mallery about the brooch that Simone gave to Telo. It belonged to Cecile and Hubert confirmed that she would have most certainly have been wearing it on the day she died.'

Izzy finished the dregs of her black coffee and watched as the boulangerie owner picked up her empty plate. 'Thanks, Maurice.'

'You need to eat. I'm afraid you're losing weight.'

'No, I didn't mean for the baguette,' Izzy smiled, 'but it was delicious.'

'Then for what?'

'I don't know… Finally realising that I'm innocent, letting me stay, just thanks.'

'But will you now?' the baker ventured, tilting his head to one side.

'Will I what?'

'Stay. There's a job here for you if you want it.'

Isobel didn't hesitate in her response. 'No, not now. Too much has happened. As soon as I can, I'll move on. I've already applied for a job in Spain, so…'

Maurice turned away, busying himself behind the counter, but tears welled up in his eyes at the thought of everything that had passed between them.

Simone Dupuis had locked and bolted the florist's shop and was inside her cottage, changing her clothes. Gone was the demure red dress that she'd been wearing that morning and in its place Simone wore a white shirt and black capri pants with flat leather loafers. She placed a headscarf around her hair, tying it at the nape of her neck, and picked up a pair of designer sunglasses.

Simone was spooked. She'd been so careful, disposing of the clothes at Salbec station where she knew nobody would find them for weeks. The porter there was such an idle man and hadn't done a day's work in his life, she noted at the time, yet this morning's visit from the young English detective had come as a complete shock. Still, she smiled. Now that she had formerly accused Telo of the murder, the police would have no choice but to follow up on it. Then the real fun would begin. Madame Dupuis was confident that she had it all worked out.

The day before Cecile's murder she'd kindly offered to trim Telo's hair, a task that Maurice had entrusted to her since his son had been a small boy. It was ironic really, as Telo had begged his father to take him to the barber's shop in Salbec, yet Maurice had been too busy in the boulangerie with his new attractive employee, giving the florist the perfect opportunity to pacify Telo with a neat haircut. It had also given her chance to collect a few hairs afterwards, as she swept up the young man's locks from the kitchen floor, and plant them on Cecile's jacket on that fateful day. Simone had been quick-thinking, too, she told herself, in snatching the brooch from Cecile's limp body as she lay bleeding out on the seat of the train. It had been her careful planning that had aided Simone in framing Isobel Gilyard, or Green, too. The Englishwoman had been stupid to leave her bag lying around in Maurice's kitchen on that first day. It had taken Simone just seconds to find something small and light in there to slip into Cecile's pocket as she lay dying.

Madame Dupuis was proud of herself. Not only had she managed to accidentally expose Isobel as a murderer – that horrendous past of hers was an unexpected bonus – but she'd also tied Telo into the scene as an added safety net. If one got away with it, then the other would surely be charged. Besides, both were a threat to Simone's long-term plans. Isobel was younger, prettier and more energetic; it would only be a matter of time before she turned Maurice Fabron's eye. And young Telo – well, the boulangerie owner would never remarry whilst he had his son to remind him of the wonderful memory of Valerie.

The brooch had been their secret, hers and Telo's. The youngster had taken the golden leaf as a sign of his Aunt Simone's trust and love and had never asked how she'd come by it. Nor did Telo realise that, if the police had ever checked, there would still be traces of blood on the pin, accidentally left on there from the murderer's fingers as she had tugged the item from her victim.

The safe-breaking had been a pure whim. Simone had given in to curiosity and just couldn't let it lie. She'd known that there was something very personal and, she suspected, lucrative in those documents and she had to find out what. Reading the notarisation had only fuelled her desire to dig her claws into Maurice, now that he was richer than she had expected and all because of Cecile Vidal's generosity.

Cecile Vidal… Madame Dupuis rolled the name over on her tongue a few times before heading down the footpath towards the river. She felt no remorse at stabbing her best friend, the woman who had everything that Simone wanted yet had failed to achieve. Wealth, happiness, children and Hubert. Lucky, dead Cecile.

Gabriella lifted the phone on her desk and listened to the speaker with wide eyes, her jaw dropping open before she replaced the receiver.

'Sir, it's a match.'

Max strode purposely across the room and grinned. 'So, we've got her!'

'Yes, but there's another problem,' the female detective replied, her voice tense. 'I'm afraid both samples were a match.'

'What? What do you mean, both samples?'

'Well,' she explained. 'The skin samples from the bloodied clothing were a match for Simone Dupuis' DNA, but the hair they found on Cecile Vidal's jacket was a match for Telo Fabron.'

'*Merde*!' Max cursed out loud as he came closer. 'They were in it together.'

'This just doesn't make sense,' Jack told him. 'Telo had absolutely no reason to become involved in the murder of his own aunt.'

'We'd better get over to Saint Margaux,' Thierry sighed, picking up his car keys. 'Gabriella, are you ready?'

His colleague nodded, stood up and tightened her long, blonde ponytail.

'Right, you two go and pick up Telo Fabron,' Max instructed. 'Jacques, you come with me and we'll find Madame Dupuis.'

'What about me?' Luc cried, wanting a piece of the action. 'I suppose I get to sit here and answer the phones, as usual?'

'Come on then!' The Inspector grinned. 'We can use an extra pair of hands today. Let's go.'

With a whooping cheer, Luc was out through the door and down the stairs before Inspector Mallery could change his mind.

Gaston Lauder had been on the riverbank since dawn. He was determined to finish his work on the field of poppies that day and stood at his easel in deep concentration. Vibrant reds clashed with the blues of the sky and he was pleased with his progress so far, but the recent meal with Isobel Green was still weighing heavily on his mind, especially as Simone had refused to speak to him since she had spotted the couple at the bistro.

He wondered whether it was time to return to Paris. Although he'd arranged to stay until the end of August, Gaston didn't want to upset the florist and, given the strained relationships amongst the Saint Margaux residents at present, he thought it might be a good idea to leave early.

There was also the fate of Isobel to consider, the artist mused, as sweeping brushstrokes flitted across the canvas. He'd felt a connection with the Englishwoman and had enjoyed her company, despite what the villagers were saying about her. Gaston felt he would let Isobel down if he just disappeared. Perhaps a few more days to see that she was okay would suffice.

As sunlight filled the skies, the young man stopped to take a drink from the water bottle he'd brought with him to the river, unaware of events unfolding in Saint Margaux. He'd been out so early this morning, intentionally avoiding the wrath of his landlady, that Gaston had no idea of the accusations and lies that Simone had been telling. He loved Simone dearly. She'd been so generous in always preparing his meals, ensuring that the guest bedroom was comfortable and warm and giving him full use of the workshop during his summer sojourns.

Seeing Simone at dinner with Maurice at the bistro had given Gaston a ray of hope that the woman who cared for him like a mother, might now have found love. The artist regretted flaunting his new friendship with Isobel in front of his dear friends, although Maurice had understood, and he wondered whether Madame Dupuis would forgive his indiscretion. Therefore, when Gaston's landlady appeared on the footpath that ran behind the village that afternoon, he expected to have to deliver an apology and to get an earful in exchange.

CHAPTER TWENTY – TO CATCH A KILLER

As Max pushed himself out of Jack's Ford Mondeo, the leather seat squeaked with relief and a shrill ringing alerted him to an incoming call on his mobile phone. He pulled it from the top pocket of his shirt and glanced at the screen. The caller ID was withheld.

'*Oui, Mallery,*' he responded, aware that Hobbs was watching him covertly from the driver's side of the car. Max lowered his voice and turned away, '*Oh, ma chérie!*'

Jack tapped the bonnet of the car to get his boss's attention and signalled that he would meet him over at the florist's shop. He couldn't help noticing the light in Mallery's eyes as he spoke softly into his phone. It was obviously a woman.

A few drops of heavy rain landed on Gaston Lauder's canvas, causing blood-red lines to drop from the newly painted poppies like macabre tears, but he was too intrigued by Simone Dupuis' words to notice.

'I have done something terrible,' she confessed in slow French, twisting her hands together in frustration. 'Please forgive me.'

'Why? What have you done?'

'I planted Telo's hair on Cecile's jacket. I think the police will soon be here to arrest him.'

The artist gripped his curly locks in frustration and took a deep breath.

'Why the hell would you do that?' he shouted, looking around to check they were completely alone. 'You were supposed to use Isobel's hair.'

Simone pursed her lips, thinking. 'I know, but I couldn't get to her and I thought, by using Telo's hair, it might solve a lot of problems for us.'

'For you, you mean,' Gaston spat. 'With Telo out of the way, you could have Maurice all to yourself. Admit it, that's the reason you've been so stupid.'

'Don't you dare put all the blame on me!' the woman countered. 'You had just as much to do with Cecile's death as I did and, if you keep quiet and accept Telo's fate, we'll get away with it.'

Gaston paced across the grass, unable to believe that his landlady would let an innocent young man get locked up. Telo didn't deserve that. They were friends and trusted one another.

'You stabbed her, Simone,' he replied, after a long pause. 'Don't ever forget that. Letting Telo take the blame won't change a thing. All it will do is eat at your conscience every day for the rest of our lives.'

'Don't tell me about regret, Gaston. You held your hand over Cecile's mouth to stop her screaming as she died. You wanted her dead, too,' came the quick retort. 'Leave well alone and let Telo go to jail.'

Jack Hobbs was peering in through the window of the deserted florist's shop as Max approached, but his boss's beaming smile was caught in the reflection of the glass door. The English detective didn't have to guess too hard to find out what had caused such a turnaround in the Inspector's mood.

'There's no sign of her here, sir,' he said, pointing at the sign and locked door, 'and no answer at the cottage. Where do you reckon she'd be?'

Mallery looked around the square. Few people were out and about, and those that were, walked quickly as they went on with their daily errands.

'Let's try Fabron's boulangerie first. Gabriella and Thierry have gone over to the house to see if Telo's there.'

'Gaston, wait!' Simone screamed, racing to keep up with the artist whose legs were pumping as he ran towards the bridge and then turned left, in the direction of the local church. His face was full of determination, blood coursing through his veins as he took the fresh afternoon air into his lungs.

As Gaston reached Maurice's 'Maison de Maitre', a small car pulled up outside and a couple got out. He could tell they were detectives straight away by the smart leather jackets and designer jeans that they wore, and Gaston took a dive into some nearby bushes to avoid being seen. Scratched but unharmed, he parted the leafy foliage and peered out. The female was ringing the doorbell, while the man walked gingerly around the back of the house, one hand on the wall as he tried not to crunch the gravel under his feet.

Behind him, the artist could see Madame Dupuis standing in fear close to the church. Her face was fixed upon the two people at Maurice's house. It appeared that Gaston was too late to save young Telo from his undeserved fate.

'Monsieur Fabron,' Max said hurriedly, giving a quick nod in Isobel Green's direction, 'we need to find Simone Dupuis urgently.'

'I haven't seen her at all today,' Maurice informed him. 'She's usually in the shop until five on a Saturday. Have you come to arrest her?'

'Yes,' Mallery admitted, 'we have.'

Jack Hobbs stood in the doorway and glanced at Isobel, who wore a satisfied smile on her face. He blushed to the roots of his fiery red hair, embarrassed that they'd put the Englishwoman through a horrific ordeal when she had, in fact, been completely innocent.

'I also unfortunately have to inform you that we're going to have to arrest your son, too,' Max went on. 'Is he at home?'

Maurice's eyes flickered to his large, foreboding house across the square. 'Yes, he is, Inspector. I'm coming with you. Isobel, please take care of things here.'

Telo Fabron opened the huge oak front door and gazed at the pretty woman. She looked vaguely familiar, but the youngster wasn't sure where he'd seen her before.

'*Oui*?' he said simply, immediately alerted to the three figures dashing across the square towards him.

Gabriella slipped a foot into the doorjamb and then followed Telo's gaze.

'*Papa*?' he was calling. '*Qu'est-ce qui ne vas pas?*'

Jack knew this meant, *what's wrong?* He'd heard his wife say it enough times.

Maurice signalled to the detectives to stand back while he calmed his startled son and then led everyone into the kitchen.

'Telo's hair was found on Cecile Vidal's jacket,' Jack explained. 'I'm sorry, Monsieur Fabron, it's a definite match.'

The boulangerie owner shook his head. 'That's impossible. Telo wouldn't hurt anyone, let alone Cecile. He adored his aunt.'

Max put a hand on Maurice's shoulder. 'I know this is difficult, but we have evidence to the contrary. We'll have to take Telo in.'

While Inspector Mallery, Jack and Gabriella stood in the Fabron kitchen, Luc had arrived in Saint Margaux on his motorbike and parked up by the gift shop.

The gift shop owner was outside as quick as lightning, admiring the long-haired man's leather jacket and gleaming Triumph.

'*Bonjour,*' she said with a smile, tossing a thick brown curl over one shoulder. '*Je m'appelle Dominique Fabre.*'

Luc, unused to attention from the other sex, told the woman that he was with the police and didn't require her assistance.

Dominique pouted and then stepped back inside her shop, unsure of what she'd said or done to deserve such a curt reply. She contented herself with peering out from behind the pastel-coloured bunting instead, determined not to miss a thing.

Luc saw no sign of his boss or colleagues, so he immediately walked towards a lone figure that stood half in and half out of the bushes in front of the largest house in the village.

'*Monsieur!*' he called. '*Suivez-moi!*'

Gaston stepped out onto the pavement, aware that he must have looked like some kind of weirdo, spying in the bushes. He explained that he'd seen a man going around the back of his friend's house and pointed to the stone path that led to Maurice's garden. Luc hesitated for a second but decided that the man looked innocent enough and strode past him to the rear of the 'Maison de Maitre.'

As soon as Luc was out of sight, Gaston ran back down the lane to the church and searched for Simone. She wasn't amongst the ageing gravestones and the artist wondered whether she might have doubled back and returned to her cottage via the riverbank. All hope was now lost of him saving his precious painting, but Gaston thought it might be prudent to return to collect his easel and paints. He'd just have a quick look inside the church first, he thought, and then return to the cottage via the river.

Meanwhile, Thierry and Luc came face to face with one another as they prowled the perimeter of Maurice's grand house, each presuming the other to be a trespasser until they almost knocked each other out as they sprang forward in surprise. Thierry rubbed his head and punched Luc on the arm.

'Where is Mallery?' Luc whispered, as though on an undercover mission.

Thierry pointed to the kitchen window and raised his eyebrows. 'Here. We'll look for Madame Dupuis.'

Gaston knew his landlady better than anyone and found her kneeling in prayer at the altar, with a bewildered Father Claude standing at her side. The artist stepped quickly down the aisle and took Simone's arm, determined to get her out of there before a guilty conscience forced her premature confession. The priest leaned to one side, watching the couple retreat out through the main doors, a feeling of great darkness falling over him.

As Gaston dragged Madame Dupuis out into the afternoon sunshine, she began to cry, a deep, wailing sound that chilled the artist to the bone.

'Hold yourself together,' Gaston commanded, pulling roughly at her arm. 'If you fall apart, you'll take me down with you!'

'We did it together, Gaston!' the woman cried, desperately trying to free herself from his grasp. 'We both murdered Cecile!'

Thierry and Luc stepped out from behind the wooden archway leading to the graveyard and could hardly believe their ears.

With Madam Dupuis and Gaston Lauder handcuffed and safely secured in the rear of Gabriella's car, Max stood outside Maurice's home and shook his head.

'I'm sorry for putting Telo through that,' he said sincerely. 'Monsieur Lauder has explained how your son's hair came to be attached to Cecile's jacket, and I'm sure Simone Dupuis will confess to her part once we interview her formerly. At the moment, we need nothing further.'

'What about Isobel?' Maurice asked, as the detectives made to leave.

Inspector Mallery reached into the glove compartment of Hobbs' car and pulled out a burgundy-coloured document. 'Yes, she deserves an apology at the very least. Let's return this passport to its rightful owner.'

Max, Jack, Maurice and Telo crossed the square, their shoulders moving in unison as they strode towards the boulangerie, each lost in his own thoughts.

Isobel watched the approaching foursome and pulled four cups from the shelf. One was for her, as she'd already prepared a chocolate milkshake with marshmallows for Telo. It might go some way to patching things up between us, she thought hopefully. At least until I leave.

In the days that followed, Simone Dupuis confessed to her intense jealousy and, most importantly, to the murder of Cecile Vidal. The hatred had burned deeply and strongly for years but, after the rebuff by Hubert, it was as though paraffin had been added to the smouldering embers and she snapped.

Gaston Lauder's story was more complex. After a brief and passionate summer fling with Cecile, they'd parted amicably, or so the woman thought. A year later, Gaston had undertaken to sketch Madame Vidal naked, the prints intended to be a gift to her husband on his birthday, and it was a trip to the framers on that fateful day that had caused her to be on the early morning train. As arranged, Gaston was already on the same train, having left his home in Paris on the first available train to Bordeaux St.Jean, travelling via Saint Margaux and Salbec.

It had been the artist's specific instruction to Cecile that she get into the last carriage, where they would meet and continue on, in order to purchase the perfect frame to match his tasteful and beautiful interpretation of Cecile's curves. What she was unprepared for, however, was the depth of Gaston's obsession with her. Ever since their short tryst, he had yearned to have Cecile for himself and refused to allow her to continue being with Hubert after what he, Gaston, had perceived to be the love affair of the century.

On Cecile's part, it had been an affair born of boredom and misjudgement, one that she deeply regretted, yet had confessed to her best friend Simone. It was that one mistake that had cost Cecile her life, for, next to Hubert, the only man that Madame Dupuis cared about was her handsome regular lodger, Gaston.

It had been Gaston's idea to travel to the nearby airport and have Telo Fabron collect him from there. And with the murder weapon concealed securely in his artist's portfolio case, nobody had given the Parisian a second glance as he emerged from the train station at Bordeaux that morning.

A stroke of good luck in the VW Beetle's overheating on the return journey, had given Gaston the perfect opportunity to get rid of the bread knife, too. As Telo got out to lift the bonnet on the motor, to allow it to cool down, his friend had opened the glove compartment, spotted the car owner's denim shirt and deftly wrapped the knife in it. Unfortunately, he'd not been quite as careful as he had intended and Gaston accidentally got a smear of blood on his favourite white shirt, a deep crimson stain that Isobel had spotted on his cuff later that day.

Gaston Lauder had confessed, of course. He'd had no choice. In the next interview room to his, the artist didn't doubt that Simone Dupuis was singing like a canary in order to pin most of the blame on him. Luckily for Gaston, he'd been astute enough to record his subsequent conversations with the florist and offered them up in exchange for some plea bargaining.

Luc, the computer genius, had been kicking himself since the arrest of Cecile Vidal's murderers. On closer inspection of the Bordeaux railway station CCTV footage, he'd spotted Gaston Lauder leaving the train with a large valise, just a few passengers behind the femme fatale, Simone Dupuis. It was a huge error on his part, but not one that Inspector Mallery had chided him for. They'd all missed it and Luc would suffer no adverse effects from the oversight, apart from having to fetch coffee and pain au chocolat for the rest of the team for a week.

Jack Hobbs had returned to Salbec station the day after the culprit's arrest and spoke to the rotund porter for a second time. Yes, he'd said, the tall man in the photo had also been there at Salbec on that morning. He'd used the conveniences and caught the next train to Bordeaux with the dark-haired woman.

'And why didn't you tell us this before?' Hobbs had hissed through gritted teeth, watching as the man's wide mouth tackled a fresh pork roll.

'You didn't ask,' came the nonchalant response. 'If you had, I'd have told you.'

Max Mallery was impressed with his team. They'd solved the first murder of his reign as Inspector on the Bordeaux force and the telephone hadn't stopped ringing with congratulations from his peers. If pressed, Mallery would admit that solving the case had taken far too long, but he was satisfied enough, and life was on the up.

The Commissioner's wife, Vanessa, was coming down to see him this weekend while her husband went off to play golf in Spain. It didn't mean anything, she'd said on the phone, they would just talk and go out for dinner somewhere quiet. Max knew just the place; a little bistro in a village called Saint Margaux.

Jack Hobbs got an official letter from the Department de Police, inviting him to join the team in Bordeaux for the next twelve months, after which there would be a review and a possible permanent position, should he desire it. Naturally, Angélique was delighted and promised to go easy on her husband, at least until the next case requiring him to work long hours came along.

Life in Saint Margaux returned to normal, with undertones of gossip and new arrivals being met with cautious stares. Dominique Fabre was fundamental in welcoming every new male visitor to the village, but never did manage to find the man of her dreams. Needless to say, she's still looking, every single day.

Father Claude held an extended sermon on the first Sunday after Simone and Gaston's arrests, warning the residents to repent and love thy neighbour, not covet feelings of lust and greed. Naturally, his words were met with murmurs of appreciation, especially by Hubert Vidal, who was heartbroken by the news of his wife's infidelity and vowed never again to take the things in his life for granted.

Isobel Green received a short visit from Gabriella a few days later. The young detective was carrying a battered shoebox full of documents that the Englishwoman instantly recognised as her own. The sight of the memories brought with it mixed emotions and she'd disappeared upstairs to the apartment to mull over the feelings that churned inside.

She'd had a lengthy and heartfelt apology from Inspector Mallery, and Jack Hobbs had called in for coffee to add a few words of regret of his own. It wasn't easy fitting in when you were an outsider, Hobbs had told her, but things would get easier every day. It was a promise that he made to himself as well as Isobel.

The pain of the past few weeks had numbed Izzy now and her anger had dissipated to a low bubble, simmering just below the surface. The Englishwoman had now begun to repair her fragile relationship with Telo Fabron, thanks to his father, and assisted in part by a rather special bake that she'd decorated in honeycomb and hazelnuts. A little bird had told her that these were Telo's favourites and might help in closing the rift between them. Izzy doubted whether Telo fully understood why she'd been arrested, but Maurice had explained, using delicate language that was neither accusatory nor harsh and his son had subsequently mellowed as the days passed. It seemed that only Maurice knew what went on in his son's head and the baker insisted that all was forgiven and forgotten on Telo's part.

One night, not long after the murderous revelations, Isobel Green stood out in the courtyard at the rear of the boulangerie with her skinny right shoulder touching the muscular left arm of Maurice Fabron. A plane ticket to Spain the next morning sat on the bedside table upstairs.

The pair stood silently watching orange and blue flames licking at the edges of the cardboard box as they danced around eagerly, devouring Isobel's secrets. A photo of Martin Freeman curled and disintegrated as the heat obliterated his face to ashes, ridding the young woman of a decade of hurt. A second image started to singe at the edges.

'Will you stay?' Maurice asked softly, touching Izzy's fingers with his own, 'now that it's all over?'

Isobel sighed. 'It will never be over if I stay in Saint Margaux, Maurice. People don't forgive easily and someone with a chequered past like mine isn't welcome in a close-knit community like this.'

'They will forget in time.' The baker smiled, his deep, dark eyes boring into hers. 'I'm sure of it.'

'The trouble is, Maurice, I won't.'

'Come away,' Monsieur Fabron urged. 'We'll go inside and drink a toast to your future.'

The following day, on the morning of her final departure, Isobel Green took her suitcase downstairs and had one final coffee with Monsieur Fabron. Maurice had realised that no amount of pleading would convince Izzy to stay. Besides, a new job and a fresh start were beckoning to her, something that Saint Margaux could no longer provide.

'These are for Telo,' Isobel announced, dropping the VW keys onto the glass counter. 'I won't be needing my car any longer.'

'Are you sure?' Maurice grinned. 'He'll be delighted.'

Izzy nodded. 'Yes, the Beetle definitely belongs in my past.'

'Why not let Telo drive you to the airport then?' the baker offered. 'As a last thank-you. A taxi will cost you a fortune. I can phone the insurance company now to get him covered.'

Isobel considered her friend's words and then the one month's salary that Maurice had given her the previous day; she wasn't exactly flush at the moment. 'Okay,' she agreed, 'that would be great.'

As they drove down towards Bordeaux airport, the lack of conversation between them filled with music from the old-fashioned car radio, Isobel turned to Telo and smiled. She was grateful for his final acceptance of her, albeit just a few days. It had cleared the air and helped her move on.

The airport came into sight and Telo steered the VW into a space near the entrance, his eyes never once leaving the road in front of him. Isobel unfastened her seatbelt as soon as they stopped, and the young man did the same before jumping out to retrieve Izzy's suitcase from the boot for her.

Isobel took the case from Telo's grip and nervously leaned forward to kiss him on both cheeks in traditional fashion. '*Merci, Telo, au revoir.*'

The young man swiftly returned the words and pressed a hand to Isobel's side, as though attempting to hug her, but the action was brief and he quickly pulled away.

'*Bon voyage, Isobel Green.*' He smiled at Izzy and climbed into the car and she waved as she watched him drive off.

Nestled into her seat at the rear of the plane, Isobel Green closed her eyes and fought back the tears. She was certainly going to miss Maurice Fabron, with his kind and trusting nature. She was also confused about her feelings for Gaston Lauder, the handsome artist who had pretended to be her friend; the man who had wined and dined her, giving not a single hint that he himself was involved in Cecile Vidal's murder. The person with the most gall had been Simone Dupuis, Isobel pondered. Pretending to offer support, collecting Izzy from the police station and lending her clothes, the woman had been more devious than anyone she'd ever met in her life.

Isobel wondered what lay before her. With the box of documents destroyed, she hoped that new beginnings were on the horizon. She hadn't found the courage to phone her parents or Viv after all, and in the end, everything had worked out. They'd never know where she was or what she was doing. That was the punishment they deserved for not believing that Martin Freeman had raped her.

Tears began to flow, and Isobel reached into the pocket of her hoodie for a tissue. Her fingers touched on something silky yet hard and Izzy gingerly pulled it out, almost dropping it as she looked down at the slightly charred photo of Martin Freeman gazing back at her.

Telo Fabron tapped his fingers to the beat of his favourite Led Zeppelin song as he drove steadily back to Saint Margaux. The sun was shining brightly and the fields on either side of the highway were filled with lavender and poppies that swayed in the faint morning breeze. Today was a great day, he thought, grinning to himself.

Telo felt no remorse at having slipped the singed photograph into Isobel's pocket as she'd kissed him goodbye. After all, she might not have killed his Aunt Cecile, but she was still a murderer and she didn't deserve to walk away from that fact as though wiping the slate clean.

The young man hoped Isobel would be far away when she found the image that he'd lifted carefully from the burning pyre. Papa had explained about Isobel's past and what she'd done, but Telo couldn't comprehend that you could commit such a crime and walk away after ten years.

A life for a life, that's how he saw it, and as long as that photograph was with Isobel Green, she'd never forget her sins.

The End

About the Author

A.J. Griffiths-Jones began her writing career in 2014 after returning to England after a decade living and teaching in China. Her passion lies within the realms of crime, both historical and current, and in particular she enjoys the research of cold cases and mysteries.

In 2016, A.J. was awarded the 'Jack the Ripper Book of the Year' prize for her work 'Prisoner 4374', an account of the life of convicted poisoner Doctor Thomas Neill Cream, which had taken years of research and unearthed some ground-breaking documents concerning Cream's whereabouts during the Whitechapel murders of 1888.

Since completing her research, Griffiths-Jones has gone on to publish a series of five cosy mysteries and a standalone crime thriller with Next Chapter Publishing and plans further crime novels in the future.

Now temporarily residing in Shropshire, A.J. enjoys swimming, cooking and the great outdoors, with a passion for exploring National Trust buildings and ancient ruins.

A move abroad is on the cards, watch this space!

You can follow A.J. Griffiths-Jones on her website:
www.ajwriter.simplesite.com

Twitter:

@authoraj66

Facebook:

A.J. Griffiths-Jones Author Page

Printed in Great Britain
by Amazon